Twisted Intentions

Twisted Intentions

By

Lew Stonehouse

HOLLISTON, MASSACHUSETTS

TWISTED INTENTIONS

Copyright © 2015 by Lew Stonehouse

Cover Art by Sam Ezzo.

First printing February 2015
10 9 8 7 6 5 4 3 2 1

ISBN # 1-60975-085-3
ISBN-13 # 978-1-60975-085-5
LCCN # 2014955596

Silver Leaf Books, LLC
P.O. Box 6460
Holliston, MA 01746
+1-888-823-6450

Visit our web site at www.SilverLeafBooks.com

Acknowledgements / Dedication

I have to say that after all that has transpired to this moment, the actual writing of the book, changes based on responses from beta readers, rewrites (upon seemingly never-ending rewrites), artist renditions and the myriad details that bring a book to publication, the last thing I had thought about was this short paragraph. It left me a bit dumbfounded. I can write a novel, but I found what to say here, elusive. I would like to thank everyone for their unfailing support in this endeavor. That would include my mother, Janet Thorna and my father, Jack Stonehouse as well as the small army of my beta readers, Arleen Benhart, Ed and Lodi Cummings, Pam Bender, Lynne Ehle, Fran Melcher, and Rick Wolf. I would especially like to thank Nancy Brown of Michigan for her professional advice and encouragement. The enthusiastic response from a literary professional such as herself had an immeasurable impact on me. To all of you, I dedicate this book.

Twisted Intentions

PROLOGUE

Detective John Livingston Harvard looked across his desk at his best friend, Detective Nick Giovanni. Sheets of paper containing reports, witness statements, and crime scene photographs took up nearly every square inch of desk space. "It's him, Nick," he snarled uncharacteristically. "I know it's the contractor and you know it's him."

Nick shook his head slowly in response. "I don't know John. I know he's in the vicinity of every one of the missing boys and none of his alibis stand up, but still, I…"

"NICK!" John roared, cutting his friend off in mid-sentence, "he's snatching up boys at the rate of one a week and the week is almost up. We know that a kid on the base-ball team he coaches reported that he felt him up after prac-tice. The first victim was from the same *team* he coaches. In fact, that's the one link we have, all the missing boys are on Little League baseball teams. The guy's own wife says that he loves boys and she says she's even suspicious about his actions sometimes. What more do you want, another miss-ing kid? We need to do it now, Nick. We need to snatch him up."

Giovanni calmly stared at his partner. "I know, I know, but I question the motives of the kid that claims the coach felt him up. As the coach says, he did release him from the team and the kid was pretty pissed about it. On the other hand, we've also got a line of people saying the guy's a saint. None of 'em believe he would do something like this," his hand waved over the pictures lying on the desk while his face twisted into a grimace. "His own wife notwithstanding." He began shaking his head again. "What's with you buddy? Why are you so focused on this guy? It's not like you."

John stared up at the ceiling as he responded, his temper cooling rapidly. "I know how these contractors are. They are low life's that got lucky and make a ton of money. They don't have any class to go with it and they think they're better than everyone else, smarter, untouchable." He returned his gaze to Nick. "My best friend in junior high school was abducted. He disappeared after Little League practice. They found his body buried in the gravel of a foundation they were about to pour. The site manager decided that the floor wasn't ready. For some reason, it turned out not to be level even though it was perfect when they left it the night before. He had a couple of his guys check it and while they were moving gravel around, they found my friend. The cops determined pretty quickly that it was the general contractor for the job that did it, but his attorneys got him off. He walked scot-free, walked out of that court room with the biggest, cockiest smile you ever saw."

"I'm sorry about your friend, John. I really am, and now your attitude makes sense. But what happened before doesn't change the facts on what we have now, on *this* case. Look, you've got an arrest record that most cops can only dream about. Your instincts are always right on, to the point where it's just plain spooky at times." Nick's face took on a sad, imploring look. "But I'm telling ya, I think that you're letting your past override your judgment this time. You know that no one here will argue with you. You go to the State's Attorney and he'll tell you to snatch him up, trusting your judgment. Maybe you are right, but I think we need to look at some of these other suspects a little closer first, especially that electrician."

John shot to a standing position, his temper rising once more. "No! I know I'm right and we don't have the time to be dickin' around with anyone else." He began to cram the contents of his desk into a huge spandex file. When he was finished he stopped and looked at Nick. "You coming?" It came out as more of a demand than a question.

Nick sighed and stood up. "Yeah, I'll come but I'm doing it under protest." He shook his head as he prepared to leave. "I'm your friend and I'm your partner and I go where you go." He looked straight at John as he slowly, loudly, let out a huge breath. "But I still think we're rushing into this." The two detectives walked out of the office, one with hurried determination and the other with obvious reluctance.

The arrest was the headline of every paper in town the next day. The contractor's wife immediately filed for a divorce, so quickly that even John questioned her motives. It was then that he had started to become uneasy, for it had been her statement, that even she had been suspicious about his relationships with boys, that had convinced him that the contractor was their guy. Her apparent conviction on the matter had arisen the specter of his dead friend and caused him to lock on to the contractor like a heat seeking missile. Her filing had suddenly snapped him into the present day, like being snapped from a dream by having a prankster throw a glass of ice cold water on his face and it had started the ball rolling in his mind. As the weeks progressed and he commenced his pretrial preparations, his usual analytical mind began to return and his uneasiness grew like a snowball barreling down a hill. He shrugged his misgivings off and bulled ahead. He couldn't possibly be that far wrong… could he? After all, the abductions had stopped after they had arrested the contractor. That was further proof they had the right guy… wasn't it?

It was months later, the night before the trial was to start, that he received a call from the county jail. An inmate had said he had information about the missing boys and wanted to talk to a detective right away. John arrived at 2:00 A.M., with mounting trepidation. As the inmate began to talk, John's whole world began to spin. He left feeling downright sick to his stomach. He drove to his office and called Nick, holding back his urge to vomit.

"Nick," he said slowly when his friend groggily answered the phone. "You were right. Oh my God, you were right all along."

It turned out that the inmate had been arrested for burglary and had been paired in the same cell with a drunk. The inebriated man had been crying continuously and the annoyed inmate soon learned it wasn't because he'd just been arrested for drunk driving. He was crying because his nephew, an electrician, had killed all those boys that were in the news. The drunk man knew that the wrong man had been arrested but he just couldn't bring himself to turn in his own family.

Based on the inmate's story and other evidence which heretofore had been pretty much ignored in the rush to prove the case against the contractor, the electrician was arrested the next day. They found plenty of evidence to back up the inmate's story. "Trophies," items taken from each of the victims, had been discovered in the electricians bedroom. The man finally confessed when confronted with the rapidly increasing mountain of evidence. He gave up the location of the remaining bodies, bragging about how clever he was to stop once the contractor had been arrested. He'd had plans to pick up where he'd left off, but in a different state and he would learn from his mistakes so that it would have been even more difficult to find him.

Things didn't go much better for the contractor. It turned out that his wife had left him for his best friend. She'd been having an affair for quite a while and when the whole missing boy thing came up, she saw an opportunity to throw more wood on the fire, use it as an excuse to file for a divorce and get quite an agreeable settlement. She'd made up the whole story about the contractor's over fondness for boys but the damage was done. No youth group would touch him. No one wanted their house built by him. He was destroyed. Two months after his release, they found him hanging from the spiral staircase of his home.

John turned to the bottle for solace. His own wife had little leeway for his drunken, bitter moods and she left him for another man. His only comfort was that she also left their only child, a daughter, with him. Her leaving and the sudden sole responsibility for a young girl shook him from his doldrums. John did not want to leave her alone with a caretaker for all the hours he knew his job would require. He decided that it was time to leave police work, but it was the only thing he knew how to do, the only thing he'd ever wanted to do.

In the end, he decided to set up shop for himself. He would become a private detective. It was the only logical conclusion. Now he didn't have to make decisions that would affect the entire future of anybody. If he made a mistake, then someone wouldn't get the divorce settlement they wanted or they might not get their stolen stuff back, a far cry from taking someone's life away from them, forcing them to hang themselves in a drunken, demoralized stupor. Now, John Livingston Harvard would merely be John Q. Citizen, just trying to make a living and raise his daughter. He told himself that life would be great, carefree and wonderfully normal and it did indeed play out that way... for a while. Given his skills and his personality, he really should have known better.

CHAPTER

1

Three years later...

John Q. Citizen, otherwise known as John Harvard, now a private detective, stood gazing intently at the entrance to the apartment building. It was cold. Very cold. He could feel the cold seeping into his bones like an invading disease and it didn't feel to him as though his heavy jacket was of much use. It was the kind of cold that stays with a person until it is forced away by a blazing fire or a long, hot shower. It was unseasonably cold for this time of year though certainly not unheard of for the Northeastern United States. The groundhog had failed to see his shadow this year so, John mused, this was probably nature's last hurrah of the season. But that did not help him on this night.

Still, he knew that if he wanted the information he sought, he would have to stay. He wished he could do this from the warmth and comfort of his vehicle. But this apartment was located in a hilly, heavily wooded area that provided plenty of seclusion and privacy. So private in fact, that most of the building could not be viewed from the main parking lot. The individual buildings in the complex were set on a steep hillside that provided each living space with a beautiful, panoramic view of the area. The apartment complex even had its own, albeit small, ski hill. Instead of huge parking lots, the builders had opted for several mini parking lots that were surrounded by trees and hidden from view, giving the entire setting a cozy, secluded feeling. It was a place to unwind and get away from the rigors of a rat race world. It was not possible to see the entrance to most of the buildings, including this one, without being directly in front of the main door. Young couples thought the hilly, forested area, was romantic, beautiful. Thieves, rapists, and cops knew it was the perfect set up for those wanting to perform activities which they did not want to be seen by others.

What John wanted was nothing more than information. Information for which he had already been handsomely paid. Information for which he would be paid even more, once it was obtained.

He had learned of this address and the apartment number from his client two days ago. Additional information had arrived just this morning with a package containing a check and a cryptic note, which among other things, directed him to this location. Not that he wouldn't have come here tonight anyway, but on the phone, his client's voice had a sense of urgency about it, and the man sounded like was used to giving orders... and one that was used to having those orders complied with instantly.

His client knew that Harvard did not have to do what he

was instructed to do but the caller also realized that money was power and a substantial amount of it was being offered. The cash sum was so great because of a perceived dire need and the fact that John was very good at what he did. Very, very good and the money that was offered made it unlikely that any reasonable request would be turned down.

So now he stood in the woods, secluded far enough back in the leafless trees that no one was likely to see his darkened figure. He watched the entrance as his breath visibly rose silently from his nostrils, into the cold and still night air. The sky was crystal clear and there were so many stars that it did not seem like there was room for any more, a dark, twinkling blanket that hung over the earth. Fortunately for him, there was no moon. The barren trees stood like dark, silent, sentinels watching over the area. John leaned against one as he watched and to the casual observer, became one with the tree.

The particular apartment that he was watching was on the ground floor and the drapes were closed. Light flickering around the edges of the window coverings told him that interior lights were on, as was a television, but that was all he could tell.

He could see people moving about through the windows of the other apartments. Being naturally curious, he wondered about the lives in those dwellings. In one apartment, a teenage boy was in a heated discussion with an older couple that were most certainly his parents. A discussion about a girl perhaps? His grades? Where he was last night?

Another apartment contained a pot bellied man in his

mid-fifties sitting in a chair, beer in hand, watching a TV. He wore a stained white t-shirt that John imagined he could smell even from this distance. The pot bellied man appeared supremely bored. A woman of similar outlook and about the same age, sat in a chair next to him, also staring blankly at the TV. Obviously a couple, they sat for hours without talking to one another. Comfortable with each other? Or just existing side by side waiting for death or some equally dramatic event to shake them from the doldrums of their plodding lives?

Was the young, beautiful blonde two doors down from the stained t-shirt on the phone with her husband? Her lover? Or a girlfriend. He had seen no one else in the apartment and she had been on the phone even as she made and then ate her dinner. She laughed a lot but sometimes her face softened into a faraway, wistful look. The kind of look a woman gets when her lover is making her think of something other than the day to day grind of living. So John supposed that it was probably a man she was talking to. But these days, even that was certainly not a given.

Harvard, himself, was forty-five. Currently, a lock of his dark hair hung aggravatingly close to his right eye. *Have to get a haircut*, he thought as he brushed it back up toward the top of his head. His hair was parted and was as dark and as full now as it had been when he was sixteen. He had piercing gray eyes, stood just over six feet and had an imposing, stocky build. Looking at him, one would suppose that he could have been an ex-football player, a fullback, maybe even a quarterback perhaps. He was not. He developed a passion for the game late in life and now regretted that he hadn't played. But, like a lot of things in life, that was water over the dam. He had been something of a loner in school and had gone into solitary sports like cross country running, skiing, and gymnastics. He had raced sailboats in high school and like everything else, he usually raced one man boats where he had to depend on no one else but himself. He was good at most things he tried. He had discovered in his early thirties that what had prevented him from being even better was mental discipline, which he started to develop with that discovery.

His thoughts were suddenly broken as a dark color sedan quietly pulled into an adjacent parking lot and stopped. What had drawn his attention was the fact that the car had no lights on. When it stopped, John noted that the brake lights did not come on, which meant either the driver was using his parking brake to stop the car or the vehicle was equipped with a "kill switch," to prevent the lights from coming on. Either way, he knew that the driver wasn't here to conduct normal activities.

The teenager, the older couple and even the beautiful blonde were totally forgotten now and the dark car held his rapt attention. As he watched, the driver side door opened. A man in equally dark clothing stepped out and looked quickly around. John noted that the interior light did not come on when the door was opened and the driver, who now stood looking around, did so quickly, but carefully. A professional. But a professional what? A cop? A burglar? A hit man? He didn't know. But he did know that the average

John Doe didn't efficiently case his surroundings in such a manner. John Doe doesn't drive with his lights out. John Doe would not know how or even think about stopping his car without the brake lights coming on. No, this man merited closer scrutiny.

Soon, the passenger side door opened and the figure that exited performed the same actions as the driver. Their facial features were obscured by the distance and the darkness. The passenger's clothing matched that of the driver. Then, they silently closed their respective doors and headed in the direction of the apartment building. Harvard noted that though they moved quickly, they did so in such a manner that a casual observer would see nothing other than two figures walking briskly. They would arouse no suspicions. He also saw that exhaust fumes from their vehicle continued to form an upward spiral of gray smoke as the car sat, apparently unattended. It had been left running.

The two figures approached the entrance to the building and walked through the main, unlocked door and into the small lobby. John could see them through the windows on each side of the main door as they approached the second, locked door. As the passenger stood looking around, the driver did something to the door and both quickly entered and soon disappeared from view. He had done a reconnaissance of the lobby area earlier and found that the second door was in very good shape and a key was needed to open it. Metal guards on the door were provided to prevent someone from jimmying it open. The door itself was made of steel and was tight fitting. It was also equipped with a very good pneumatic return so the odds of the door not fully closing were slim indeed. That meant they either had a key or someone was extremely efficient at picking locks.

John was undecided as to what to do next. It was obvious that the occupants of the car were up to some sort of skullduggery. Their reason for being there might have nothing to do with the apartment he was watching. Might have. But he felt that the coincidence would be astronomically high and he was not a big believer in coincidence.

He had not been hired to take any action on this case. Only to observe and report back on what he had seen. He had not come armed. He had spent most of his adult life carrying a gun and found it was useful only in very few situations. Most of the time, all it did was tear up the clothing of the one carrying it. Besides, he was just John Q. Citizen now. What did he need a gun for?

It occurred to him that now might be one of those situations where it might indeed be needed. No sense in second guessing it now. Taking his own quick survey of the area, John moved out of the woods and approached the still running car. He carried a small digital recorder in his pocket and he used this to record the license plate number, make, model, and color of the vehicle. He also noted the time. Keeping one eye toward the front door of the apartment, he inspected the car for any information he could uncover. He found a small sticker on the bumper and another on the windshield. The car was a rental. There was nothing inside the vehicle. Not a thing. Not a wrapper. Not a newspaper. Not a coffee cup. None of this was doing anything to alleviate his fears that something bad was happening.

Deciding that there was nothing more to be learned from the car, John hurried to the ground floor window of the apartment he had been watching. Anyone seeing him at this point would be suspicious of his actions and may call the police. Nothing to be done about it now. The cold snow squeaked in the still night as he moved to the window. It sounded to him like blaring trumpets heralding his arrival to anyone who might be interested.

When he got to the window, he quickly looked around again. No one seemed to be looking out their domiciles in his direction. No dog walker had stopped their nightly ritual to stare curiously at him as if to say, "Who the hell are you and what are you doing?" No dog, for that matter, was barking furiously inside or out to attract the attention of its owner. He did not like moving in the open so quickly and in such a totally unplanned manner. He liked to scope out the situation well ahead of time and to plan each move carefully to optimize his chances of not being discovered. He was sure that the occupants of the car had thoroughly checked this area out well in advance of their little operation and had planned every move. They would also know of the teenager, the older couple, and the beautiful blonde.

But what, exactly, was their operation? Nothing his client had said indicated that this would have anything to do with an unlit vehicle, driven by professionals who obviously did not want to be seen and who, equally obviously, were not planning to be long in their endeavors. Their actions were not the ones of common burglars. He had seen plenty of those. They were usually kids, stupid ones at that with none of the foresight or professionalism displayed by the occupants of the sedan. Besides, this was prime time for residents to be home so no, burglary was not a likely motive.

What else? If they were there merely to demand something of an occupant of the apartment building, that would mean a certain amount of time. Why leave the car running? No, talking was probably not on the menu either.

The ex-detective could only come to two conclusions. Either they were here to kill or do serious bodily harm to an occupant of one of the apartments, or to kidnap an occupant. If they were going to kill someone, why not wait until later when most people, including their target, would be asleep? They did not have to worry about the noise of everyday life drowning out their actions. They had already displayed more than enough proficiency to convince him that they could move in undetected silence.

John had another thought. Even if they were going to kidnap someone, why now? Why here? At this exact point in time? Surely there were better places to do either one. No, because of their assured actions thus far, he was sure the individuals from the car had planned something to do with someone in this building and thus had checked the area previously. But some event demanded that they take action tonight, immediately. He decided they were probably as uncomfortable about moving around in the open at this hour as he was. It gave him little comfort.

Further thoughts about the motives for their actions tonight were cut short by a muffled cry and then a thump from within the very apartment he had been watching. Though obvious enough to him, now standing directly outside the apartment window, it was doubtful that anyone else, even in the adjacent apartments, would have heard anything.

Obviously, something untoward was happening in the apartment. But what? And what should he do? He had been told specifically not to have contact with the occupant of the apartment or to have his presence known. However, he didn't imagine that his client had anticipated tonight's events. In any case, he didn't think he could stand by while someone was being kidnapped or worse.

John pressed his ear against the window, straining to hear anything he could. He heard nothing. The cold glass was numbing his ear and he didn't know how much longer he could stand the painful, stinging feeling. The outside entrance door suddenly flew open. He immediately recognized the general form of the driver. Unfortunately, the driver saw him at almost the same time. There was nowhere to go and the look in the driver's eyes that were peering out from a newly donned ski mask in the brightly lit area, told him that the time for stealth was over.

John continued to study his opponent's eyes, looking for a hint as to what his actions would be. He knew from experience that a gunman looks at the point where he is going to shoot, a subtle give away to those who know what to look for. If the other man dropped his piercing gaze to look at John's chest, gunplay would likely soon follow. Thankfully for the weaponless private investigator, the driver did not avert his gaze.

Instead, without taking his concentration off from Harvard, he mumbled something to his companion who was just out of sight behind the door. Then the driver launched himself at John and a strange sort of silent combat began. Except for the squeaking snow and the dull sound of blows landing, some muted grunts, there was absolutely no sound. It was soon apparent that both men had studied martial arts and it was equally apparent that neither man was going to quickly gain the upper hand. That was bad for John, who was out of shape and would tire quickly. It was also bad for the driver. Time worked against him in the form of attention from others. The driver knew that cops would quickly follow that attention and cops were definitely not on his list of desired people to see.

The rapidly tiring private detective saw indecision creeping into the body language of the driver. The driver was also realizing that something was going to have to happen very quickly. The driver's head darted to the side in a futile attempt to find his partner in crime. Neither combatant had seen where the driver's companion had gone. Each had been too busy trying to disable the other. But the current attempt by the driver to locate his cohort, quick as it was, was long enough and John was able to land a glancing blow to the front of the man's neck.

The driver staggered back, briefly clutching his throat. This enabled John to also look past his opponent for the driver's companion. He saw him putting a limp form into the back seat of the dark car. But he could see no more because the driver had recovered and now it was John's turn to fend off a revitalized blitz. His opponent was coming at him with a simultaneous attack of hands and feet. The initial attack succeeded only in driving John backwards in exhaustion but the driver continued to press his assault. Harvard heard a car door slam and a moment later heard the tires of the dark vehicle spinning as they desperately tried to grip the icy pavement.

Just then, the attack by the driver had success as a well placed foot landed in John's groin. As was the blow to the throat of the driver, it was a partially deflected strike but effective enough to allow the driver to stun John and give him the opportunity to quickly move toward the dark vehicle. His companion had stopped the car near them and had opened the passenger side door. The driver jumped into the passenger seat and the car sped away and was lost from view almost instantly. The diminishing sounds of the squealing tires and the surging engine were the only trace of the dark car as it wound its way out of the wooded complex.

John could barely stand, let alone run. He could not hope to get to his vehicle in time to catch the kidnappers. He looked around. Hell, they were almost to the main road already. No one seemed to be aware of the exchange. He gingerly walked to his SUV and got in, a dull ache in his groin. He sat there a moment, catching his breath. He was no longer cold. He did not work out regularly and it now showed in his overheated body and lack of breath.

They say that one should be able to fight for one's life for three minutes. He reckoned that he had been fighting for about two minutes, probably less. His arms quivered from his body's left over fight or flight chemicals, but at the same time they felt like lead and he considered himself lucky to have lasted so long. He had once been a second degree black belt in a form of martial arts originally designed to take on multiple attackers and protect a palace. One man taking on more than one attacker meant that the defender had to dispose of assailants as quickly and efficiently as possible. Therefore, most of the moves were designed to kill or maim, quickly. They were not the sort of moves that could be used in a common bar fight, but good in a life and death struggle. However, he had not gone to a martial arts class for many years and only adrenaline, coupled with instinct honed from hours upon hours of practice had allowed him to go toe to toe with the driver. A few years ago, the driver would really have had his hands full. He was grateful that there had been no gunplay since his own weapon was sitting at home in his night stand. It would have been a pretty one sided gun fight. That thought made him grin in spite of his pain and weariness. Sort of one upped the old, "don't bring a knife to a gun fight," routine. He would have been grateful for a knife.

But now the driver of the dark car, his companion, and the occupant of the apartment he was supposed to be watching, were all gone. As he sat there, the man wanting to be John Q. Citizen began to get angry. This was not anything like what he had expected. There was much more to this than he had been told. In spite of what the papers, movies, and crime novels would have one believe, this sort of highly professional kidnapping rarely happened in the U.S. And these men were professionals in every way. The only thing they had not counted on was ex-detective, John Harvard.

He dug a piece of paper from his briefcase, picked up his cell phone, and dialed the number that had been written on it. It had come with the certified check this morning. He tried to calm his breath further while he waited for the connection to be made. It was answered almost instantly.

"Hello," a voice calmly answered.

"This is John," he said, and unlike his client on the other end of the phone, he was not so calm. Not so calm at all.

"Oh, what do you have to tell me," said the client, with more interest.

"I have lots to tell you. But first I want some answers, and I god damn well better get them." John retorted.

"I can see something has happened to upset you," answered the client with a mixture of amusement, but increasing interest.

Recognizing the tone, John could hardly contain his anger. The adrenaline from the fight was subsiding, replaced by a deep rooted rage, fueled by the left over body chemicals that welled up almost uncontrollably. "Listen, asshole, you told me to come here and report who came and went and to particularly watch for an old, beat up Jeep CJ5. Well guess what? The Jeep never showed. What did show were two guys in a rented Ford Crown Vic. They were pros. And do you wanna hear the fuckin' icin' on the proverbial fuckin' cake? THEY TOOK HER!" he yelled.

There was complete silence on the other end of the line. John angrily shouted out, "You there?"

"Yes," came the terse reply, followed by more silence.

"Are you gonna fuckin' say something?" John spat out angrily and without waiting for an answer, "I'm gonna call the fuckin' cops."

"No!" came the instant reply.

Johns eyes furrowed in a mixture of surprise and confusion. "Why the hell not?"

"There's more to this than you know," said the client.

"No shit, Sherlock," yelled John. "But we still have a case of kidnapping, at the very least. I don't know what kind of shit you're into here, but that girl is gone and it didn't look very voluntary to me."

"John, please believe me when I tell you that most likely, all isn't as it appears. We need to talk. Please don't call the police. I don't believe any harm will come to her at this point. If you call anybody, it most assuredly will."

"And how do you know that? You some sort of kidnapping expert now? I don't like this," John stated flatly. "Why should I believe you? You obviously have not leveled with me yet."

"I know. I thought that your involvement would be minimal and I didn't think this would get out of hand." Though obviously shaken by the news, the owner of the voice was quickly getting his wits about him. "I'll double, hell I'll triple your fee if you just stay quiet and work with me on this."

John thought for a moment. "I won't be a party to someone getting raped or murdered," he said a little more calmly as the anger began to leave almost as quickly as it had come.

The client said, "Rape has nothing to do with this John. And if we play this right, no harm will come to her. Just please listen to what I have to say before you do anything, for her sake if nothing else. You are said to be the best in your business. That's why I called you. Now don't you think that the least you should do is to get all the facts before deciding a course of action?"

The adrenaline was fully gone now and the anger with it. Thoughts of the contractor suddenly welled up from the mental vault that John had buried him in. As much as he hated to admit it, the voice was right of course. He was just tired. He felt all used up. A bottle of wine and some soft blues music sounded really good at this juncture. It would give him time to think this out.

"Obviously you have a lot to tell me. You're sure that nothing will happen to her?" asked John in a resigned voice.

"Well, I didn't take her so I can't be one-hundred percent certain. All I can tell you is that based on what I do know, I really don't think so. Otherwise, I would be the first one calling the police. You know my stake in this. I believe it's in Sue's best interest to sit tight until we can come up with a plan. Will you wait and talk to me?"

"Where?" John asked.

"Do you know where Russo's is on Grand and 51st?"

"Yeah, by the river," replied John, both tired and exasperated.

"Be there at 7:00 A.M. tomorrow morning. There is a booth in the corner at the back of the restaurant. We can there talk privately," said the client.

"I'm not sure I like this," said John. "Nothing better happen to her."

"It won't."

"Tomorrow then." He paused and with a sudden, increased ferocity, "And you better have a damned good explanation."

"Trust me," said the client. "It will be. I just hope you're prepared because at this point, it seems I've chosen my team and if my team doesn't get it done, well, let's just say that Sue's not the only one who's going to have a very bad day."

CHAPTER

2

John broke the connection on this cell phone, started his vehicle and winced as the radio instantly blared out at him. He'd been in a great mood and listening to a pop star as he pulled into the apartment complex earlier that evening. He had been really blasting the radio. It was an upgraded system and he liked it loud. His ex-wife had been constantly complaining about the volume but she, like his previous joyous mood, was gone and no longer relevant. Now the sound only irritated him as the anger and frustration returned and he couldn't reach the control knob to get the volume down fast enough. He briefly mumbled to himself that he was glad he didn't have his gun at the moment. It flashed through his mind that he probably would have given serious consideration to the thought that shooting the radio would have been the quickest way to stop the noise. Not really, but sometimes he felt like such drastic measures would be an appropriate response.

He lived about forty minutes away, most of it expressway. As he drove, he thought about the night's events and what had brought him here. As an ex-cop, his instinct was to call this in and bring the full force of the law to bear. As were most crimes involving women and children, time is a precious commodity. What could he and his client hope to accomplish by themselves? For that matter, what could his client have gotten into that would involve kidnapping Sue? John thought that his client, her father, was taking this very well, even willing to wait until morning before having their little, "meeting." Though his client and his daughter were estranged and hadn't seen each other for years, she was still his daughter and as such he should be frantic in his efforts to get her back. That added to his growing apprehension about his client's involvement in all this.

John had a daughter of his own. She was six years old and was the solitary light in John's life. He split custody with his ex-wife and hated it when his daughter was not with him. The thought of someone taking her against her will brought some very dark thoughts to his head indeed. He couldn't imagine being as calm as the voice on the phone just now.

His client owned a software company that John had never heard of. However, judging from the money that his client was willing to pay, it didn't appear that he was worried about where his next meal would come from. John had done some background on him before cashing the man's check.

He found that his client, Peter Browning, the Third, no less, had cheated on his wife numerous times. She had forgiven him time after time. Eventually, he met a woman almost thirty years his junior and had been totally captivated by her. Though his wife knew of his affairs, she'd suffered in silence, consoled by the fact that he at least attempted to be covert about it. But this particular young woman caused Peter to throw caution to the wind. He began to miss parties and other social events. The final straw came when Peter had brought her to a party under the guise that she was a programmer that he was interviewing. A very lame excuse at best. His wife was at the party as a co-hostess.

So when they got home that night, his wife quietly informed him they would no longer be sharing a bed. Two days later, Peter was served with divorce papers and a court order removing him from the house. He went willingly, relieved that he could be with his new woman without restraints. Except, as is often the case in life, it didn't quite work out that way. It turned out the younger woman was quite content to be a kept mistress on the side. Peter had paid for her upscale condo. She was lavished with gifts and an occasional trip when Peter went out of town on business. But now Peter wanted to marry her and be with her forever. To actually live, with her. That, had not been on her agenda. So she left him.

Peter attempted to return to his wife, but being away from Peter even for a short time had given her a clearer view of the life that she had been living, and she didn't like the picture. She was disgusted with herself for putting up with him for as long as she did. She wanted no part of it. Period. End of story.

His daughter, who had been old enough to understand about her father's philandering ways for some time, never forgave him. She became aware of his many affairs as she was entering into puberty. To that point, she had had a good relationship with him. He was always loving and attentive when it came to her. But as she began to figure out the whole boy-girl thing in her own life, she realized what it was her father was doing and she didn't like it. It also dawned on her what this was doing to her mother and she was smart enough to know that she herself could one day be in the same situation. That was the beginning of the end of the relationship with her father. She was a freshman in college when he began his affair with the "floozy." When he so willingly moved out, in her mind, he had chosen this floozy over her and her mother. So that was that.

She rarely spoke to him afterward and never went to his house to visit. Oddly enough, she chose her father's profession and became an accomplished computer programmer in her own right. She had just started her own business and in a lot of ways, was a lot like her father. The area of dating was the large exception. She was now thirty-eight years old and had never been married. She'd had plenty of men knocking down her door to get at her. She was very attractive and kept herself in good shape. However, understandably, she had some serious trust issues when it came to men. She had come close a couple of times, but when they plopped the ring down in front of her as they proposed, she panicked and at least figuratively, ran for the hills.

So, since his daughter would not let him have a real relationship with her, Peter did the next best thing. He truly loved Sue and wanted only the best for her. He had told

John that he had a friend, Tom Weaver, who was a private investigator. He had him keep tabs on her over the years. Though she didn't know it, each one of her boyfriends had been thoroughly checked out. A few of them had been discouraged in various, mostly discreet ways, from continuing a relationship with her.

Tom Weaver had died of cancer recently. During one of his last conversations he had told Peter that John Harvard was an excellent P.I. and could be trusted. Tom had been checking out a new man that had come into Sue's life and had found... nothing. He couldn't find so much as a credit card or even a valid driver's license that registered to him. *That* was extremely unusual. Before he could pursue it further, he became ill and went into the hospital. He remained there until he died, which mercifully, hadn't been long.

That had been a couple of months ago and now Peter Browning wanted John to find out if Sue was still seeing this mystery man. He was the driver of the CJ5. It had been some months since his friend had actively worked on the case. Peter thought a logical place to start would be to find out who owned the Jeep. His friend had never revealed what the license plate number of the Jeep was. Peter was sure he must have obtained it at some point so that he could find out who the registered owner was. His friend's wife had given him permission to go through his files but Peter found that his "office" was in total disarray and Peter, whose own desk and office were spotless and always in order, could not understand how anyone could work in such conditions. In any event, he decided it was time to find a replacement for his friend.

So that was how John Harvard came to be standing in the woods just outside of Susan Browning's apartment. By now John had arrived home. He activated his garage door and pulled in. Next to him sat his, "toy," a gleaming Audi TT. Since the breakup of his family, John found pleasure in few things. The Audi came as a consolation prize to himself and he loved it. He would put the top down and cruise the countryside, imagining himself to be nineteen again, driving around in his Triumph TR4 and completely carefree, his only worry being if he could afford the five bucks it would take to fill the tank. Ah, but once again, that was water over the dam and four wives ago. Still, it was nice to remember.

He got out of his truck and after taking a moment to glance at the car, walked into the house. Throwing his coat over a chair, he grabbed a bottle of Merlot from the wine chiller and a glass. Then he headed out to a sun room that overlooked a small lake with steep wooded hills on the opposite side. He intentionally did not turn on the lights. He wanted to sit in the dark and gaze out over the lake and think. He started to sit but realized he was missing something. He walked over to a laptop computer sitting on the counter in the kitchen. It was hooked up to a small, but powerful speaker system that did nicely for most occasions. He brought up a music program and selected an album of Native American Music. He had been given the album as a gift and it sat unopened for months but one night he couldn't find anything in his library of forty thousand plus songs that suited him. So he selected the long forgotten album and cued it up. He was rewarded with a different kind of music altogether. A lot of flute, which he liked, and not much singing. It was mellow and very relaxing.

He pressed the "Start" button, adjusted the volume and returned to the sun room. He opened the wine, poured himself a glass, took a sip, and sat back. For a moment, his mind went blank as he savored the taste of the wine and let the music wash over him like a soothing blanket. Eventually, he returned to the here and now.

The first thing he noticed was that his forearms were sore. He rolled up his sleeves and saw in the dim light that they were red and tender to the touch. They were caused by blocking the blows from his opponent tonight. He knew from experience that in a few days, his entire forearm would be black and blue. He could remember when they would practice blocking for a whole class during his marital arts training. Though he always enjoyed his instruction, he like everyone else, dreaded the blocking classes. The first few times you blocked an opponent with your arm, it didn't really hurt. But after a few minutes of doing nothing but that, the pain would begin and every blow seemed like it was harder than the previous and if the instructor thought that either one of you were holding back, well, suffice it to say the alternative was worse.

He rolled his sleeves back down and began to analyze his next move. Given his current knowledge of the case, his logical place to start was Sue's apartment. He thought about how the intruders got into the apartment. Did they break in? Did they have a key or did they pick the lock? As he had at the time, John thought that they would have to be awfully efficient to pick a lock that fast. He suspected it was more likely they had a key. But from who, and having a key to the front door is vastly different from having a key to an individual apartment.

The other possibility was that Sue herself had let them in. Did she know them? He realized that one of the first things he would have to do tomorrow would be to check out Sue's door and find out if there were any signs of forced entry. He doubted they had done anything as crass as to kick it in. Even jimmying the door with a crowbar wouldn't have been a good alternative. Either of those choices would have made noise and a passer-by seeing the broken door or frame would most likely call the police or at least knock on her door. Neither was something the intruders would want.

He got up and retrieved his file on this case from his truck in the garage. He opened it and removed a picture of Sue that had come with the package this morning. She was a pretty woman with a wholesome look about her. Her eyes were green and her dark hair was cut in a short "bob." She wore a white turtleneck and generally gave the impression that she was older than she really was. He studied the picture, imploring it, as he had done on so many homicide investigations when he was a cop, to speak to him. Of course, it did not. But John imagined that her eyes were responding to him. They spoke of a generally good life, wanting for nothing, at least materially.

But emotionally, life had not been so kind. What was going on in her little world when this picture was taken? It was a studio portrait, probably from her college yearbook. Though she was smiling, her eyes seemed sad. It was as though she was there for the picture only because that was what was expected of her and not because she wanted something to remember that time, that place. He doubted that Sue herself had this same picture.

He removed other pictures from the file. These were more current and obviously taken without her knowledge. She looked much different than she had in the yearbook picture. Her hair was quite a bit longer. Her facial features had sharpened but not to the point where they detracted from her looks. John thought that some women actually become prettier as they age. Sue Browning was one of those women. The photographs had a time and date stamp in the lower right hand corner. In the various pictures she was shopping, talking to an unknown couple and one where she appeared to be at a party. She was laughing but again, John imagined her eyes were talking about a different story.

The last picture in the file showed her outdoors with a man. John judged the man to be in his late thirties to early forties. It was date stamped six months ago. He hadn't noticed it this morning but then again he was in a hurry. He was trying to check out Peter Browning, cash the check and run some errands before going out to Sue's apartment. Tonight was supposed to be a fairly quick recon mission and nothing else. He had just wanted to get a feel for the place at night. He made a quick, mental comparison of the man in the picture and the man he had fought with earlier tonight. Though the man had been hooded, he could tell from the general shape of the body and head that they were not the same. The hooded man had a large head with matching torso, more like a football player. The man in the photograph was more the soccer type, long and lean.

He wondered where the picture was taken and who the man was. He was laughing. Sue was not and she didn't appear to be in the laughing mood. Her body language spoke of tension. John had gotten very good at reading body language as a cop. He could walk into a room and have a feel for what was going on in seconds, many times before anyone had uttered a word. His arrest record attested to his uncanny ability to read a situation. Seemed like the only times his ability failed him was when it came to his own relationships, but in this case, he was sure he was right. Why was the man laughing when Sue was so serious?

After thinking about that for a while, John suddenly decided that he was very tired. He corked his bottle and returned it to the wine chiller. He turned off the music, the lights, and went into his bedroom. He briefly considered a hot shower to wash the sweat and the tenseness off him, but decided he was too tired and he had to wash his sheets anyway. So he undressed, turned out the light and within seconds, was in a deep, dreamless sleep. He would need it.

CHAPTER

3

He arrived at Russo's at 6:30 A.M. It was a Greek restaurant and a pig was turning on a spit in the front window. A cooking grill, further removed from the window but still in plain sight, was filled with a variety of cooking meats. A young man in a white uniform stood tending the food and was in constant motion turning the various pieces meat, taking some off, while putting others on. Though young, his movements said that he'd been doing this job forever. John guessed he was a son or some sort of relative of the family who owned the place.

Inside, a small counter stood at the front of the restaurant facing another grill and front window. This was obviously a secondary grill, not where they prepared most of the food for their eat-in guests. There were a few fixed stools so that customers could eat a quick bite or, as was most often the case, wait for their pickup food. A wall separated this area from the main eating area. It felt like a nice place. He imagined that many families ate here and the walls were full of laughter and good times. As soon as he had walked through the door he was greeted with the smell of gyros, bacon and a veritable cornucopia of other mouthwatering odors. He had-n't really been hungry before but that was changing fast.

A waiter hurried over to him. "How many of you will be eating with us this morning, sir?"

"There's only me and one other," replied John. "He said he wanted to sit in a booth in the back."

"Ah, your part of Mr. Browning's party then?" asked the waiter.

"Yes, but party?" said John.

"Mr. Browning reserved a table for three," said the waiter and began to move toward the back of the restaurant. John followed, wondering who the third person was. Then he remembered that Peter had used the term, "team," last night. John hadn't really given it much thought, but now it appeared that Peter meant the term in the literal sense.

The waiter motioned for him to sit and asked if he would like anything to drink while he waited. John ordered a large glass of tomato juice and took a seat facing the front door. Some old cop habits die hard.

Peter Browning arrived at precisely 7:00 A.M. He carried a briefcase and was accompanied by a slender, attractive blonde woman in her late thirties. John stood up and helped her into the chair on his right. Peter took the chair across from him. His mood was serious and there was none of the calm indifference John had heard in his voice the previous night. He wasn't nervous, but he was very serious and ap-peared tired. The waiter was upon them almost as soon as they were seated, giving them all menus and quickly leaving after asking if anyone wanted coffee.

John asked, "Have you heard anything?" John was wondering if the kidnappers had contacted him. He didn't think they had or he probably would have received a call from Peter.

"No," came the terse reply from Peter. Then he added in a slightly lighter tone, "I trust you had a good night?"

"Yes I did as a matter of fact," and hesitantly added, "and you?"

"Not so good," replied Peter. "It was my daughter that was taken last night after all."

"Yes, but last night you appeared to be taking it rather well. So well in fact, that you had me a bit concerned."

Peter looked him directly in the eyes. "When I get upset or I'm seriously thinking about something, my whole demeanor changes. I'm one of those people who can barely contain a bout of laughter at a church or other serious occasion. It's not that I think anything is funny, it's just a nervous reaction. My reaction last night was one of shock. I shut down. After all, having your child taken is one of a parents' worse nightmares. Mine came true last night. As I told you over the phone, I love my daughter Mr. Harvard. Do not ever doubt that. I have many faults, not caring about my daughter is not one of them. I would gladly exchange my life for hers, even though she may not appreciate it."

It was a speech straight from the heart and John could instantly tell it was true. He was relieved. Last night he had considered the possibility that Peter Browning was somehow involved in his daughter's abduction. He didn't think Peter actually knew she was going to be taken. His reaction to the event told John that, but he did wonder if he had somehow set up a situation where this could have occurred as a result of his actions.

Now, John was pretty sure that wasn't the case. He didn't throw the idea out completely, merely shelved it for possible consideration in the future. If there was one thing he had learned, it was that an investigator needs to keep his mind open to other possibilities, no matter how farfetched they may seem. His mind flashed to the contractor hanging from his staircase. It was a harsh reminder that sometimes even experienced investigators can get tunnel vision to the point that it was obvious to everyone but them that they were on the wrong track. But they refused to see other possibilities. He did not intend to fall prey to that error in judgment again. His police days sometimes felt like a lifetime ago but no matter how much time passed, that hanging man would not let him forget.

Peter spoke, "John, you're probably wondering who she is." nodding toward the woman that accompanied him.

Shaken from his thoughts, John turned and looked at her. She raised her right hand out to shake John's and said, "Hi, I'm Emily Stone and I work for Peter."

John turned to Peter with a quizzical expression on his face. "No, it's not what you think," said Peter. "I'm sure you looked into me and found that I've been a bit of a naughty boy in the past. There's no sense denying it. But I'm happily married now. Sue and her mother taught me that there is a price to pay for everything. In my case, the price, among other things, was a life with my wife and my daughter. It was a stiff bill and not one that I wish to pay again. Emily works for me as a programmer and that is as far as the relationship goes."

Peter turned back to Emily, took her still out stretched hand and started to say, "My name is..." but was cut short when Emily said, "I know who you are Mr. Harvard. As well as being a programmer, I'm a bit of an information freak. I can hack into most any information system there is. Peter has been using me for years to ferret out information about Sue. There are only so many ways you P.I.'s can get information legally. That and Tom, Peter's friend, didn't have the patience to sit for hours behind a computer screen, first trying to get, then scrutinize reams of information to find something useful. I'm sorry, but I probably know much more about you then you would like."

As John looked at her, he realized she really was quite beautiful. Not at all the sort one thinks of as a computer geek. Her skin was naturally pale, but currently tanned. *She must visit a tanning salon*, he mused. Her hair was very long and very blonde. She wore no makeup and John thought she appeared to be a very natural person, no dying of hair and probably rarely wore makeup. She didn't need to. As was his custom, he looked at her eyes, trying to read what was there. They were pale blue and there was a warmth in them that seemed to radiate outward. The mythical Medusa's look could turn a man into stone, a look from Emily Stone could turn a man into water, though hot water it would be. He felt feelings course through his body that he had not felt in a long time. John was amazed that Peter had not fallen victim to her gaze. That spoke volumes about his commitment to his new wife. He thought he saw something else in her eyes. Admiration? But if she knew about his past, he could not figure out how that could be so. He must be misreading her.

He suddenly realized that he was staring and was still holding her hand in his. He quickly let go and turned back to Peter. Peter looked back at him with a knowing smile on his face as if saying, *I'm right there with you pal. She's something, isn't she*? John shook himself a bit. "Alright, so what is it that I need to know and why don't you think Sue's in any immediate danger?"

"As I told you over the phone the other day, Sue has her own company called "Demotic Software," said Peter.

Frowning, John looked at him. John liked things to make sense. He liked to understand everything, even the name of a software company. Some names came into being just because they sounded good to the ear. "Demotic Software," sounded like it had meaning. To John, it sounded awfully close to, "Demonic," and he certainly wanted to know why someone would choose a name like that. "What did you say the name was again?"

"Demotic Software," said Peter.

Emily spoke up and John turned to look at her. "The name comes from Greek origins. It refers to language spoken by common people. You would probably know it as a 'colloquialism.' Basically, what she's saying is that she's producing software for the common person software that anyone can readily understand and use. Quite clever I thought." John nodded his head in agreement.

"Anyway," continued Peter, "she started this company a couple of years ago. She got into it slowly while still working for her previous employer. She wrote up some free-ware and shareware programs that really took off."

Though he didn't know a lot about computers other than how to turn them on and navigate through various windows, John knew what that meant. "Free-ware," was software produced by some geek in his basement and distributed over the internet free of charge. "Shareware," was produced by the same people, but there was a nominal charge, usually around ten dollars. "Shareware," was set up in different ways if you didn't pay the fee. Sometimes you could only use it for a limited period of time, say thirty days. Then, the program simply stopped working. Other times, only some of the features of the program worked until you paid and received an unlock code in return. Occasionally, "Shareware," was set up on the honor system. The entire program worked for as long as you needed it with only your undocumented promise that you would pay for the program eventually. John could see how producing these programs might be intellectually rewarding, but one could certainly not become financially independent from them.

Peter continued, "Do you know anything about computer encryption John?"

"Not really," he replied, "other than I know that when I pay for something over the internet, my credit card info is supposed to be encrypted so that no one else is to able to read it."

"Exactly," Peter continued. "For what you're talking

about, most internet sites use 256 bit encryption. That means that your computer sets out a string of 256 characters as a password that protects contents of that file from being opened and understood by anyone other than it's intended recipient. Those characters can be in any order. That's a long string for someone to try to put back in the correct order. Given current technology, some people say that the sun would burn out before the fastest supercomputer in the world could crack the code on a 256 bit encryption. However, there are even people who are now working on 1028 bit encryption."

"Why would they want to do that if the encryption they have now would take so long to break?" asked John.

"Notice I said 'current,' technology," said Peter. "As computers and programs get faster, so too will be the time it takes to crack the encryption."

Emily interjected, "More to the point, the problem is everything has an Achilles heel. In this case, it's the password used to initiate the encryption, the 'key.'"

"Key?" questioned John. "What kind of key? I thought we were talking about software."

"We are," Emily continued. "This is a software key. As with any code, if someone wants to encrypt something, they have to have a way of deciphering it once it's scrambled, to put it back the way it was originally. They would create a key to unlock the code. But if you created a key that could decipher something and left *that* unprotected, anyone gaining access to your computer system could simply find the file containing the key and use it to unlock your encrypted file. So, you need to protect *that* key with a password."

"Makes sense." replied John.

"And therein lies the problem," said Peter. "Unfortunately, even those of us who know better frequently use passwords that mean something to us. That way it's easier to remember them. Hackers know this. What they do is to find out as much about the person who created the password and start entering that information as possibilities, such as your birth date, the birth dates of your spouse, children, etc. Maybe the name of an old lover, your mother, something that is familiar to you, anything to help you remember. They have hacker programs that will continuously try different combinations until they hit the right one. Some are crude and just randomly keep on trying until they hit. This is called the 'brute force,' method.

Other programs are far more sophisticated. The Secret Service is currently using a program they call 'DNA.' This program searches a target computer's hard drive. It looks at all the plain text there, date books, address books, letters and so forth. It also looks at the web browser logs for that computer and searches the visited internet sites for key words there as well. After all this, it takes the key words it found and uses the 'brute force,' method in an attempt to unlock the key. A few years ago, authorities in England used a similar method to find the password of a white collar thief. The man was into show horses. The password turned out to be the name of a part of a spur."

Emily now picked up the conversation again, "Sue was trying to come up with a better method of encryption. To do that, she was attempting to learn all of the weaknesses of current configurations. In computer school, they teach the students how to hack so that they might prevent hackers from hacking them. Sue was using the same line of thinking. The more she looked into this, the more immersed in the hacking culture she became."

"And now we come to the crux of the matter," said Peter. "What Sue was developing, was the ultimate hacking program. This program silently goes out over the internet and spreads to where ever you tell it to go. It can sit for days, months, if need be. Eventually, it finds its way to the target computer. There, it collects key words, similar to the Secret Service's DNA. But it goes a few steps further. It automatically begins to query databases all over the world, looking for any reference to the creator of the key. That means, birth and death records, real estate records, college records, financial records, even newspaper references. It automatically hacks into those databases *on its own*. Simultaneously, it brute forces random combinations, in case they didn't use a password with meaning. It continues until if finds the password for the key. Then it relays the password back to the originator and self destructs."

John sat for a moment letting this set in. Then he concluded, "But I thought you said the sun would burn out before even a supercomputer could do that."

Peter and Emily looked at one another and smiled grimly. "He listens well," said Emily. She looked back at John. "Other than the fact that I was talking about pure random attempts, you are quite correct. But here is the thing that makes Sue's program so utterly devastating. Besides sending a hidden program out to the target computer, it uses the internet to send out hidden working drones to an unlimited number of computers on the internet. It links them together as one, massive, supercomputer! The Secret Service's system does this to around four thousand computers. Imagine the power of four *hundred thousand* computers linked together, or even more?"

"Are you beginning to understand what this means John?" added Peter. There is virtually no electronically linked institution on earth that would be safe, for years to come, while they attempted to find a counter measure to this program."

John sat in dumbfounded silence and contemplated what he'd just heard. His mind was reeling as Peter continued. "The only system that would be safe, would be those that were on a completely closed network with no access point to the outside world."

John didn't have the knowledge of computers and networks to know how each system could be hacked. But he knew intuitively that the user or users, of this program would have power beyond imagination, especially if they kept it quiet and used it judiciously.

Emily interjected. "The users of this program could quietly move money from any bank account to an account of their own choosing. They could obtain information about almost anything or anyone and as I'm sure you know, information is power. One could use it to make or sell investments before anyone else. It could be used for corporate espionage, to learn of new developments and products. Hell, for that matter, international espionage. The secrets of every security agency in the world would be an open book. It would be a terrorist's dream come true. That alone, would make Sue a much sought after person."

Peter and Emily sat quietly, letting John sort his thoughts. Eventually, he turned to Peter and was about to speak, when the waitress returned. Everyone ordered and when the waitress was out of hearing range, John looked at Peter and stated flatly, "We're in way over our heads. Your daughter could have been taken by anybody, not the least of which is some terrorist group. We need to call the Feds and I mean *now*!"

Peter shook his head and replied, "I think I know who took her. I've had dealings with them in the past through an ex-partner of mine." A grimace crossed his face and John could tell that he was dredging up some unpleasant memories. He continued, "A few years ago I went into business with a buddy of mine from high school. His name was David Hickler. Dave was one of those guys who, though extremely intelligent, was carefree and more than a little reckless. If there was a quicker, easier way to do something, he would take it, and if it wasn't quite ethical or even legal, so be it. Understand, he was basically a good guy, just always looking for the easy way.

I hadn't talked to him in years. Then, I met him at a software conference in Vegas. He too was a programmer looking to shed the constraints of working for someone else. He seemed to have mellowed over the years and came across as a mature, thoughtful person who just wanted to perfect his craft. Well, we talked and he told me that he was working on a program that would compress video to a fraction of its original size and would be completely loss-less."

John interrupted, "Loss-less? What the hell is that?"

Peter smiled and Emily explained, "I'm sure you have seen movies and pictures on your computer." John turned to her and nodded, "Yeah."

Emily continued, "Well those things take up huge amounts of memory space. A single raw movie would take up several DVD's. To counteract that, software engineers came up with programs that would take out some of the information so that it could be 'compressed.' In other words, the less information there is, the less memory space is needed.

The trade off is the more information you take out of an image, the less space it takes up. Unfortunately, the more information you take out, the less quality you have. It's like building a brick wall. Some of the bricks can be removed and the wall still retains its integrity and still looks basically the same from a distance. But, the more bricks you take out, the less stable the wall is and the more noticeable it is. Continue to remove the bricks and eventually you begin to change the look of the wall, the gaps become much more obvious."

Peter chimed in, "I'm sure you've seen movies and pictures that are very small on your screen. Some of those are grainy even then, too much information has already been taken out. But if you try to enlarge the images to make them easier to see, the pictures become blurry and even more difficult to make out. My partner was trying to come up with a video compressor that would allow you to record a two hour movie that would take up very little memory and not lose any information."

"Did he do it?" asked John.

"No, but that's not the point here," said Peter. "I'm telling you this so that you will understand that he potentially had a program that would be worth a lot, and I mean a lot, of money."

"Okay, so where are you going with this? What does this have to do with Susan?" asked John with a puzzled look on his face.

Peter continued, "Dave felt that he was getting close and being typical Dave, he began to get very worked up and excited. He would tell everyone who would listen, even those who did not want to listen, all about his new program. Also being typical Dave, he would exaggerate just how close he was to completing this not so little program and how much money it was worth. I begged him to keep quiet about it, for a variety of reasons. However, the best reason never even occurred to me."

John looked at him, a little bored, a little confused and more than a little exasperated about this apparent running around in circles. "So," John said, "What was the best reason?"

"His son was kidnapped," replied Peter.

CHAPTER

4

John had been looking about the room as he listened to Peter. His eyes scanning the restaurant, mostly subconsciously as he looked for anything out of place without even realizing he was doing it. The building was filling up and the general din was getting louder. But Peter's last statement about his partner's son being kidnapped snapped his attention fully back to Peter.

John's eyes widened. "What? By who?" He had begun to get a queasy feeling about where this was going.

Peter sighed, "There is a loose cadre of individuals, collectively called 'The Coeptus Guild.' It is a group of 'investors,' that specialize in computers, both on the hardware and the software side. Sounds innocent enough. But if you were to look into this company, you'd find that everyone involved is a ghost."

John cocked his head and his eyebrows furrowed. "Not literally of course," continued Peter. "But the names are obscured by a variety of methods. Try to look into it to any depth and you find nothing concrete, like trying to capture smoke in your hands. They do this for a reason." Peter looked briefly at Emily who returned his look with a face so devoid of expression that John couldn't read it. John felt that they were talking to one another without saying anything, the way some people do when they've been together for a long time.

Peter continued, "One night, Dave called me around one o'clock in the morning. He was frantic and so emotionally distraught that I could hardly understand what he was trying to say. He and his wife had been asleep when they were suddenly awakened by a slamming door. They were understandably groggy and if only one of them had been there, it would most likely have been passed off as being nothing more than a dream.

Eventually Dave decided to get up and check the house. He first went to his son's room. There, he found a note taped to the door. The note stated that his son, Billy, was safe as long as he didn't contact the police. The note further instructed him to call a phone number contained in the note.

He placed the call and was informed that he was to go to a designated spot underneath a bridge in the city. He was to be there within twenty minutes or the meeting would be cancelled."

"Smart," said John. "That gives him little time to make plans or to call in any troops."

"Oh, it gets better," said Peter. "They also told him that the person he was meeting with not only didn't know the location of Billy, he didn't even know Billy existed and Dave was informed that he was not to bring Billy up or again, that would be the last he saw of Billy. He was to discuss certain matters with this unknown person and only those matters. The person would then give him another phone number to call. He was to wait ten minutes, then call the number. That number was only good for fifteen minutes."

"Wow," John said. "Those guys were really good. So what happened?"

Peter went on. "Well, he called me and I told him that it didn't sound like he had a choice at that point. His best bet was to do what they said until he knew more about what was going on. The gist of it is, he met with the mystery man. He was informed that they wanted his program. Dave explained that it wasn't completed yet. Like a typical geek, he started to explain all the intricate details of what he was trying to do and the problems he faced. It soon became apparent that the mystery man knew nothing about computers. He was just a walking, talking message box.

When he called the number ten minutes later, he was informed that he was to finish the program and he would not see his son until he did."

John asked, "I thought you said he never finished it."

"He didn't," returned Peter. "After a week, it became evident that something would have to be done. Billy was in kindergarten at the time and his absence couldn't be explained much longer. Eventually, it was agreed that Billy would be returned, but Dave was to complete his work. He was told in no uncertain terms that Billy could be taken again if Dave failed to live up to his part of the agreement or if he tried to bring the authorities into it.

Dave worked like a fiend for months, but he couldn't make it function as advertised. I worked on it as much as I could. After all, I was now the sole income for our little company.

In time, it became apparent that Dave could not make his program work. He received one final call telling him that as long as he mentioned this to no one else, the matter was dropped."

"That's it?" asked John incredulously. "After all that, they just let him go and let the matter drop like nothing happened? That doesn't make sense."

"Like I told you," said Peter, "They are, after all, businessmen. Strong arm, despicable businessmen, but businessmen. Killing Billy and or David would have alerted the authorities and brought on a massive investigation. Especially since they probably figured that I knew about it and god knew who else. A boy, or even a man turning up dead was one thing. A killing of a boy and his Dad on an extortion gone wrong is an entirely different matter. As long as everybody was left unharmed, with the expressed threat of future harm hanging over their heads, chances were excellent it would progress no further."

John said, "So you think that this group is responsible for Susan? Why?"

"After that whole thing went down and appeared to have gone away, I had Tom, my investigator buddy make some discreet inquiries," Peter continued. "It took him a long time and a lot of this is speculation, but eventually he began to turn up some information. Some pretty strange stuff. Turned out, Dave wasn't the first person they had strong armed. Usually, things turned out okay. Some of the people they targeted actually made some good money off from them. Nowhere near the money they would have made of course, but enough to keep the natives quiet, so to speak.

However, as Tom dug further, the more it became apparent how badly it could have gone. He found that though things usually had a safe, if not so happy ending, it could just have easily gone the other way."

"What do you mean?" John queried. He was listening intently now. His exasperation had evaporated and his mind was whirling as he began to form a picture of what had happened to Susan. Though still very concerned about her well being, he was starting to understand Peter's reluctance to involve the authorities. Even now he was formulating a plan that he hoped would lead him to Sue, quickly.

Peter said, "Tom found some situations where people just vanished, off the face of the earth. Did you hear the story of the successful programmer that was found living with homeless people in Texas recently?"

"Yeah," John replied. "He lived in Albany, New York. His wife called him on his cell phone as he was leaving work to ask him to pick up a pizza on his way home. He never arrived and no one had a clue as to where he went. They never even found his car."

"Right," said Peter. "Then a few months later, in a immigration raid on some slums in Brownsville, Texas, he was arrested, along with others. Obviously, he didn't fit in with the rest of the group. The authorities questioned him and found that he had no idea of who he was or how he got there. Fingerprints identified him."

"The Coeptus Guild did that?" asked John.

"Tom could never get anything concrete on it, but it had all the earmarks of one of their shenanigans. That programmer had also been working on a project that was worth a lot of money. He spent months in therapy and eventually got his life somewhat back to normal, but he never marketed his program. There was no point, someone else had just released a program that was almost identical."

"Let me guess," said John. "Someone who worked for the Coeptus Guild."

Peter nodded. "Well, not for them directly, but a company funded by them."

Again, very clever. They didn't miss much. If, by some chance the kidnapped programmer had raised a stink about it, the Coeptus Guild could claim no knowledge of how the company that released the program had acquired the code. Given his memory problems, John suspected that the kidnapped programmer would not be able to provide any details about his strange disappearance. Even if he could, a good attorney would be able to tear the man's story apart in a court room using those same memory deficits. John further suspected that the Coeptus Guild had a team of very good attorneys.

At this point the waitress arrived with their food. They ate in silence, which was fine with John as it gave him time to digest all that he had learned. As they were nearing the end of their meal, John looked at Peter. "Okay. I can see why you think that the Coeptus Guild may be involved and why you don't want to run to the authorities. But what if you're wrong? What if this is nothing more than an abduction for other reasons?"

"John, you are an ex-cop and an extremely competent investigator. You actually saw the abduction go down. Did it look like the sex crazed actions of rapists to you?" asked Peter.

"No," John admitted. "It didn't. As a matter of fact, it was the most professional operation I've personally ever seen. From the time I saw their car enter the parking lot until the time I saw them leave, it was no more than four minutes I know that I upset their time schedule a bit, but they dealt with me and the whole situation in a proficient manner and unfortunately, I was not much of a stumbling block as a whole. More like a hiccup."

"I doubt anyone could ever think of you as a 'hiccup,' John." Emily rejoined with an amused look in her eye. She had not spoken for some time. She was smiling and John was again struck by her soft beauty. He found himself lost in her eyes once more. As before, he could swear he could see something there that had nothing to do with this case. Was he really interpreting this right? Or did she have this effect on all men and they all thought she was interested in them. If that was the case, her life would be hell, constantly fending off the advances of hopeful, unwanted suitors.

Peter spoke and he broke his gaze from Emily and turned to listen. "I'll grant you that there could be some other explanation, so it is imperative that we move on this quickly.

Money is not an issue. Tell me what you need and you'll have it. Do you want me to hire more investigators to assist you?"

"No," John replied. "Not yet. One of the first things I need to do is to check out her apartment. Do you have a key?"

"I don't have a key nor do I know of anyone who does." Peter said. "I think Tom was probably in her apartment from time to time. But I have no idea if, in fact he was, or how he got in, if he did. I pretty much let him do his thing and didn't ask too many questions about how he obtained the information. I was more interested in what he found, not how he got it."

"Okay," said John. "What about an office?"

"Yes," Peter answered. "She rented a cubicle over a bank. It's one of those deals where they take an entire floor and turn it into one room offices. They provide a secretarial pool, fax machines, etc. Depends on what you pay for. You want someone to answer the phone, done. You want your own fax machine, done. They're all add ons. You start with a one room office and go from there. Spartan, but it meets the needs of many budding entrepreneurs with little money perfectly, and no, I don't have a key for that either. I have the address though."

He reached under the table and removed his brief case. He balanced the case on his legs and removed a thick file folder. He handed it to John and said, "Here is a copy of everything I have on Sue that I think is pertinent. Some of Tom's notes are in there as well. At least, as much as I could find in his office. I have more, but it takes up several boxes. You can go through them if you like. I also took the liberty of speaking to Tom's wife and you have permission to go there too and see what you can find.

John took the file. It was heavy and quite thick. Peter said he had boxes of information. John imagined that considering he'd kept tabs on Sue for her entire adult life, that would make sense. But it was kind of scary that anyone's life should be so well documented, even if it was well intentioned.

He opened the file and briefly went through it. He found the name of a bank with an address. "Is this where her office is?" asked John as he showed Peter the paper.

"Yes it is." he replied.

Emily and Peter looked on silently as John continued to peruse the file. He absently heard as the waitress asked if anyone wanted anything else. He vaguely heard them order more coffee and then heard dishes and silverware clink as she cleared the table.

He continued to examine the file for some time, knowing he'd have to go through it again when he had more time. He had to take some notes and he hadn't brought enough paper. Besides, this wasn't the place to do it.

His concentration was broken by the sound of Emily quietly laughing. From somewhere off in the distance, he'd heard Peter telling a computer related joke. The kind that would only be funny to a computer geek. He looked up, feeling a little out of place, like he'd been rude or something. "I need to get back to my place and go through this again," he said.

"That's fine," Peter said. All traces of whatever laughter he'd just been sharing with Emily were now gone. He was deadly serious once again. "Just let me know what you need. Emily is also at your complete disposal. Remember, she has an amazing ability to obtain information. You can have her 24/7, if that's what you need. I'm sure I don't have to tell you, speed is of the utmost importance. I really don't care what you have to do to get Sue back. I'll support anything and I mean anything, you do to get my little girl back safe and sound. That's *all* I care about."

John reached into his breast pocket and removed a piece of paper. He handed it to Emily. "Here is the license plate number of the car they took her in. I tried running it through my normal sources, but it doesn't show up. I'm pretty sure it's a rental. The other number on there is the number off from the bumper sticker that was on it. If you could find out what address the car is registered to, it would be a start.

Emily looked at the note and said, "I can probably do one better. I'm pretty sure that I'll not only find out what address they rented it from, I'll find out who rented it."

John looked at her and thought, *This woman is going to come in very handy*. "Great," he told Emily. "Let me know as soon as possible." He stood up. "Alright," he said. "You'll be hearing from me by noon at the latest. I'm going to go through the file again and probably head over to her apartment. What about your ex-wife, Sue's mother? Would she have the key and would she cooperate?"

Peter looked at him and for once, appeared a little indecisive. "I really don't want her mother to know the extent that I've been keeping track of Sue," he said. "She'd blow a gasket. But I guess her gasket rather than a casket for Sue."

John thought that was a little bit of gallows humor, but he could see from the look on Peter's face that he had no idea of what he'd just said. "I'll try to come up with something and keep you out of it as much as possible," returned John. "I won't tell her about the extent of your involvement."

A look of relief crossed Peter's face. "Thank you."

John turned to Emily and put out his hand. She took it in hers and they shook. "It was nice to meet you," he said.

"It was nice to meet you, too," Again, that softness. Again that look in her eyes. *I could be in serious trouble here*, John thought. "I'm sure I'll be calling you once I get into this."

"I'll be waiting for your call," she replied. "Please don't hesitate. My home phone and cell number are both in there too. Though I've never met her, I feel like she's my sister or something. You've got to find her."

"I will," John replied, though in reality, he wasn't so sure how this would turn out. It didn't appear that these guys made too many mistakes. It looked to him like everything went pretty much according to their timetable. Not that he would have anyway, but the worried look on both of their faces prevented him from saying what his feelings on the matter truly were. "I'll talk to you later." and with that, he turned and strode out of the restaurant.

CHAPTER

5

As John walked back to his truck, he began thinking of what he would do next. He decided to return to Susan's apartment building. Though he couldn't get into the actual apartment right now, he at least wanted to give the place a once over in the daylight. Maybe he could find some evidence that would help him unravel this bizarre case. He really didn't think he was going to find anything useful outside the building but he wasn't sure when he would get inside and it had already been several hours since the abduction. It was probably safe to assume that no one would be entering the apartment anytime soon so whatever was inside would most likely stay intact until he could get in there. At least he could search the outside.

When he arrived, he parked in the same place that he had the previous evening. It was a couple of buildings over from Susan's. His police training had taught him to set up the, "staging," area some distance from the actual crime scene and this, truly, was a crime scene. By parking this far away, he could be reasonably assured that he would not destroy or alter any evidence or clues. "Start on the outside and work your way in." he'd always been told.

The natural inclination of most people would be to go immediately to the source of the action. In the case of a homicide, the body. But one had to keep in mind that the perpetrator had to arrive at the crime scene and they had to leave it. By rashly proceeding directly to the body, valuable evidence could be destroyed or altered. One might drive up the driveway and destroy tire tracks or footprints left by the offender and his vehicle. The offender may have dropped fibers from his clothing or perhaps trailed droplets of blood from himself or the victim as he returned to his car. John had seen bodies left where they lay for hours as technicians painstakingly worked their way to the victim, collecting evidence and photographing their way "in." Only after they were sure they had cleared a path that was free from any such evidence, would the body be picked up and taken away. Even the bag into which the victim had been placed would be in turn, placed into a new, sterile bag that would itself be collected as evidence, in case anything had fallen from the body as it was transported.

Before getting out, he reached into the back and retrieved a digital camera, a small six inch ruler, some plastic baggies containing some swabs and his digital voice recorder. He stepped from the truck and began walking in the direction of Susan's apartment. He slowed as he approached the parking lot and began looking at the snow covered ground. Though it had been very cold last night, it was warming fast. It was still below freezing, but the salt that had been spread on the pavement was beginning to do its work. Most of the tire tracks that were still visible were melted beyond recognition. The few that he could make out were filled with slush tossed up by passing cars. So much for tire and foot impressions.

He moved to the spot where the dark car had been parked. Fortunately, no other cars were presently parked there and he looked around carefully for anything that may have been dropped. There! What was that?

He bent down and looked at a small white cloth that had been folded several times. He looked around him and realized that it was in about the same position as the rear passenger side door would have been in last night. Could they really have dropped something? John wasn't sure if it was from them or not, but decided to collect it anyway. Normally, this cloth would be photographed with and without a scale and measured to at least three of the nearest fixed objects, before collection. But he wasn't a cop anymore and this case would not be going to trial. All he was interested in were clues to help him find Susan.

He reached into his pocket and retrieved one of the baggies. He removed the cotton swabs and used the bag as a glove to pick up the cloth. He knew plastic wasn't the best container for evidence of this sort. The lack of air could cause mold and would cause anything biological to degrade quickly. But it was convenient and he didn't plan on keeping it long. He sealed it and inspected it closer. There appeared to be smudged lipstick on the cloth. Susan's?

He remembered that after the muffled cry and the thump, there had been no other noise. He also recalled that Susan appeared to have been totally limp when she'd been placed in the car. She had given no resistance and had obviously been rendered unconscious. John realized that she'd most likely been drugged and this cloth could have been used to administer the dosage.

He stood up and looked around the immediate area some more. He could see black patches where the tires had bitten into the pavement as the dark car had hastily sped off. At a real crime scene, he would collect the patches in an attempt to chemically match the rubber with the tires of the vehicle. But again, this case was probably not going to court and he already knew what they had been driving. He looked around for Sue's car, a blue two year old Lexus. He saw that it was parked in the same spot where it had been on the prior evening. He didn't see anything that appeared to be out of place or changed since last night. He tried opening the doors but found that they were all locked. He would have been surprised to have found it any other way. John could not see anything else of use in the immediate area, so he began retracing the steps of the abductors.

He found nothing until he got to the front door of the apartment building. He began to carefully look over the area where they had fought. The snow was pushed away in several places, revealing the almost unnaturally green, frozen grass beneath. Obviously the lawns at this place were well taken care of. John could see his footprints leading up to Susan's window. His gaze returned to the area of the fight. Paw prints and a patch of yellow revealed that some dog owner had thought it an inconvenience to walk their dog away from the building. He didn't imagine that the other residents appreciated it. *Just went to show that there are assholes everywhere, even in an upscale place like this*, he thought.

As he surveyed the area, he noticed a few, small, droplet sized, discolored patches of snow. He walked over to them and bent down. It appeared to be blood! He didn't remember any blows that would have caused this and there had been no blood on his own hands. The droplets were near the edge of the grass, in the area where the dark car had stopped last night to pick up the man he'd been fighting with. Could John have possibly caused some damage to the man to make him bleed. A scrape perhaps or a bloody nose?

John noticed the dog prints were also in the immediate area. The blood could also have come from the dog. He looked around at the area again. There were no other drops. He reached into his pocket again and retrieved another baggie. He used a swab to help push the discolored patches into the bag. He knew the swabs weren't the sterile ones normally used to collect DNA evidence, but they were all he had. He just hoped that no one at the factory had sneezed on them or handled them with their hands. After he retrieved the stained snow, he reached in his coat for yet another bag. He used this to retrieve a sample of snow that was not stained.

The slam from a car door caused John to look up. A woman had just parked her car and was heading toward the building. She was looking down and paying no attention to anything but where she was walking. Like most people, she was oblivious to what was going on around her. John quickly stood up and slowly ambled toward the door. As he had planned, the woman got there just before him. He followed her into the vestibule and toward the locked door that allowed entry into the resident area.

"Hi," he said to her, realizing it was the woman he'd seen talking to the teenager last night with her husband. He almost felt like he knew her. He wanted to ask her if she thought her son had absorbed anything from their talk last evening. Instead, he smiled and continued, "Beautiful day, isn't it?"

"It sure is," she replied, while opening the door with her keys. "Maybe spring will be here soon. I heard it's going to be in the upper forty's by the end of the week." She opened the door fully and stepped in.

John grabbed the door and held it open as she entered. Then, he stepped through while saying, "I heard that too. The ten day forecast is predicting, may I dare say it, fifties."

"Oh wow," she laughed. "Well enjoy the day." and with that she walked to the elevator and pressed the button.

"You too," John answered and walked down the hall, out of sight. When he heard the elevator arrive and the door close, he returned to vestibule area to make sure she was gone. He then walked to Susan's door. Being this close to the elevator and vestibule, she must have quite a bit of noise as people came and went. Her apartment most likely had the lowest rent in the building.

He inspected the door and frame around the area of the lock. There were no signs of forced entry. He looked quickly around and then tried the handle. As expected, it was locked. He put his ear to the door and listened. Nothing. He remembered that the television had been on last night. Someone must have turned it off.

He decided he could learn nothing more here so he returned to the area of the vestibule and looked around. It was a good sized area. It had a small table with stuffed chairs to either side. A phone rested on the table and a monitor was located directly above it. Directions on the monitor informed the user to type in the name of the desired person by touching the appropriate letters on the screen. The extension of the person was then displayed and the user utilized the phone to call the apartment. There was a video camera in the corner, near the ceiling. It was pointed down and probably covered almost the entire area. John noticed that the co-axial cable that transmitted the images from the camera, was dangling from the wall, disconnected. It didn't take a rocket scientist to figure out who had disconnected it. It had probably been done some time before the kidnapping, but not too long before because it would have been fixed otherwise. As a matter of fact, John was surprised it wasn't fixed already. That meant that the kidnappers had indeed been there at least once before. If the system was hooked up to a recording device, and John thought it most likely was, that meant that the image of at least one of the men, had to be recorded! He could see no way they could get to the camera without that happening.

He used the monitor and punched up Susan's name. Her extension was displayed and as expected, was not her apartment number. John picked up the phone and called the extension. After four rings, a female, mechanical voice answered, stating that the person called was not available at the moment and gave the option of leaving a message. *Nice system*, John thought and hung up the phone.

Just then, the front door opened and a man in a blue jumpsuit walked in carrying a large toolbox. Patches on his arm indicated that he was from an alarm company. He looked quickly around before centering his gaze on the disconnected video camera. John saw an opportunity. "Hi," he said.

The man looked at him and smiled, "Hi. You live here?" he asked.

"No," John replied. "Just visiting a friend. She's not here. This is a really nice place. I've been looking at apartments and this place looks pretty cool. Pretty good security."

"Much better than most," answered the man, whose jump suit displayed the name 'Pete,' in white letters. "Unfortunately, we occasionally get kids in here that goof around." He pointed up at the camera. "It's been disconnected. It's tied in to the paging system so that the residents can see who's calling them from the phone over there. Some kid was probably talking to his girlfriend and thought it would be funny to disconnect it so she couldn't see him."

"Is that the only time it's active," asked John.

"No," replied Pete. "It's active all the time. But when the paging system is used, it ties into it. The residents can actually see the image whenever they want. There is a small screen right on the paging systems in the apartments. It can also be tied in to their television. They could be watching their favorite show and suddenly get the urge to see what's going on in the lobby. They change the channel and wham, there it is."

"Wow. That's pretty sophisticated stuff. When people do things like that," John pointed to the camera, "I mean, is it live? Do you have someone monitoring it?"

Pete nodded, "Well we can. But we have a lot of these systems in place. We don't monitor them all. We have a guy that sits in a room and if we think there may be trouble, he can call up the screens and get a live feed. Most times though, it just gets recorded. If there's a problem, we can pull up the recorded feed and look at it."

"Can't you go back and see who disconnected the camera? After all, you would think you could see someone walk up to it, then it goes blank."

Pete had put his toolbox on the floor directly under the camera. He stood on it while John was talking and began to screw the cable back in. He looked over at John and shrugged his shoulders, "Eh, sometimes. But usually not, unless there's a break in or some sort of disturbance."

John nodded. "You guys really seem like you're on the ball. I'm assuming you do houses too?"

"Yeah, sure. We'll put these things in a RV if you want. We hook it up with satellite."

"No!" John laughed. "I don't have that kind of money. But a buddy of mine is building a new house and I think he'd love a system like this. Do you have a card?"

Pete stepped down off the tool box and opened it. He retrieved a business card and handed it to John. "If your buddy decides to do this, please have him mention my name. I get a commission if he puts the system in."

John took the card and looked down at it. It bore the name of the company, its address, telephone number and web site. It also had an email address for Pete and his cell phone number. He looked up at Pete, "Thanks." he said. "Well, I've got to get going now. Nice to meet you."

"No problem," replied Pete. "I hope your buddy takes it." He smiled, "It's called job security. No pun intended."

"I understand," said John. "See ya." He waved and left the building.

CHAPTER

6

When John got back to his truck, he used his cell phone to call a number he knew by heart. The police dispatch was answered by a cheerful voice who announced that her name was, "Jenny."

"Hi Jenny," John responded, "Captain Giovanni please."

"Sure," Jenny replied. "Is this John?" Jenny had been a dispatcher starting way back when John was on patrol. She was a very nice person and a top quality dispatcher with a way better than average body. Though she had always, quite obviously, been attracted to him, the feeling wasn't mutual. He enjoyed talking to her, but for some reason, she did nothing for him sexually. It didn't help her crush on him that one night, at a party, things had gotten pretty hot and heavy between them.

Like with all party's involving cops, the liquor was plentiful and free flowing, as were the sexual innuendo's involving the women there. Cop parties attract women like bees to honey and this one was no exception. One thing led to another and the next thing John knew, he was involved in a game of strip poker. He was doing rather well, or to phrase it better, Jenny was doing rather poorly.

John's current marriage was on the rocks, a familiar state to him and to most cops. He was still living at home, but he knew it was over and had already made plans to move in with Nick Giovanni, his partner at the time. Jenny was down to her very brief panties. Unlike most men, alcohol did nothing to curb his sexual appetite. Every time Jenny removed a piece of clothing, she would look John directly in the eyes, letting him and everyone else in the room know that she was doing it for him. John's alcohol sodden brain suddenly could not find a reason why he was never attracted to her for at that particular moment she looked like the goddess Aphrodite, come to life.

John had the winning hand that would have removed her panties. But instead of complying, she announced that she would only remove them for John, in private. This was followed by many guffaw's and much drunken laughter. Jenny stood up, walked over to John, took his hand and led him to the nearest bedroom. She closed the door and was on him in an instant. John responded eagerly. The last vestiges of clothing were removed and hands went to genitals. But right at that moment, there were angry voices and suddenly it sounded like a herd of elephants had entered the living room, bent on destroying it. John dressed hurriedly while Jenny looked for something to put on.

It turned out that one of the girls at the party had been invited by a cop who had stopped to give her assistance when her car had run out of gas. She was an aerobics instructor with a body that one would expect of someone in her profession. She also had a very jealous boyfriend who had followed her to the party. He had watched for a while and quickly figured out that she and the cop would shortly become the beast with two backs. The bad thing for him however, was that he didn't know he was watching a houseful of cops.

But he did know that there were a lot of men in there. So he called a few of his buddies and together, they literally crashed the party. They opened the door, rushed in and the jealous boyfriend immediately planted one on the jaw of the surprised and very drunk cop. That was it. The place went up for grabs. The neighbors soon called the police, who recognized the house immediately. Eventually, one living room, a lot of blood and several broken bones later, the much worse for wear intruders were in custody or rather, quiet enough to be transported to the hospital.

John, had watched the fight from the sidelines, the odds were already way against the invaders and there was no need to get involved. But it had been a cold dash of water on his amorous intentions. He didn't notice Jenny until the beaten amigos had been taken out on gurneys. The victors were busy giving each other the high five, congratulating themselves and as all cops do, reliving the event and their roles over and over, which as everyone knows, is thirsty work. That meant, of course quenching their thirst with even more beer. Jenny wore a man's bathrobe and if anything, the event seemed to make her hornier than ever. John looked at her and knew the moment was gone, not likely to come back. She could see it in his eyes and didn't argue when he told her he was tired and left shortly after.

They had remained friends and occasionally Jenny would make exploratory comments to see if John was coming round. He never did.

"Yeah, it's me," he now told Jenny over the phone.

"How ya doing stranger? Haven't heard from you in a while," she said.

"You know, this and that, trying to make a living," he replied.

"Well, if you need anybody to talk to and all that."

He laughed quietly and said, "I know who to call."

"Alright, hold on, I'll connect you," and John heard himself being transferred.

"Captain Giovanni," Nick answered shortly after.

"Hey Nick, you working hard or hardly working?" said John.

"Hey John, what's up with you?" Nick answered. "What do you want now? You only call me when you want something. You don't even send me flowers anymore." Nick laughed and so did John.

"Well, if you didn't whore yourself out to everybody else who asked, I might be a little nicer to you asshole."

"Yeah, yeah, yeah, that's what they all say." retorted Nick.

"Now that we're done with the preliminaries, I need a favor."

Nick snorted, "I figured you did. What is it this time?"

"I'm on my way there now. I've got some stuff I need

analyzed and I need it right away."

"I don't know John. We're pretty busy right now. We just had a rape/homicide home invasion and the Chief's under a lot of pressure to get this guy. It was up in the Goose Lake subdivision."

John whistled. Homes in Goose Lake started at around five million. That was a large tax base for the city. Not only that, but the residents were big contributors to local politicians as well as various charities. There would be a lot of pressure on a case like that. "I understand Nick. But the case I'm working could easily result in the untimely death of what we hope is still a very much alive woman."

"This sounds like something we should be involved in John."

"You're right. You definitely should be. But at this point, my client wants no police involvement and I reluctantly agree. I'll explain the details when I get there. I need your help Nick because I think this could go very bad, very fast. Not only do I need some stuff analyzed, but I would just feel better if you were aware of the whole thing, just in case."

"Just in case what? I don't like the way that sounds. I'm not used to hearing you talk like this."

"It looks like there are some very bad, very powerful people involved here Nick. It appears that they have the power to just make people go *poof* and disappear. If something unexpected were to happen, I'd feel better that someone else knew about it."

Nick was quiet on the other side. He'd known John Harvard for a long time. He'd been through a lot of shit with him and he knew that John did not scare easily. He'd seen John walk into a bar that was about to erupt in a good old fashion, western type shoot out, where the tables would be turned on the side for protection and the lead would start flying. John walked in like he owned the place. A reliable informant had called the information in just minutes before it was to go down. It was before the days of SWAT, Special Weapons and Tactics teams, and even if they had been in existence, there was no time to get them there.

He and John were just blocks away when the call came through to go to a pay phone. Some information was just too sensitive to put out over the air and it was before cell phones were so common. So John knew before he walked through the door, what he was dealing with. But he was the first one through. It turned out the snitch was right. John stood there and talked to the bar tender, waiting for backup to arrive, hoping nobody would start shooting before they did. The backup did arrive in time and all occupants of the bar were put up against the wall. Every man in the place had a gun and pockets bulging with ammunition. This was not going to be a quick shootout. It was intended to be a shoot-out that was going to last until the losing side were all dead.

John's bravery could not be called into question. So if he was concerned enough to want Nick to know about it, it was serious. "When will you be here?" asked Nick.

"In about twenty minutes."

"I'll be waiting."

John broke the connection on his cell phone and reached into his brief case as he drove. He removed the file Peter had given him earlier and found Emily's number. He dialed it and waited for her to answer.

A moment later, Emily's voice came over the line. "Hello."

"It's me. I've got some information for you. Let me know when you're prepared to copy." While he waited for her, he explained what he had found at Susan's apartment. When she was ready, John read the information off from Pete's card.

"So I take it you want me to hack into their server and try to get the video of whoever disconnected the camera?" Emily questioned.

"Yeah. It was sometime yesterday, almost for sure. It would be long enough before they took her that someone wouldn't readily connect the two incidents, but not long enough that there would be time to fix it. I think they were pretty hot to trot on this, so I would say start maybe a couple of hours or so before the incident last night. I had been there around an hour and a half. So it was some time before that."

"Alright. They probably have their server at the same location as their website. So it shouldn't take long to find it. The question will be how good their firewall is. Considering what they do, it's probably pretty good, so it may take me some time."

"Okay, just let me know as soon as you have something. Anything on the rental car?"

"Not yet," she answered. "I just got into their server when you called so I should have something soon."

"I'm going to be in a meeting for a while, so unless it's earth shattering, wait till I call you. Oh, and one more thing, is Peter in?"

"Yes, but he's on the phone. Do you want me to tell him you're on the phone?"

"No, that's alright. Do you know if he'll be in the office all day?"

"As far as I know." replied Emily.

"Good. Just let him know I'll be in there in a couple of hours. I'm going to want a sample of his DNA."

"To match with the cloth you found?" asked Emily, already knowing the answer.

"You got it," answered John. "I'm going to pick up a kit in a few minutes. I'll be stopping in right after that. I want to get it into the lab I'm using as soon as possible. Anyway, I gotta go now. I'll talk to you later." John broke the connection and rummaged through his file once again. He didn't tell Emily that he was going to lay the whole situation out to Nick. He wouldn't tell Peter either because he was certain they wouldn't approve. But he was going to need Nick's help on this, if for nothing else than a quick turnaround of his evidence. John knew he could trust him. But all Emily and Peter would know was that Nick was a cop and they were more than a little paranoid about cops right now.

He continued going through the file. He was looking for the number for Peter's ex-wife. He was just getting ready to pull to the side of the road in frustration when he finally found it. There were two numbers listed. Neither was marked. He dialed one and received a voice mail message for his efforts. It was a woman's voice and John noticed that she said, "We're not in." Was she remarried? He hadn't thought to ask and the notation in the file merely said, "Dana- Sue's mother," and showed the phone numbers.

He dialed the second number and a woman answered. "Hello."

"Hi, is this Dana Browning?" John asked. There was a pause on the phone.

"Who is this?" came the reply in a suspicious tone and John thought to himself, *I'll bet she's remarried and wants to know why someone is calling her by her old name. Shit! Not a good way to start.*

"My name is John Harvard. I'm a private investigator and I would like to talk to you about your daughter, Susan."

"Why do you want to talk to me about Susan? What's going on here and where did you get this number?"

This was going downhill fast. He had promised Peter to keep his name out of it as much as possible. Given the way things were going already, John had doubts that he'd be able to pull that off. He'd had a cover story planned out before he even picked up the phone. But he hadn't counted on Dana Browning's immediate hostile attitude or her suspicious nature. First he decided, he needed to find out the reason for the hostility.

"Mrs. Browning," he began, wanting to see if that got a reaction.

"It's *Pittman* now, thank you very much," she said in a stern, clipped voice.

Good, he thought. *Now we're getting somewhere.* "I'm sorry, my mistake, Mrs. Pittman. Look, it's obvious we've gotten off on the wrong foot. If you don't mind, let's start over," he requested in his most charming voice. There was a quiet chuckle from the other side and John instantly felt more relaxed.

"I'm sorry Mr... 'Harvard,' did you say your name was?" she asked pleasantly.

"Yeah, John Harvard."

"I'm sorry Mr. Harvard." she continued. "But the name 'Browning,' brings up a part of my past I would just as soon forget. Now, what is this about?"

"Well," he began, "I'm afraid that there's a problem with Susan. I've been hired to look into it. Look, it's very complicated and I would feel better if we could talk about this in person, as soon as possible."

The hardness began returning to her voice. "Who hired you? Why are you investigating my daughter? What's this about? Does she know about this?" The questions came out with the speed of a machine gun and John felt like he was being physically pummeled. He decided it was time to go straight with this woman, as much as he could and still try to keep his word to Peter.

"Your daughter is missing Mrs. Pittman." he said flatly, tired of beating around the bush. He didn't have the time to dance with her on this and it sounded like she was too intelligent and straightforward to fall for any concocted story, at least right now. If the conversation had started differently, before her guard was up, he might have been able to pull it off. But now, all her senses were working at full strength and

John felt that anymore mess ups on his part would turn this into a total debacle.

"What are you talking about? I just talked to her last night. What do you mean she's missing?"

Again, the machine gun questions, with no chance to answer them separately. But now, he heard a note of panic creeping into her voice. Time to counter. He had to get her off the offensive and get her listening. More importantly, he had to get her cooperation.

"Okay, here's the story. She was taken from her apartment at approximately nine o'clock last night by two men. I know because I saw it. I had been hired to find out where she was living and how she was doing. My being there was pure coincidence. I tried to stop them, but unfortunately, I wasn't able to. Now, you need to calm down so you can help me find your daughter."

"My God!" she said quietly. "Are you kidding me? Please tell me this is some sort of demented joke... please." John could hear her beginning to sob. "Why were you there?" she asked quietly, choking back another sob. "I don't understand. It doesn't make any sense." He could tell she was desperately trying to get herself under control. He admired her fortitude.

He'd arrived at the police department parking lot and now he sat in his truck, his mind racing to choose the right words. "Like I said, I was hired to find out where she was living and how she was doing..."

"By who?" Her words were getting sharp again.

"By your ex-husband." he said at last. "I'm sure you

know that Sue won't have anything to do with him. But he really, really loves her. He regrets what he did, but he knows there is no fixing things with you. He also knows that he probably can't fix things with Sue either. But he is concerned about her and wants to know she's all right. So from time to time, he hires someone that can at least tell him where she's living and you know, if she's even married or not. That type of thing. You can agree or disagree with his methods, but if I hadn't been there last night, we wouldn't even know she was taken. So in the end, it was a very good thing for your daughter."

Silence dominated the phone line. Then, quietly, "Why haven't the police called me?"

John let out a sigh of relief. Okay, on to the next step. "Because," he said, "Peter thinks he might know who has taken her. They are a group of men who are always looking for cutting edge technology that they can make a profit on. Their methods for obtaining this information are sometimes brutal and well beyond the law. But I want to stress, a good outcome is quite possible, if we play by their rules and calling the police is definitely breaking the rules."

"How does Peter know about these men?" she asked.

"Because he had a partner who inadvertently got involved with them." John replied.

"And how did that turn out?"

"It was a draw, Mrs. Pittman. The important thing is that no one was hurt. In this case, a draw is not a bad thing. So we have to play this cool. Okay?"

She hesitated a moment before answering, "Okay… for

now. I have to assume that if Peter hired you, you must be the best there is and you know what you're doing He only works with the best."

John didn't know if he was the best or not. But now wasn't the time to quibble over the details. "I'm an ex-cop and I am very good at what I do. Now, will you help me?"

"Yes," she replied. "I'm going to call Peter as soon as I get off the phone you know and *before* I meet you."

"That's fine," he said. "But can you do me a favor and hold off for a couple of minutes? To be frank with you, he didn't want me to mention his name unless I had too. He was afraid of what your reaction would be. By the way, do you have a key to Sue's apartment?"

"He is afraid, huh? Well, it sounds as though he may have learned *something*, from me. Even if it was a little late," she said with a tone used by an exasperated teacher when talking about a student that keeps making the same mistake over and over.

"Now, about that key, Mrs. Pittman…"

"Yes, I have a key, and please," she said, "call me Dana. It looks as though we may be spending some time together. Do you mind if I call you John?"

"No, that would be fine." he replied. "Can I meet with you soon to get the key? I have to get into her apartment and see if there are any clues as to where she may be and who took her."

She gave him an address, in the Goose Lake subdivision, of all places. Looks like she married into money again, though John didn't think that was her purpose in marrying.

He didn't know much about her, but she had all the signs of a classy, strong woman who wouldn't demean herself by marrying for money. They agreed on a tentative time and hung up.

John looked at his watch. He was late for his appointment with Nick. But first he called Peter and told him what had just transpired. "I didn't tell her you have Sue under periodic surveillance," he told him. "Just that you wanted to know if she was even married and how she was doing."

"Thanks," he answered. "I was hoping to not let her know I was involved at all. But believe me, I understand your predicament. When she gets going with that staccato questioning, she's relentless and it's difficult to withstand." With that, they exchanged good byes and hung up. John got out of his truck and walked into the police department.

CHAPTER

7

After walking through the front door of the city Police Department, he stood looking around. Memories flooded back. Though he stayed in pretty regular contact with a few of his old buddies, he didn't come here very often. His nostrils filled with the smell of the building. Sweat, leather, shoe polish, brass polish, gun oil, paper, and a myriad of other smells unique to a building that had served the public in such a manner for so long. There were as many sounds, phones ringing, someone shouting in a room somewhere in the back, hushed conversations, a place of life, of vitality.

He remembered seeing a news story of a structure that was being torn down and replaced by an office building. The place was a police station that was over seventy years old. John had been saddened by the news. He had never been there, it wasn't even in his state. But he thought of all the busy activity that building had witnessed. All the laughter, the tears, the anger, the joy. The stories those walls could tell. After all those years of service, it was being taken down like so much unwanted trash. He imagined that the officers that had served there were probably upset as well. He understood the need for modernization, but did the old have to be totally discarded? Couldn't they have made it a library, a half way house? Something that would have allowed the building to go on living.

An officer was escorting a half naked black man into a back room. The man was handcuffed from behind, sweaty, numerous welts and scrapes over most of his upper torso and a large lump on his forehead. Judging from the way the officer was escorting the man, John figured that at least some of those injuries had been caused by the officer. John smiled and shook his head, some things just don't change. They may have better, fancier equipment, but when it comes right down to it, it's still *mano y mano*, one man trying to do his job. The other, trying desperately to prevent that man from doing so.

He walked up to the front desk and announced to a radio room operator that he didn't know, that he was there to see Captain Giovanni. He was buzzed in a moment later. He walked down the hall to Nick's office and entered.

"Hey John," greeted his old friend. "Shut the door. Why don't you explain to me, exactly, what's going down here."

John spent the next twenty minutes explaining what had transpired. Nick asked a few questions, but mostly listened. "So," John commented at the end of the story, "I think it stinks and I don't like it. But I think Peter's request not to get the police involved may have some merit."

"You realize that if this all goes to hell in a hand basket, you and I could be in a world of shit? I have to tell you, I don't like it. We're accepting an awfully big responsibility here."

"Gettin' a little careful there in your old age?" John sighed with the merest hint of humor. "I know Nick. But what would you do?"

His old partner let out a breath of pent up air and turned his chair to look out the window. He absentmindedly held a pen in his right hand and was quickly clicking it, in and out, in and out, in and out. Finally, he turned back and looked at John. "It sucks!" he declared. "It just fuckin' sucks. I was having a good day. Hell, things have been just peachy for a long time now. Count on you to screw it up."

"Sorry." John responded. "I take it that means you didn't come up with any alternatives?"

"No. As usual, I can't fault your logic. If we do bring everyone else in and the woman turns up dead, we're off the hook, but I sure will have trouble sleeping at night. If we go it alone and she still turns up dead, we're screwed, but I'll at least sleep better knowing we did what we could." After a few moments he added, "I'd say we could try to bring a few guys in that could help us. But if this guild is as powerful as your client thinks, they may well have someone working for them that's on our side. That would screw things up royally."

"I know. I thought of that too."

The two men sat in their chairs contemplating their options. "Alright," Nick rejoined at last. "Where are these samples?"

John reached into his coat pocket and retrieved the three baggies. Nick grimaced as his eyes rolled back. "Oh Lord

John. What kind of evidence gathering is this?"

"Hey, listen asshole, it was the best I had. I didn't think I'd be collecting any blood evidence. It's not what I normally get involved in. The one with the red water is the blood and now melted snow. The clear one is the control sample."

Nick shook his head and reached for his phone. He dialed some numbers and after a moment spoke to whoever had answered. "Ask Tom to come in here, will you?" He hung up. A minute later a kid in a uniform came through the door.

"Yes sir?" asked the kid to Nick. "Tom," Nick responded in a conspiratorial tone, "We need some help here. We've got a very hush hush investigation going on. It's on a need to know basis. Can you keep this to yourself?"

The kid looked at John and then back to Nick. With a serious, but very eager look on his face he replied, "Sure Captain. What do you need?"

"I need you to take this evidence." Nick handed the baggies to the kid. "First, I need you to properly package and process this blood. It is mixed with melted snow. The clear bag is a control sample of the snow. Then you need to take the cloth in that baggie and properly process and store it as well. I'm sure you know this, but keep both of the baggies in case there's any evidence inside them. Then I want you to log them in and get them processed ASAP."

"What case number do I log them in as?" asked the kid.

"Use your imagination," replied Nick. "Chain of evidence isn't as important here as the results. We merely need it as an aid to an investigation. Run trace on both items as well as DNA. Watch and make sure it goes through the system quickly. Report the results *only* to me. Tell no one else, not even your mother. Understand? Oh, and leave a few collection kits out front for me will you."

The kid nodded, took the bags and walked out. "That kid is an officer?" asked John in wonder. "He didn't look like he was more than sixteen.

"He is." laughed Nick. "He's twenty-two and a father already. He served with us as an intern. Once he graduated, with a degree in chemistry, he applied and with a little help from me, was accepted right away. He's very bright and I think he's going to make a first rate Crime Scene Tech." His look and tone grew more serious and he said to John, "What are you going to do next? I take it you want the results run through CODIS?"

CODIS, which stands for Combined DNA Index System, was a national databank of DNA samples. The biggest contributor to date, was the U.S. military. Most states were now adding convicted felons to the database as well. Similar to the strides made when the advantages of having fingerprints on file were discovered, a DNA sample can be run through CODIS, even though the submitting agency may have no idea who the sample belongs to. A computer sifts through all known files, looking for a match. Many cases recently, some of them very cold indeed, had been solved because of CODIS. There were some who felt that this was Big Brother coming to life. John and many victims, as well as their families, strongly disagreed.

"Yeah, run it through CODIS. How soon can I expect something?"

Nick grinned, "There have been some pretty amazing advances in DNA work in the last couple of years. Computer chips are now doing the grunt work. Pretty soon you're gonna have field kits that can analyze DNA pretty much instantly. So to answer your question, I'll probably have something by tomorrow.

"Great!" said John. "I'm going to pick up a key from Sue's mother. Then I'm going over to her apartment and see what I can come up with there. After that, I want to try Sue's office."

"Okay. As you heard, I'm having Tom leave you a few kits, in case you want to try your hand at collecting again." He looked at John with a wry smile. "And as far as your hacker friend goes, I really don't want to know anymore about her. I'm going to assume that any information you obtain was by perfectly legal means. Right?"

"Of course Nicholas," replied John with a smile, shrugging his shoulders and displaying his open hands in front of him in a display of youthful innocence. "You know me, I wouldn't have it any other way."

"Watch your back on this one John. You and I both know that this thing with the Coeptus Guild is probably blown way out of proportion. But if it's not... just watch yourself. Now get out of here asshole, I have important work to do."

John stood up, turned and started toward the door. "Thanks Nick, later."

"Hey!" His friend's voice stopped him and he turned back. Before he could respond, Nick continued. "Thought you said when you left here that cheating wives and husbands were gonna be the height of your excitement." There was not a trace amusement in Nick's countenance.

John grunted, "Humph! God does have a sense of humor, doesn't he?" Without waiting for a response, he turned and left the room.

He picked up the collection kits at the front desk and walked back to his truck. He got in and started driving toward Dana Pittman's house. His stomach growled and he realized he was hungry. But he wanted to get that key first. He wondered how the conversation between Dana and Peter had gone. He smiled and thought, *Better him than me.* John couldn't imagine Dana putting up with any man cheating on her even once, let alone several times. But, as they say, older and wiser and all that.

John picked up his phone and dialed Peter's number. He wanted to ask him how his conversation with Dana had gone. He didn't want to say anything to Dana that would contradict what Peter had told her. There was no answer. He then called Emily and didn't get an answer from her either. *Must be in a meeting together*, he thought. Then he reached down, turned on the radio and listened to some Yanni as he drove the remainder of the way.

CHAPTER

8

John arrived at the Goose Lake subdivision and pulled up to the guard shack that marked the entrance while recalling that the security was known to be pretty good. The entire subdivision was walled in and the streets were patrolled by armed, private security guards. They were supplemented by several off duty police officers who worked the exclusive neighborhood as an extra detail. He stopped at the gate and rolled down his window.

A fat, obviously bored security guard in his late fifties looked at him with a, *What do you want? Can't you see I'm busy reading my paper?* look. "I'm here to see Dana Pittman," John announced. The guard punched some keys on a keyboard. Then he picked up a phone and spoke quietly into it. He hung up and said to John, "Go on in." A security bar raised and a row of tire spikes lowered as the guard was speaking.

He proceeded into the subdivision and began searching for the address. As he drove, he looked around in awe at the homes, which could rightfully be called mansions. Though he'd been through there on many occasions, it never ceased to amaze him that there were so many people that could afford houses like these. But still, they lived and died like everyone else. He thought of the Rape/Murder home invasion that Nick had told him about. The woman had lived a life most people only dreamed of. But now, she was just as dead as any low-income drug addict. Death didn't care what your station in life was. It was the ultimate in equal opportunity.

He found the address and stopped at the gated entrance. An intercom system was provided so that drivers did not have to get out of their vehicles. He pushed the button and waited.

He soon recognized Dana's voice. "Hello John. Please come in. Park near the front door and I'll meet you there." With that he heard the intercom click off. The gate in front of him rolled smoothly open and he drove through.

True to her word, she stood on her front porch waiting for him, arms clasped in an attempt to stay warm. She was dressed in a black sweatshirt with matching pants and white jogging shoes. Instantly, John could see where Susan had gotten her wholesome good looks. Her mother was an older version. Though past her prime, she was still a very attractive woman. He knew that she had to be at least in her early sixties, more likely pushing seventy. But as he approached her, he was hard pressed to see any evidence of that age. She moved with the easy grace of an athlete, and John could only hope that he could move as well at that stage of life. He imagined that she had a smile to match her looks, except she definitely wasn't smiling now.

Concern showed on her face as she spoke, "I talked to Peter and though I wasn't happy with his snooping around in my daughter's affairs, I understand why he did it. I suppose in this case, I should be happy about it. Let's go inside and sit by the fire."

John listened carefully to each word as she spoke in an attempt to figure out how much she knew about Peter's 'snooping,' as she put it. He would have to tread lightly here. He needed this woman to trust him and if she found out that he was misleading her about anything she would most likely close up like a clam and at best, would be antagonistic toward him and his efforts.

They entered a two story foyer area with marble floors. They walked through and turned right in to a magnificent library. He was awestruck. John tried not to let his feelings show as he took it all in. The room was two stories tall with cherry paneling from floor to ceiling. Ornate wood engravings decorated a cornice that ran along the top edge of the walls. A large, warming, fire was burning in a fireplace that was as massively proportioned as the room and sat directly below an equally large painting of Dana and a man about her age. He supposed it was her husband. Though gargantuan in scale, the room had a welcoming ambiance of warmth and security and John felt he could spend a lot of relaxed time here.

Dana saw him staring at the painting. "That is my husband," answering his unasked question. "I think it's a bit garish myself but he insisted. Every married couple in his family is expected to display one." She motioned for him to sit down in a chair in front of the fireplace. "Please excuse my appearance but I decided to get some time in on the treadmill before you arrived. It's a great stress reliever and I can think much more clearly after a good workout."

"No, I understand," replied John. "I feel the same way. Unfortunately, I don't work out nearly as much as I should. So, what are your thoughts now that you've been brought up to speed on everything that's happened?"

"I'm more than a little scared. I don't like calling the police. But I guess I understand why we shouldn't involve them. What do you think John?"

"I'm right there with you Dana," he replied. "Being an ex-cop myself, I have a very strong urge to get them involved. But, when you sit down and analyze it, you find there are few options. Could we be doing the wrong thing? Sure, but based on the information of their past activities, it looks like it's the best course of action, at least for now. Do have anything you want to ask me?"

"Yes," said Dana, "I would like to hear your version of everything and what you think about all this."

So, for the next twenty minutes, John reiterated the story, pretty much exactly as he had just told Nick. Leaving out the fact that he *had* told Nick the whole story as well.

Dana listened quietly, occasionally asking questions. When John was finished, she picked up two keys from an end table and handed them to John. "Here are Dana's apartment keys. The normal looking one is for the main entrance door. The funny looking one is a high security key and that opens her apartment. Do you want me to come with you?"

"No," answered John, "That's not necessary. Thank you anyway. I also want to go to her office and look in her car. Do you have keys for them?"

"Unfortunately, I don't have keys for either one. I've never had a reason to go to her office or drive her car. She may have them at her apartment," she replied in a shaky voice. She shook her head. "I just can't believe this is really happening. She's just a programmer for god sake! I can't think of a safer job. Who would think?"

Her last words had come out as a barely audible croak, her eyes brimming with tears. John wanted to take her in his arms and console her but didn't know how she would react and he didn't want to make the problem worse. Instead he said soothingly, "I'm sure everything will be alright Dana. These people are businessmen. They don't want to complicate matters by harming people unnecessarily."

"But what if she doesn't agree to give them the code? I know her. She can be extremely stubborn. Why did she create such a monster anyway? Why didn't she take more precautions? Didn't she know how dangerous that would be? Why...?"

She was teetering on the edge of hysteria and he was afraid she might fall off. He couldn't afford that, he needed her to remain lucid. "Mrs. Pittman!" John said loudly. She stopped talking and he said in a much quieter, but firm voice, "It will be alright. We'll get her back. I understand that you're upset, but we have to concentrate on the job at hand." He could see that she was working herself into a frenzy. Tears were flowing freely down her face and her shoulders shook as she went into uncontrollable sobbing. He could take it no longer. He got up from his chair and walked to hers. He knelt down on one knee and took her into his arms.

He held her while she cried. He said nothing. *She just has to cry this out*, he thought. They stayed that way for what seemed like hours. In reality, it was only a few minutes. After a while, she moved away from him and said, "Thank you. I'm better now. Can you excuse me for a moment?" John nodded and watched as she got up and left the room.

John returned to his chair and sat, staring at the fire, waiting for her to return. *I just have to get Sue back*, he said to himself. He felt sorry for Dana, for she did not appear to be a women who lost her composure very often. To have lost control in front of a complete stranger must have mortified her. *Oh lordy*, he thought, *Nick's right. This really sucks. Big time*. He studied the fire once more and was soon lost in thought.

"I'm going to have some coffee, would you like some?" Dana's words had startled him. She was standing in the library entrance, looking at him.

"No thanks," he replied. "I really should get going... if you're alright now."

She walked over to him and took both his hands in hers. Her eyes were red, but her self control had returned. "Thank you so much for your understanding. I'm sorry I put you through that. You have enough on your mind without tending to a hysterical woman."

"Mrs. Pittman... Dana, it's no problem. I understand.

Really I do. I have a daughter of my own and I know if something like this happened to her, I'd be a complete basket case. I could only hope I could handle it as well as you."

She smiled ruefully. "I very much doubt that John, but thank you for saying so. Now, is there anything else you need?"

He shook his head. "No. If I do, I'll call you. Will you be at the number that I got hold of you at?"

"Yes. That is my cell phone. Do you have my home phone?"

John retrieved her numbers from a notebook he had brought with him. He had written the numbers in it earlier because he didn't want Dana to see the full file on her daughter. "Is this it?" he asked as he showed her the number. "Yes it is." she replied.

"Good. I'll keep you informed. I'll let myself out, if that would be alright. You go pour yourself a cup of coffee and relax in front of that wonderful fireplace of yours."

John walked back to his truck and got in. He started it and tried Peter once more. Hmmm. No answer. He looked up Peter's cell phone number and tried that. No answer there either. He tried Emily again and this time she did answer.

"Hello?" she said.

"It's me. I just left Dana Pittman's house. I've been trying to get hold of Pete. Do you know where he is?"

"No," she replied. "I haven't seen him since this morning. I don't know where he is."

"Crap!" retorted John. "I have some things I wanted to

discuss with him. Do you have anything back on the rental car yet?"

"As a matter of fact, I do," she answered. "The car was rented at the airport to a man by the name of Leonard Sipolski. He rented it yesterday morning and brought it back last night. He used the agency's express return so I can't give you an exact time. He paid in cash. It was actually rented for three days and that's what he paid for."

"Didn't he have to give them a credit card for a security? What about a driver's license?"

"Yes. He gave them both. I've run down the information on them and you're not going to like it."

"Let me guess, there's no such person as Leonard Sipolski," John asked with an air of resignation. He really hadn't expected anything less.

Emily responded, "It took me quite a while, but I found that there is a Leonard Sipolski. The bad news is that he is three years old."

"That figures," replied John. It was the newest rage with scammers. Use the social security number of infants to create false identities. The chances were good they wouldn't find out about it until they were old enough to get a job and apply for credit of their own. Then, they would find out that not only did they already have an established credit rating, but in most cases, it was bad.

"What about the video feed from the alarm company?"

"I was able to get into their server and I pulled the file for that day. I'm going through it now, but when that cable was pulled, it just went blank. Nobody approached the camera."

He thought about it a moment and said, "I can only think of one way for that to happen. Someone must have entered the resident area of the building, then waited for a while before coming back out into the vestibule. If they stayed close to the wall, it would be possible for them to get under the camera without being seen. That camera was mounted with the assumption that anyone that would disable it, would have to first enter the building and disable the camera before trying to get into the resident area.

"But, if they're *already* in the resident area, it wouldn't pick them up until they were a couple of steps from the interior door. Whoever disconnected that camera is on that video. It's a matter of going back far enough and then figuring out who."

"Somebody thought this out. How do we know which person on the video is the one who came back out and disconnected the camera?" Emily asked.

"I don't know," said John flatly. "Let me think about that. Do we have a copy of the file so you don't have to go rooting through their machine again?"

"I'm almost done, but it's still downloading. It's quite a large file."

"Good! I'm on my way to Susan's now. When you see Pete, ask him to call me."

"I will. Good luck at Susan's."

"Thanks," said John and broke the connection.

CHAPTER
9

John disconnected his call and proceeded to put his truck into gear. As he did so, his gaze fell upon the DNA test kits Nick had given to him and a thought came to him. He put the truck back into gear and redialed Dana. She answered on the first ring. "Hello."

"Dana, it's John. I'm sorry to bother you again but I was wondering if you could do me a favor?

"Sure," she replied. "Anything I can do to help."

"Thanks. I'd like to come back there and get a DNA sample from you. I was going to have Pete do it, but I'm having trouble getting hold of him. I'd like to get this to the lab as soon as possible so they can compare any DNA on that rag I found with yours. I'm sure you know that a relative's DNA is similar enough to tell us if it was used on Emily."

"I understand. Did you try him on his cell phone?" Dana responded.

"Yeah, I did, a couple of times. Emily doesn't know where he is either."

"That's very odd." said Dana. "He always carries that

cell phone with him. He even takes it to bed at night. He's one of the easiest people in the world to get hold of. Did you try Patti, his administrative assistant?"

"No. To tell you the truth, I didn't even know he had an assistant. He always answers the number he gave me. It was my impression that Emily was his right hand. How do I reach this Patti? Do you have an extension or something?"

"That number you have is his direct line. Most people don't have it." She then gave him Patti's phone and extension. "When will you be here?"

"I'll be there in a moment. It should only take a minute of your time." They hung up shortly after. John was beginning to get an uneasy feeling about Peter's dropping out of sight. It was probably nothing. But apparently, Peter was always accessible and with everything that was going on right now, he thought it strange, at the least, that Peter should do a disappearing act now. It could be he was in a hurry to go somewhere and simply forgot his phone. It'd happened to John occasionally. Could be just a coincidence. The problem with that line of thinking, however, was that John was not a big believer in coincidences.

He stopped at Dana's and collected the DNA sample. He then drove to the station and dropped it off with Nick. He sat in Nick's office and brought him up to speed about his meeting with Dana and his difficulties in getting hold of Peter. "This thing just keeps going from bad to worse." Nick said to John. "What do you think it means?"

"I'm not sure," replied John. "One of three things. One, he simply forgot his phone. Possible and the option that I hope is the correct one. Two, He's involved in this somehow and took a powder. Given the effort he's put into finding her, I don't think that it's likely. Three, the big one. He's been taken as well."

Nick looked at him, his eyebrows furrowed in concentration. "That would make sense," he said, "if Sue wasn't cooperating and they needed someone to use as leverage to make her see the light. But, assuming they know at least something of her background, why not take her mother? She'd be an easier target and she would mean more to Susan."

John spoke, "Dana Pittman would not be as easy a target as you might think. You know the security at Goose Lake. Her house is no slouch on security either and there are a lot of people working in and around the house. Peter, on the other hand, is out in the open. He has his own entrance to his office and he's constantly out and about."

"Do you know if his car is in the parking lot?"

"No," John replied. "I don't know what he drives, for one thing. This is all just coming about. I've been concentrating on finding Sue. It never occurred to me that they might snatch Peter. Look, let's not put the cart before the horse. I'll drop by Peter's office on my way to Sue's apartment. If his car is there, he's most likely, innocently, in the building, unaware of the panic he's causing. We'll do a search of the building and try to locate him. If his car is not there... well... he may be out running errands, forgot his phone and doesn't want to bother going back."

"Yeah, right!" Nick snorted. "And you'll be receiving a phone call from Sue any minute now asking you to pick her up."

John shook his head, "I'm just trying not to jump to conclusions. With our suspicious nature, we know how easy it is to do. I also know that I know very little about Peter's habits and even if I did, this incident could throw anybody's routine out of whack.

"The problem with that theory," replied Nick, "is that Dana told you he always carries his phone with him and that he's the easiest person in the world to get hold of." He picked up his phone and while he was dialing, said to John, "I'm going to run his name for plates."

A moment later, Nick jotted down a list of plate numbers and vehicle descriptions. He hung up the phone and handed the information to John. "I'm betting he drives the BMW."

John stood up and took the paper from Nick's outstretched hand. "Yeah, you're probably right. Alright, I'm gonna to get going. I've got a lot to do today. I'll keep you posted."

Nick remained seated and said, "You're carrying your gun today, I hope."

"Nah, not yet. Didn't see anything that I would be doing yet that would necessitate it. But now that it looks as though this may have been taken to the next level, I guess I'll stop by the house and pick it up. See ya."

John left Nick's office and walked to his truck. He had told Nick that he was going to stop by Peter's office first but as he walked, he decided that Peter's office was too far out of the way. He wanted to check out Sue's apartment first. Besides, he was thinking that he would see if Emily would go with him to Sue's office. She was the computer guru after all and would be the one to make the most sense out of whatever was on Sue's work computer. So he could check on Peter's car when he picked up Emily.

As he approached Sue's building, he once again scanned the lot for anything out of the ordinary. He didn't see any familiar vehicles with the exception of Sue's car, which remained where it had been parked earlier.

He walked into the vestibule and began selecting the proper key. He glanced up at the video camera as he was reaching for the door. It was disconnected again! He stopped short and stared at the camera, trying to decide what it meant. Had they come back? But why go through the trouble of disabling the camera again? They'd already pulled off the most ticklish part of the scheme. They'd already shown they could get into the apartment without any obvious signs of a break-in. He remembered that the security guy had said that it was not an uncommon occurrence for someone to unplug the camera. He stared at it a little longer while weighing the importance of the detached cable.

John finally decided that it was probably nothing and unlocked the main door. He shook his head, if this happened all the time then the security wasn't all *that* great after all. He proceeded to Sue's apartment and opened that door as well. After closing it behind him, he stood still, surveying the area in front of him.

The living room was a large area with wood floors and a fireplace located on the left side. The fixture was encased with marble and had an ornate, stone mantel that gave a modern, upscale feel. The rest of the room was an eclectic mix of new and old. The furniture was composed of modern teak, metal and glass, while the wall coverings, window treatments and picture frames, gave the feel of an old English mansion. A large grandfather clock stood on the wall opposite the fire place, between two doorways that John assumed were bedrooms.

Beyond the living room was the dining room, that was decorated in a modernistic fashion. To the right of the dining room, only partially revealed from this viewpoint, was the kitchen. As John walked further into the room, he could see that the kitchen also had a clean, modern feel with cherry wood cabinets, marble counter tops and a ceramic tile floor. *Very nice for an apartment, must be a condo*, he thought.

He looked at the dining room window that faced the door. That was the window that he had tried to hear through last night. He stopped walking and looked around, trying to spot anything that was out of place. Anything that would give him a clue as to what had happened. He looked for blood. If the blood he had found actually was from the man he had fought with, maybe his injury had been sustained in the apartment. Nothing. Where was the television that had been giving off the flickering light last night?

He found it in the kitchen. It was attached to the underside of one of the cabinets and was a seventeen inch LCD model. He noticed that it was not on. He looked for a computer, a briefcase or papers. He didn't find anything. He decided to look in the bedrooms. She probably had one of them set up as an office.

He entered the first bedroom. It was large, with a separate bathroom and a large, walk-in closet. A small desk sat in one corner along with the peripherals of a computer, but no computer. *She must have a laptop computer*, he thought. He walked to the desk and began rummaging through its drawers.

His cell phone rang. As he was reaching down for it, he saw a motion out of the corner of his eye, coming from the direction of the closet. He immediately saw that it was a man and the man was raising a gun! John unclipped his cell phone and with one, smooth motion, sent it sailing in the direction of the intruder.

This caused the man to avert his gaze to the flying phone and caused his reflexes to point the gun upward as well. John knew that he couldn't outrun a bullet and his only chance was to try to grapple with the intruder. He took advantage of the distraction by rapidly closing the gap between them. The man quickly recovered and fired a shot in John's direction. There was a dull "Thwap," from the silenced weapon, but he felt no searing pain to indicate that he was hit.

The man didn't have time for a second shot before John was on him. With his left hand and forearm, he used an outward blocking motion to strike the attacker's right wrist in an effort to dislodge the gun or at the very least, change the direction of the barrel. Then, while continuing his forward progress, he used the protruding knuckles of the fingers of his right hand and struck a direct blow to the intruders throat. John felt the knuckles bury themselves in the man's larynx. A good, solid blow.

But the attacker did not lose control of the gun! Instead, he finished the arc caused by John's blow to his wrist, by continuing out and then upward motion that finished by the intruder changing the direction of his gun hand again and bringing the weapon down directly onto John's head.

Both men went down to their knees in agonizing pain. John saw through a hazy film that the man was slowly bringing the gun upward once again and was aiming directly at his chest. With what little strength he had left, John fell back onto his left elbow. At the same time, he managed to snap his right foot up in an arcing motion and struck the attackers right wrist once again. Success! This time the gun flew from the man's hand and into the wall of the walk-in closet.

John fell to his side and rolled toward the gun. He retrieved it and tried to bring it up toward the assailant. But he was half laying on it and John was having trouble summoning the strength it took to roll off the gun and then raise it. He looked up at his attacker. The man was wheezing and gurgling. Both men looked each other in the eyes and both knew that the proverbial hunter was about to become the proverbial hunted.

The man decided it was time to get out. While clutching his throat, he stumbled to the bedroom door and disappeared. A moment later John heard the front door open and close. As he began to drift off, he realized that the man's face was familiar. But from where? His last thought as he lost consciousness was, *I'm going to have to remember where I know him from*, and then he thought... nothing.

CHAPTER
10

From a million miles away, John heard his cell phone ringing. He opened his eyes and looked around. A fur coat dangled directly above his head. He attempted to sit up, but the movement made him dizzy and a wave of nausea overcame him. He laid back down again. Where was he? Why was he here? Why did his damn head ache so bad? And who the hell was calling him? Then, blackness.

That damn phone again! This time, he made no attempt to answer it and eventually it stopped. He just laid there collecting his thoughts. Gradually, it began to come back to him. By the time the insistent phone rang once again later, at some indeterminable amount of time, he remembered where he was and what had happened. Unwilling to face another wave of nausea, he decided to roll over to where the phone lay instead of attempting to raise himself off the floor. The spinning motion almost caused him to go to blackness land once again but he balled his fists, gripped tight, held on and answered the phone before it stopped.

"Hello," he croaked.

"Daddy, where have you been?" asked his daughter, Mary Kate. "I keep calling, but you don't answer."

He desperately tried to collect himself. He couldn't let her know his condition. "I've been working angel. You know that Daddy sometimes doesn't answer his phone when he's working." He paused, summoning the strength to push himself upright, pulling his knees up and began massaging his head with his free hand as he spoke. He had a huge welt just to the left and forward of the center, close to his forehead. Lucky there. The very top of the head isn't too good at stopping things. Apparently, nature decided that most people would face their attacker head on and therefore reinforced the forehead accordingly. His daughter began speaking again.

"I know you don't answer if you're working." said a very dejected sounding six year old. "I'm tired of being at mommy's. She said we were going to do lots of fun stuff, but all she does is talk on the phone." His ex-wife, Shelby, was on vacation and had taken Mary Kate for the week. John had a nanny that came in to get Mary Kate off to school if he had to leave early. She also cleaned the house and sometimes even stayed there if John had to go out of town. But it was convenient that this case came up when Shelby had her.

His voice was getting stronger, "Mary Kate, do you mean to tell me that you've done nothing fun since you've been there?"

"No!" she replied. John collected his thoughts and said, "Wait a minute. Didn't you tell me that you went to the zoo?"

"Yeah."

"And didn't you say that you rode the roller coasters all day yesterday," he continued.

"Yeah."

"Well then, how can you say all she does is talk on the phone?"

"Well, she's been on the phone a lot *today*," replied Mary Kate.

John grinned in spite of his pain. Oh the energy and the patience, or lack thereof, of a six year old. "If mommy's on the phone now, then how are you calling me?"

"I'm using her cell phone, of course," she responded indignantly, as if the answer were obvious. Which of course, it was. But John's muddled brain still had a lot of cobwebs in it. He softly chuckled to himself. *I'm using her cell phone, of course*, she had said. It never ceased to amaze him that this little girl that he had first seen as a completely helpless, bloody, tiny creature, was able to say such adult things in a mere six years.

Not long ago, he recalled, he had gone through the house, looking for her. When a six year old is quiet for more than a couple of minutes, it would behoove one to find out what they were doing. He found her in her room. She was laying on the floor, her head propped up on a pillow. Her knees were raised and she had them crossed. She had the cordless phone propped between her shoulder and her cheek and she was laughing while talking to one of her friends. "Who are you talking to?" he asked.

"Nina." came the reply. Nina was one of her best friends from school. "How did you get her number?" he had asked. He received look of complete exasperation as she replied, in the same indignant voice she had just used a moment ago, "I looked it up in the school directory! Daddy, can we talk later?" He knew then, that this stage of life, where she was his baby and completely dependent on him would be over way too soon.

His thoughts returned to the present. "So why are you calling me now?"

"Because I'm bored." came the answer.

"Well, angel, I'm sorry, but I'm kind of busy right now. Can I talk to you later?"

"I guess so." she said dejectedly.

"Okay, I love you." he said.

"I love you too, Daddy." came the reply and she hung up. He felt a little guilty, but he had to get moving.

The gun! He just remembered that he had the man's gun. He slowly rolled back over to where he had awakened. There, amongst the shoes, he found it. It was an old Charter Arms, six shot, revolver. It had a much newer looking, hand fashioned silencer attached to the front end. He imagined that the shooter had most likely purchased the silencer from some guy who made it in his basement. It really wasn't all that difficult for a person with even rudimentary metal working skills.

It was a .22 caliber revolver. Most people think of a .22 as basically a toy, which for the vast majority of people, it most certainly was. As a Boy Scout, John himself had learned to shoot with a .22 rifle. He had found that he loved it! There was no recoil to speak of and the smell of the cordite, the sharp, "crack," of the gun going off, was exhilarating to him.

But once he became a policeman, he learned what a deadly round the .22 really was. True, it didn't have the mass of the larger rounds. But it had the speed. The speed, coupled with the lightness of the round, caused the bullet to behave erratically and had the potential of causing tremendous damage. Sometimes the bullet would enter flesh and go straight to its target. Sometimes the bullet would enter at, say, the shoulder and would wind up in the leg, causing damage the entire way as it tumbled through the body. Still other times, the bullet would strike a victim's waistband, catch the elastic material of the underwear and travel around and around inside the underwear like an orbiting planet, until it finally stopped, causing no discernible damage to the victim.

But professional hit men loved it. It was cheap, easy to conceal, light and could be silenced easily. If used efficiently, it was a deadly killer. The emphasis here is on the word, "efficient." Some years ago, a high profile Chicago mobster had been walking to his car one day when two men approached him. They used a .22 and put several bullets in his head, then walked away.

What they didn't realize however, was that though the .22's had entered his outer skull, they didn't penetrate the tough sac that holds the brain. So, just like the example with the underwear, the bullets whizzed around between the skull and the sac until they came to rest. The mobster went down and played dead.

After they left, he got back up. The people who had ordered the hit thought that the mobster had been talking to the Feds. He had not been. But after he arose from the dead, he began singing like a canary, albeit a canary with a really bad headache. The two guys who had botched the shooting were found a few days later, in the trunk of a Mazda. They were dead of course, shot once through the heart with... you guessed it, a .22. The people who had taken out the two guys in the trunk, *they* had been efficient.

He held onto to the gun as he crawled toward the doorway of the closet and used the frame to pull himself to his feet. He felt sick, but shrugged it off as he slowly moved to the chair in front of the desk. He put the gun down, sat there a moment before renewing his search of the desk. His fingers felt like they were the size of sausages. Because of the presence of the intruder, he doubted that there would be anything of interest in the apartment anyhow. The intruder! *That's right*, he remembered. *I've seen him somewhere before. But where?*

He finished his search and moved into the kitchen. He was getting control of his nausea and now found himself extremely thirsty. His tongue felt like it was twice it's normal size. He poured himself a glass of water, brought it to his lips and hesitated. He was afraid that if he drank it, he would be sick. He decided, instead, to use the water just to wet his tongue and lips. He took a little sip, savored it's coolness, it's wetness, and spit it out in the sink.

He decided that there was nothing of use in the apartment and left. As he approached the front door of the building, he stopped. Looking out through the side door windows, his eyes searched the area for any sign of the intruder or a backup. He didn't see anything. He began walking toward his car and somewhere along the way, decided that if there was a second shooter waiting for him, so be it. He felt like shit and if the guy was any good, he wouldn't feel a thing, not even this wracking headache or his upset stomach.

As he drove to Peter's office, he briefly thought about calling Nick. Nah, wasn't worth the effort. Besides, Nick would just bitch at him for not getting his gun first as he had promised to do. Then he thought about calling Emily, to let her know he was coming and to tell her what had happened. Nah, not worth the effort either. What he really wanted to do was lay down somewhere and go to sleep. But he knew he couldn't. First of all, there were things to do. Sue and possibly Peter, were out there somewhere. Second, he didn't know if it was true, but he had always been told that concussion victims should stay awake.

So he spent the rest of the time driving, trying to force his poor brain into remembering where he had seen the intruder's face before. He replayed the entire incident in his mind and eventually came up with some nagging questions. Had he interrupted the shooter's own search of the apartment? Or, more worryingly, was the shooter there waiting for someone? Like John? If the shooter was there for him, how did he know when he would or even if he would, get there? The word "coincidence," came to mind once again, and everyone knew what John thought about coincidences.

John pulled into the parking lot and used the makeup mirror in the truck to check himself. There was a trickle of blood on the top of the welt. Not much and he used a tissue to clean it up. He didn't want to walk into an office full of computer geeks looking like a movie extra from "Fright Night." Fortunately, his full head of hair hid most of it.

Before getting out, he put the truck into gear to check the parking lot for Peter's car. He'd almost forgotten to look. It told him his brain was still not firing on all cylinders. A moment later, his heart skipped a beat when he saw the car parked in a spot labeled, "President." *Shit*! he thought. *Well maybe he'd gone out and was now back.* He parked his truck again and walked into the building. It was a four story structure with lots of mirrored glass. He discovered that Peter's company took up the entire first floor.

He found the reception area and approached a pert blonde sitting behind a desk she greeted him warmly. He put on his best smile to cover up the fact that he was in no mood for pleasantries. "Hi, my name is John Harvard and I'm here to see Peter Browning."

She smiled back and said, "Just a moment." She picked up a phone and dialed it. A moment later she softly spoke into the phone, "Hi Patti, there is a John Harvard here to see Mr. Browning." A few seconds later, "Okay, I'll tell him." She looked up at John. "His assistant is going to let him know. Someone will be with you shortly."

John felt some relief. They seemed to know where Peter

was. "Okay," he answered. "Could you tell Emily Stone that I'm here?"

"Sure," and the receptionist dialed Emily. A moment later she told John, "She'll be right here."

Emily walked into the reception area with a shocked, ashen look on her face when she saw him as she said, "My God John, are you alright?"

He gave her one of his most charming smiles and as normal as he could, replied, "A little worse for wear, but why do you ask?"

"Well," she stuttered, "No offense, but you just look terrible." John walked over to her and put his hand on her shoulder.

"I'm fine," he said softly. Their eyes locked and he was again taken aback by her quiet beauty. "Let's go to your office and talk." They walked down the hall and as he closed the door behind them, he continued, "I didn't think I looked that bad." She sat behind her desk and he took a seat in a chair on the opposite side. He told her what had happened at Sue's apartment. When he finished, she started to say something, but he cut her off, "Where's Peter? His car is in the parking lot, but he's not answering his cell phone or his direct line." He realized how gruff he sounded and added, "Sorry, you were saying something?"

"I was just going to ask if you knew who the man was?" she responded.

He shook his head, "No, I don't. When's the last time you talked to Peter? I'd really feel better if I knew where he was."

"Why?" she asked. "Do you think something has happened to him too?" A worried frown creased her beautiful face. As she talked, she picked up the phone and dialed. A moment later, she spoke into the phone, "Hi Patti. Do you know where Pete is?" She listened to the response and looked up at John. "She says they're looking for him, but he doesn't seem to be here. Patti says that's strange because she called his cell phone and heard it ringing in his office. She went in, but he's not there. They're going to look in the building's cafeteria."

John bolted to his feet. "Where is this cafeteria? I want to..." he suddenly felt very faint. His legs folded beneath him as he fell back into his seat. His fingers tightly gripped the arms of the chair as he fought to remain conscious. He was vaguely aware that Emily had rushed to his side. She knelt down and was saying, "John, John, are you alright? I'm going to call an ambulance." She stood up and moved toward her desk.

His head was beginning to clear. He reached out and grabbed her hand, "No, please. I'll be fine. Just give me a minute." She turned, knelt in front of him again and placed her other hand over his. Her thumb caressed his hand while she waited. He closed his eyes and they remained in that position, holding hands, while his brain continued to sweep aside the cobwebs. Her skin was so soft! Eventually, he looked at her and smiled. "Whew. I guess I won't do that again anytime soon."

"I still think you need to go to the doctor," she responded as she pulled his head forward and gingerly parted his hair to examine the wound with one of her hands. leaving the other in his.

"I probably do, but I don't have time. Now it looks as though Coeptus Guild has two people."

Emily stood up and John let her hand slip away. He wanted it back and was thinking of a way to accomplish that mission when Emily declared, "Then you at least need to sit a while."

"Fine," he replied. "I want to go to Sue's office. Will you go with me? After all, you're the computer expert and you know her pretty good as well. We're burning daylight here and if you come with me, you might be able to pick up on something that I would not. It would save a lot of time."

"Okay, but I really think you should sit a while. I could have some food brought in. Maybe that would help. Do you think you could eat something?

He shook his head and said, "No, but I might as well do something constructive. Have you finished looking at the surveillance video of her apartment?"

"Yes," she responded. "I didn't find anything. No one approached the camera. It just went to snow. Any chance that the connection was loose and it just fell off?"

"I really doubt it," he answered. "But I have a theory on that. Can I look at the footage?"

"Sure," she said. She reached over her desk, turned her monitor around and moved the keyboard so that John could reach it. She brought up the file and punched a few keys. Soon the video began playing. The time displayed was 11:02 A.M., hours before the abduction. He could see the vestibule area. A woman came out of the resident area at 11:33 A.M. He couldn't see her face as she walked away from the camera, but he could tell it wasn't Susan. Emily fast forwarded the tape, stopping when he asked her to. Suddenly, as John looked on, the picture went to snow. The last time recorded was 4:59 P.M. No one else had come or gone from the building. Quiet building!

"How do you operate this thing?" he asked. She showed him the controls and John moved the controller so the movie would start where she had started it, at 11:02 A.M. He started the movie and then hit the rewind button. The effect was to play the movie backwards. It began to do so, but in real time. He pushed another button and the movie sped up.

"Do you really think it's further back? That's a long time for someone to be standing in the hallway," she said.

"What if they weren't standing in the hallway? What if they were in Emily's apartment, waiting for the right time to disconnect the cable?" he responded. "I found a flaw in the system. If you come out of the resident door and keep your back tight against the wall, it's possible to slide over to the camera without being seen. The system assumes that anyone disabling the camera would come in from the outside. It doesn't take into account that someone who's *already* inside would want to circumvent the camera."

He continued playing the tape backwards, periodically stopping when a blur told him that someone was entering the vestibule area. He looked carefully at each person. She showed him how to take a, "snip," or a still picture of the person on the video. He didn't know who he was looking for, exactly, or what. He hoped that eventually, one of these faces would turn up again in his investigation.

When the tape displayed a time of approximately 9:30 A.M., the going got slow. All sorts of people were coming and going and it was painstaking work. It took a lot of time to study each face, grab a picture and save it. Suddenly, at a display time of 7:47 A.M., John froze in his seat. There was a man in the frame. He was not looking at the camera, but straight ahead, moving from the main door to the door leading into the resident area. There were several people coming out at the time, blocking the man's face from the camera for the most part. Probably planned it that way. But there were a few frames that clearly showed the man's features before he disappeared from view. John Livingston Harvard recognized the man immediately.

It was not a face he would soon forget. It was the man with the gun in Susan Browning's apartment! What's more, it suddenly clicked where he had seen that face before. He remembered the pictures in Sue's file. It was Susan's mysterious boyfriend.

CHAPTER
11

"Holy shit!" he exclaimed. "I know that guy."

There was a sharp intake of breath as Emily said, "Really? How do you know him?"

"He's the guy that tried to shoot me in Susan's apartment. What's more, he's Sue's mystery boyfriend. This explains a lot. This guy's in it up to his eyeballs. He knows her schedule, has access to keys to her apartment and probably knows what she's working on." He went on, his adrenaline pumping to the max, pushing his brain to full capacity. "I need to go over that file again, try to find that Jeep. I need to go back to that apartment and see if I can recover any prints that can help identify this guy. I should probably go over Peter's friend's files too."

He had been talking slowly, more to himself than to Emily. He hadn't even been looking at her, but at the picture frozen on the monitor. He looked at her now and saw that she was just sitting there, with a strange look on her face. She suddenly smiled and said, "Whoa there boy. Remember your head? You need to slow down a bit. Do you really think he's involved? Maybe he just happened to be there and thought you were a burglar. Tom Weaver never said anything about that guy being suspicious or dangerous, just that he didn't know anything about him."

"Too big a coincidence!" John stated flatly, "and why would he try to kill me? And you don't need a gun with a silencer to stop a burglar. I need to make a phone call. I've got a favor to call in. Is there someplace I can go? I don't want to bother you."

Emily stood up. "You can stay here. I'm going to check with Patti to see if they've made any progress in locating Pete. Take your time."

After she left, he closed the door and used his cell phone to make a call. A male voice answered, "Hello?"

In a loud and happy voice, John said, "Hillbilly! How's it going?"

"Great," replied Hillbilly jauntily. "Good to hear from ya. What's going on with you?"

William—Bill—Swanson was another ex-partner of John's. They had ridden together when John did a brief stint on a mounted horse patrol. The man seemed to know everything about horses and had an uncanny way with them. He was their "Horse problem" guy. Periodically, one of the horses on the patrol would have what could only be described as, "mental," problems. Hillbilly was the horse's last chance and he never failed. He could walk into the stall of a totally insane horse and within minutes have the horse calm and snuggling with him. A few minutes after that, he would be riding the horse as though nothing were ever wrong. The fact that he was originally from Georgia just added more reason to his nickname. Though he had moved north when he was ten, he still retained a bit of the southern twang. The accent, his way with horses, thus, the name, "Hillbilly," and since his name was Billy anyway, emphasis was on the "Billy," part.

But he got out of the horse business when his superiors found that he was as equally talented at finding evidence. Now he was in charge of the Crime Scene Investigations unit, CSI for short. John had done Hillbilly a huge favor a number of years ago, just before he left the department.

John had been assisting on a drug raid one night and was in charge of making sure that no one ducked out the back. He was standing in the dark alley behind the house when he noticed a basement window quietly slide open. A figure squeezed out and silently ran toward the alley. John waited until the unknown fugitive ran out from behind the garage. Then he pointed his gun at the small form and yelled, "Police Officer. Freeze!" To his surprise, a scared, female voice said, "Mr. Harvard?" It was Karen, Hillbilly's twelve year old daughter. He immediately lowered his gun and said, "What the hell are you doing here?"

She explained that she had been recently hanging with a couple of older girls from school who were into drugs, big time. She admitted to John that she had taken some, but had just started experimenting. She and her so called friends had come to this house to purchase more. Bad timing, or good... depending on your point of view.

"Please don't tell my father," she tearfully begged.

"You have a choice," John replied. "You can be taken

down with the others, or you go home right now and tell your father everything, before I do." She chose the latter and quickly disappeared from the scene. A few days later, Hillbilly walked up to him and said only, "I owe you. Big time and I won't forget." Then he walked away and nothing was ever said about it again. His daughter turned out just fine.

Now John said into the phone, "Hillbilly, I need a favor."

Only slightly more serious, Hillbilly replied, "Sure John. What do you need?"

"Well," John continued, "I can't go into details, but I need an apartment gone over for fingerprints, ASAP. It's rather sensitive and I'm sorry I can't be more forthcoming with details, but I need to know who a certain man is that's spent a lot of time there. I'd do it myself, but time is of the essence. Also, there's a gun on the desk in one of the bedrooms that I need to get to Nick. Think you can help me with that?"

"No problemo," came the quick, unquestioning reply. With that, John gave him the address and made arrangements for him to pick up the keys at Peter's office.

He hung up with Hillbilly and called Nick. He brought him up to date on what had happened. "When are you going to pick up your god damn gun, John," came Nick's angry retort.

"Right after I leave here," John replied. "I'm going to send you an email of this guy's picture. Maybe you could work some of your Photoshop magic on it and see if your fancy facial recognition program can pick up anything."

Photoshop was a popular program used to enhance digital images. He had seen some pretty amazing stuff done with it.

"You had good timing with your call. I've got a response from CODIS. The blood is probably from your guy. He was a Master Sergeant in the military, a Ranger in the Army, served in Desert Shield, the first Gulf war. He was honorably discharged a couple of years ago. Nothing on him since then. He's a pro and would certainly be an asset in a situation like this."

"What's his name?" asked John.

"Gregory T. Harris," Nick replied. "He would now be thirty-four. Is this the guy in the apartment that shot at you?"

"No," said John. "Not the same guy. Have you run a check for license, vehicles and stuff?"

"Jeez, give me a break," Nick answered. "I just got this stuff back. I'll do that and let you know. Now on that rag you turned in. You were right, DNA indicates a match to your vic. Also, there were traces of chloroform on the rag, so that's how they got her out without a fight. Could your shooter have been the other guy that grabbed her."

"I never really got a clear look at him, but I don't think so," came John's reply. "So we're looking at a minimum of three guys, none of whom are probably decision makers at Coeptus Guild. Quite an operation. Can you send Harris's ID photo to my phone?"

"Sure, I'll do it right now while we're talking. You still think you should handle this by yourself? Now there are two missing people and you've been shot at," said Nick's concerned voice.

"I'm not ready to call it yet. Can you to try to track down credit card transactions, bank accounts, run background, anything that might tell us where our Ranger is?"

"Sure thing. Keep me posted, John."

John said, "I will. Later," and hung up. He pulled up Emily's email account and sent the photograph of the shooter to Nick. His cell phone beeped to let him know he had a message. It was the photo of Harris.

He was a good looking guy that could have graced the cover of GQ magazine. He had short blonde hair and a square jaw. He reminded John of some no nonsense hero in a video game. There was a toughness in his eyes that would be intimidating to most folks.

He brought his phone back to the main menu and had just sat back in his chair to think things over when Emily walked back in the room. He looked up at her, "Any luck?"

"No," she replied. "I think you might be right about Pete."

"I'm pretty much resigned to it. How are we going to handle this so that no one calls the police?"

Emily rolled her eyes, "I told Patti that we have to wait at least twenty-four hours before the police will take a report. Is that true?"

"Not really. Most of the time when an adult disappears, it's of their own volition. But try telling that to an upset parent or spouse. So the cops pull the old twenty-four hour trick out of the bag. However, in this case, they'd be here in a heartbeat. If they didn't and something bad did happen, wow, lawsuit heaven. You ready to go?"

She reached in her drawer and took out a silver box with cables attached to it. He recognized it as an external hard drive. He gave Emily a questioning look.

"This is an external hard drive with a huge capacity," she explained. "I'm hoping it will be big enough. I'm going to make what's called a clone of Sue's hard drive. That means I'll make an exact copy of whatever is on her drive. Then, I will be able to examine it, but leave the original information intact."

John nodded and opened the door for Emily. They walked to John's truck, got in and he told her that he was going to stop by his house first. They said little on the way. He wanted to, but damn, his head hurt.

When they pulled into his driveway, he looked at her and said, "Do you want to come in? I'll only be a sec."

"No thank you. I'll wait here if you don't mind," she answered.

The first thing he did was walk to his gun case. He had three guns that he'd purchased when he first became a cop. A Colt Python .357 Magnum revolver, a Colt .45 model 1911 Mark IV semiautomatic and a Walther PPK .380 semiautomatic. He researched each gun carefully before buying and found that over the years they'd served him well. He never felt the need to buy anything else.

The rage these days, which was just beginning when he'd quit the force, were 9-mm semi-auto's with a huge capacity for carrying ammunition. But John had seen and heard many stories of 9 mm's failing to bring down their intended target. In one such incident, a state trooper, who was riding with a rookie, stopped a guy on a motorcycle. The guy got off the bike, pulled a gun and started shooting. The troopers returned fire, emptying both of their fourteen round clips. They reloaded and dumped most of the next twenty-eight rounds into the biker. Though neither of the troopers were hit, many of their rounds hit the biker. The man did in fact die... of a heart attack! John had never heard of a guy being seriously hit with a .45 and not going down. He may not have fourteen rounds in the magazine of his .45, only seven in fact, but it usually only took one to do the job.

But he didn't think he would need such firepower today. The disadvantage to the .45 was its size. It was massive, heavy and hard to conceal. Instead, he selected the Walther PPK. It was a .380 caliber, kind of a 9 mm short. Like the difference between a .22 long and a .22 short. It was a 9 mm and so had all the inherent failings of typical 9 mm. It's milling tolerances were tight, so it was prone to jamming. Not a good situation in a gun fight. But he found that if the round wasn't too high power and the gun was kept very clean, jamming was kept to a minimum. To combat the poor stopping power of the 9 mm, John purchased aluminum hollow points. The aluminum was soft and prone to deforming anyway. Couple that with the hollow end and, well, the effect on flesh was devastating. In fact, it opened up so well on impact, that it created the problem of not having enough stopping power if it had to pierce multiple layers of clothing, bone or building material. To take care of that problem, he alternated each aluminum round with a normal round, thinking that something was bound to get through and bring the target down.

The Walther was a very well made German weapon. It was small and therefore easy to conceal, disassembled very easily and was reasonably accurate. John had carried it as a backup piece when he was in uniform.

He checked a clip to make certain is was full and inserted it into the gun. He pulled back the slide and inserted one round into the chamber. Then he removed the clip. It now held only six rounds instead of seven. He put a fresh round into the clip and reinserted it. He retrieved a second clip, made sure it was full and put it into his pocket. He put the gun into a small belt holster that held it on the inside of his waistband. He then pulled his shirt out of his pants enough to cover the small, protruding bulge. It would be difficult for anyone to spot that wasn't trained in such things. As an afterthought, he grabbed a spare box of ammunition as well.

He then walked to his office and retrieved an electric lock pick. He wasn't very good at it, but he could, eventually, get into most locks. It worked by vibrating the pins on the lock into position. All one had to do was insert it, turn it on and apply a slight amount of torque so that when a pin locked into place, it stayed there. After they were all in position, just turn the pick like a key and the lock would open.

He quickly downed a couple of Tylenols and returned to the truck. He got in and put the box of ammunition in the center console. Emily's eyes grew wide. "Sorry, but I'm not going to anymore gunfights without a gun. Has a tendency to ruin your whole day, to say nothing of the headache."

"No. It's okay," she said in a shaky voice. "It makes sense. I've just never seen real bullets before. It's kind of creepy. Kind of scary. I assume you have the gun on you?"

"Well," he grinned, "I wasn't planning on throwing them at the guys." She looked a little hurt and very vulnerable.

"Hey, It'll be okay. We probably won't even need it." She gave him another of her strange looks, turned her head and gazed out her door window. It was obvious that the conversation was over. He put the truck in gear, backed out of the driveway and headed toward Sue's office.

It was a silent ride. At one point, he reached down and turned on the radio. He asked, "Like any music in particular?"

She looked at him briefly and replied, "Doesn't matter. I like all kinds of music, except rap and opera." Then she turned and looked out the side window again.

The woman is beautiful… and weird, he thought. He wondered if it came with the brains. He selected some Roy Buchanan from his built in iPod and rode the rest of the way just listening to Roy's talking guitar.

They arrived at the building and parked. John couldn't take her silence anymore and asked, "What's the problem? You had to know at some point that guns would be involved, especially after somebody tried to shoot me." He looked at her and waited for her answer.

She looked back at him, her lower lip quivering. "Actually, when this all started, I didn't think it would come down to this. I certainly never thought anybody would get seriously hurt. These people, according to Pete, don't want violence, it attracts attention. I kind of thought that by now, they would have convinced Susan to give her the program and she would be back in her apartment. This whole thing was a little exciting, secret meetings, private investigators, you know, mystery. For someone who sits behind a computer all day, it was a much needed bit of excitement. Don't get me wrong, I don't want anyone to get hurt. It's just that, the excitement is gone and all that's left is the reality of it… and it's not very pretty."

He could see her eyes brimming with tears. "Hey," he said softly, "Let's just take one thing at a time. We're making progress, a little slow perhaps, but progress. You're not used to these things. Most cops carry guns for years and never fire them at anyone."

"Have you?" she asked bluntly.

He rolled his eyes and gave her a wry grin. "I'm not a good example. Look, the point is, like Peter said, these people don't like violence. Things have gotten a little out of hand, but that doesn't mean that the guy in the apartment acted under orders. He's probably in a world of crap right now for using a gun."

He didn't believe that, he'd seen the look in the guy's eyes and he didn't looked surprised or panicked. Which meant that the whole thing was most likely planned. But he was trying to calm her down. On impulse, he suddenly reached for her and she for him. He held her in his arms while softly, slowly rubbing her back. The smell of her perfume wafted into his nostrils. It smelled good. He hadn't held a woman for a long time. Today he had held two. He smiled. Things were looking up. Of course both women were in need of consoling, but one had to start somewhere.

They separated after a couple of minutes. "Thank you," she said quietly. "Let's go." They walked into the building together. There was a bank on the first floor. They entered an elevator and took it up to the second floor. The door opened and they saw a woman seated behind a desk. She was typing and didn't appear to even notice them.

John leaned over and softly spoke into Emily's ear, "Just walk in like you belong here. Don't say anything. Follow me. If she says anything, just say 'Hi,' and keep going. Let me do any talking." With that he stepped out of the elevator with Emily right behind him. The woman didn't even look up and they kept moving.

The secretary's desk was centered between two hallways, one went to the left and the other to the right. He knew Susan's office number, but didn't know where it was. He went right and quickly saw that it was the wrong way. He stopped and quietly said, "Okay, her office must be the other way, but I don't want to go by that woman again right away. She must be the one who does the typing if they need it and answers the phone, if they need that. She probably doesn't know everyone who comes here, but I don't want to take a chance." Emily nodded in response but didn't say anything.

A moment later they moved back toward the elevator. This time the woman looked at them as they passed. She smiled and said, "Hello."

"Hello," both Emily and John said together as they

walked by. They found Susan's office. John looked around to make sure nobody was looking. Then he took his keys out of his pocket, as well as the lock pick. Emily looked at his keys with a questioning look. "In case anybody walks by, I want them to see the keys and assume I'm having trouble with the lock," John said as he answered her unasked question.

He put the pick into the lock and pushed slightly. The door opened a few inches and stopped. Emily looked at him and said, "That was fast."

John's eyes were wide as he said quietly, "I didn't do anything. Stand to the side of the door and stay here." With that he looked around quickly to make certain that no one was in sight and drew his gun. He clicked off the safety, glad now that he had chambered that round at his house. With the safety off, the gun was ready to fire.

He stood to the side of the door and pushed it open with his free hand. It swung open the rest of the way. He pushed it further until the door came to rest against the wall with a quiet thunk. He did this to make certain that no one was standing behind the door. The office consisted of one room. It had a desk, a couple of tables and a couple of filing cabinets. There was nowhere for anyone to hide.

He looked around the hallway again and holstered his gun. Then he took Emily by the arm and quickly led her into the office. He closed the door and studied the room. The place had obviously been ransacked. Susan was a programmer and this was her office. *What's wrong with this picture?* he thought. *Oh yea, there's no computer.*

"Shit," he said to Emily. "They're one step ahead of us again."

"Where's her computer?" she asked. The monitor was there, but no computer.

John replied sarcastically, "That's my point. It isn't here."

"Now what John?"

"Let's go through the drawers and see if there's anything useful." They began rummaging through the drawers and cabinets. John was going through a bottom file drawer when he found a picture in a small frame. It was a picture of the mystery man. He used his cell phone to snap a picture of the photograph and send it to Nick's email address with a brief note, "Sue's boyfriend." Then, he put it back in the drawer, stood up and immediately felt woozy. He walked over to the chair and quickly sat down.

"John! Are you alright?"

"Yeah, we're done here. Let's go." He slowly stood up and began walking to the door. He wobbled slightly as he walked. Emily took his arm and helped him. He let her do so until they approached the woman near the elevator. Then he shook her off and picked up speed as he walked the rest of the way. He pushed the button and suddenly turned.

"Hey," he said in the direction of the woman.

"Yeah?" the woman replied.

"I just wanted to ask. I'm kind of in a hurry. I've got a lot of computers in my office and I didn't notice. My computer guy was suppose to pick up one of them for repair. Did you notice anyone walking out of here with a computer recently?"

"Yeah," she replied, "Just before you got here, some guy walked out with one. I don't know if it was yours."

"Short chubby guy, kind of balding, about fifty?" John asked.

"Oh no," she answered. "This guy was tall, short blonde hair, very muscular and he was only in his thirties." John could tell the woman was a bit smitten with the tall blonde man. But what really got his attention was the fact that she had just given a near perfect description of the man that John had fought with last night. This was the man who had kidnapped Susan, Gregory T. Harris.

"Hmm," John said. "Could've been his partner. Did he say anything."

"No. He was through here so fast, I never even had a chance to talk to him. I sure wanted to. If you see him, maybe you could ask *him* to bring your computer back when it's fixed?"

The elevator arrived. "Sure," he replied with a knowing smirk. "I'll tell him." He and Emily stepped in. When the door closed, she looked at John, smiling, "That was smooth."

"Thanks," he grinned. Then his face became more serious, "She just gave me a description of one of the guys that took Susan. He took her computer too. Busy guy."

They rode the rest of the way in silence. When the door opened, they walked to the truck and got in.

"John, you really look beat. Why don't we call it a night."

He'd been so involved with this, that he hadn't noticed that it was dark. Where had the day gone? He never did have lunch. Now he realized that he was once again hungry. He looked at Emily, "Are you hungry?"

"A little," she answered. "But I don't feel like a restaurant right now. I want to relax."

John thought quickly. He didn't feel like going home to an empty house and he really did want to spend more time with her. "If you would like, we could go back to my place. I've got a fully stocked refrigerator and a wine chiller full of wine."

She smiled, "That sounds nice. Okay."

"How's your head?" she asked a little while later. He noticed that her mood seemed to have changed for the better. He was certainly glad about that.

"It's pretty good. I took some Tylenol before I left the house. I am feeling a bit tired though."

"Then you'd better get to bed early tonight," she responded with a smile. John looked at her, trying to decide if she meant the obvious hidden meaning in that. He wasn't sure and elected to play it safe by saying, "We'll see how my head feels. Could be some good company, dinner, nice wine and relaxing music will bring me around." Now it was his turn to smile and see how she responded. *Oh the games we play*, he thought.

Emily's eyebrows raised and her smile took on a playful, mischievous look, "So you're looking for someone to help nurse you through this are you?"

"Hey, I'll do whatever is necessary to bring me back up

to my full potential, so that I may perform my duties to the best of my abilities," he chortled as he pulled into his driveway.

She laughed, "So the man does indeed have a sense of humor." Her face went to a half smile as she quietly added, "It feels good to laugh like that."

He stopped the truck and got out. As they proceeded up the walkway he said, "I have an idea. Unless you think of something strikingly important, let's just enjoy the evening I don't see that there's much more we can do tonight. I've got some irons in the fire that most likely won't be ready until tomorrow. What do you say?"

"Agreed!"

They walked in and he led her to the kitchen. "This is beautiful," she exclaimed. The room was quite large with cherry wood cabinets, marble counter tops, and green tile floor. Not unlike Susan's kitchen, but much larger. It was equipped with an island and an additional breakfast area. A small fireplace sat on the wall next to the breakfast table. She noticed an electronic dart board next to the fireplace. "Lose many darts in the fireplace," she asked?

He laughed, "Not really. You'd have to be a pretty bad shot or pretty drunk to be off that much."

"You haven't seen me play."

"You shoot darts?"

"A little," she replied with that mischievous grin. He suspected that grin was telling him that she played more than little. This was shaping up to be a pretty good night.

They chose a wine and he poured a couple of glasses.

They agreed on steaks for dinner so he went out onto the deck and fired up the grill. She followed, carrying her wine with her.

"It's a little cold for grilling isn't it?" she asked.

"Yeah, but it's the best way to cook steaks." They stood together, looking out at the frozen lake. Like the previous night, it was clear and the stars were out in all their glory. Even more so from here because of the lack of ambient light. The lake was small and there weren't many houses, so it provided a peaceful haven for the few residents.

"So where do you live," John asked?

"I live in a condo over in Brighton Ridge."

"Those are nice."

"Yes, but nothing like this. If I lived here, I'd probably work from home and never leave. You're lucky to have this. By the way, where's your little girl?"

"She's at her mom's for the week. I'm going inside, unless all you want for dinner is steak."

She laughed, "I've had worse dinners, but okay." They went back in and John prepared the rest of dinner. He lit a fire in the kitchen fireplace, using real wood. He didn't care for the fake gas logs that a lot of homes had. Not that they didn't have benefits. But he liked to hear the crackling and the smell that only a natural wood fire can give.

When the steaks were done, he lit some candles on the breakfast table, turned out the rest of the lights and they sat down. They found they could talk to one another easily and he was surprised when he realized they had polished off two bottles of wine.

The conversation had grown quiet when a soft Louis Armstrong song began playing. She looked at him and said, "I love his music, this song in particular. It was just meant to dance to."

Taking the hint, he asked, "Would you like to?" She gave him a smile that said, *thought you'd never ask*, and stood up. They moved to a clear area closer to the fireplace and he took her in his arms. As they danced, she began to move closer and seemed to flow into him. His pulse quickened.

She looked up at him and there was no mistaking the yearning in her eyes. "I'm no prude, but I don't think I've ever felt this comfortable with a man this fast before."

He smiled and shrugged, "Don't know what to tell you. We agreed that we were going to relax this evening. I guess we're doing a pretty good job at that."

Her face tilted a little further back in that classic, *kiss me, you fool*, pose. He complied. The kiss rapidly grew in intensity until both suddenly realized there was no turning back. "Time to take this someplace more comfortable?" he queried.

She nodded. Still holding one of her hands, he moved to blow out the candles, before leading her to his bedroom. With a frenzy that comes from pent up passion too long ignored, they removed each other's cloths and fell into bed. They never even turned the bedroom lights on and he found that his head didn't hurt one bit. Not once.

CHAPTER
12

His cell phone was ringing. John's eyes fluttered open and looked at the clock on his night stand. The glow from the LED numbers showed that the time was 2:16 A.M. He untangled himself from Emily, fumbled for the phone and made the connection, but before he could utter a greeting, a mirthful voice spoke to him instead.

"This is supposed to be *your* case and here I am at two in the morning while you're all snuggled up safe and sound in your bed. I used to defend you when people would tell me that you're an asshole, but no longer."

"Nick?" John croaked.

"Who else would be gracious enough to make sure you don't drop the ball on this?"

"If it makes you feel any better, I'll be an eternally grateful *asshole*, okay?"

"Good," Nick replied and his tone turned much more serious. "Now that I have your attention, I found your shooter."

A jolt of adrenaline instantly brought John wide awake.

"Really? That was quick, how'd you find him?"

"Actually," said Nick, "I didn't. A fisherman down by the Harrison Street bridge did. He hooked the biggest piece of crap in his life, or should I say carp?"

John sat up incredulously and asked, "He's dead?"

"As dead as they come. Hung up in the eddy around one of the abutments."

"I didn't realize that much ice was gone already."

"Yeah, well, it's pretty clear in that area, except for the last couple of days, it's been pretty warm. Anyway, he's casting his lure from shore when he gets a call from his wife. He lets the lure drop down to the bottom while he talks. Went to reel it in and it had snagged on something. He tugs hard as a last resort and suddenly it pulls free. He brings it in and finds something that looks an awful lot like a piece of face. He decided to call the police. The responding officer looks at it and calls a detective. He looks at it and brings in the divers. They go down and bring up a body, attached by chains to some dumbbells. We get called in and I'm standing there on shore looking down at this guy and suddenly I realize that his face, minus the patch torn out by the treble hook of the lure, matches the picture you emailed me. It's your guy!"

John listened in rapt attention. "Holy shit," he said when Nick was finished. "Any idea how he was killed?"

He replied sarcastically, "I'm not sure, but I'm thinking the 9 mm sized hole in the back of his head might have had something to do with it," Nick continued somberly, "this changes things you know. I have detailed information on a homicide victim. My ass is in a sling if I don't say anything and they find out later. I can ignore it for a little while, 'I didn't realize it was him,' and all that. But your time to keep this amongst ourselves is running out."

John sighed and rubbed his face with his hands as he thought about the implications. Did they do this to the shooter because of his botched attempt to kill John? Or because of the fact that the shooter tried to kill him in the first place? Or maybe because John had seen his face and could identify him. He wasn't sure, but one thing was obvious, they didn't appear to be a very tolerant group. Now what?

"Nick," he said slowly as he stood up. He didn't want to wake Emily. He put on a robe walked out of the room, closing the door silently behind him. "Have you been able to ID him yet?" He went into the kitchen as he talked and sat by the still glowing fire.

"I'm heading back to the lab to run the prints collected by Hillbilly against our mystery boy. My guys are at the Morgue now getting prints off from him, which they'll get to me forthwith. Since he was in the water, it's going to take a while to get them. You know how it is."

Yes, he did know how it was. A body in the water begins to get wrinkly, just like a live person who is in the bathtub or swimming pool too long. The wrinkles are not very conducive for obtaining fingerprints. He was aware that they now had scanners that could make the job easier. He didn't know if Nick's department had one or not, but he thought they most likely did. In the old days, a syringe would be used to puff up the fingers with water or formaldehyde. That would stretch the finger out enough to get usable prints. Depending upon the stage of decomposition, things could get much more gruesome than that. It was a part of the job he didn't particularly miss.

"Anything back on that Harris guy?"

"I've been able to come up with an address just outside of Nashville. He owns a home situated on several acres of land. Since I'm trying to keep a low profile here, I did some phone pretext work and found that his electric bill is extremely low. Either he has an alternative form of energy other than the electric company or he doesn't spend much time there. Oh, and I also found that he's the proud owner of a two year old Mercedes Benz, fully paid for by the way."

"Mighty expensive car for an ex-army guy. Sounds like a man for hire to me," said John.

"Exactly what I was thinking."

"Does he have a land line?" asked John.

"Of course not," Nick responded. "I know what you're going to ask next and the answer is no. I have not attempted to get his cell phone records yet. Like I said, I've been trying to fly underneath the radar." Nick added, "Please try to remember Sir John, that I am gainfully employed by the good people of this state, county, and city and I do, occasionally have duties outside of your requests that I must perform if I am to continue to meet their expectations."

John rolled his eyes and laughed at his friend's retort. But as for the phone, more and more people were doing away with the use of a normal land line telephone, opting instead for a cellular phone with a lot of minutes. It had the advantage of always being with them no matter if they were at home or at the grocery store. This was especially true of people that did not want to be found because one couldn't simply call a subject's house phone to see if they answered. In addition, obtaining phone records from a house phone could place a person at a particular location at a particular time. However, no house phone, no way to tell where a person was by merely dialing up the home phone or by comparing times on a bill. No doubt about it, a cell phone definitely helped to hide a person's location. Mr. Harris was definitely one of those.

"What about you John, have you come up with anything since we talked last?"

John told him about Emily's office and what he had found there, including the fact that Harris had ransacked the office just before they got there.

"Did you have your gun this time?"

"Yes," replied John defensively with a hint of sharpness. He suddenly realized that he was still very tired. "Harris is a very busy guy. Let's see, in the space of twenty-four hours, he kidnapped a programmer and her father, probably killed my shooter and cleaned out Sue's office. Not a bad days work. He's our link Nick. He's obviously an integral part of this. Find him, we find Sue."

"Agreed," Nick rejoined. "He has to become the focus of our investigation. John, I think at this juncture, we have to consider bringing the chief into this. I can explain the situation and stress the need for this to remain low key. This has escalated way beyond where it was when you first came to me. We now have a second kidnap victim, an attempted murder of you, a completed murder on lover boy turned shooter, and a burglary of Susan's office. Things are moving way too fast for either of us to handle efficiently. I need the full resources of this department to find credit card transactions, cell phone records, and God knows what else."

John listened to Nick silently. He was right of course, but he was still haunted by the fact that these people were powerful, intelligent, appeared to have unlimited resources, and most likely had tentacles everywhere that made strategic sagacity. This would have to include the police department. It would make sense if they were going to conduct operations in a given area, to have a mole at whatever police department would respond. He wouldn't be surprised to find they had sleepers at key departments like the F.B.I. and most major police departments.

He could use Emily of course. But he was starting to feel rather protective of her. He didn't know how much they knew about her existence. The way this case was going, it was obvious that if they decided she was too much of an impediment to their plans, they would have no qualms about taking her out. They had already been within a few feet of her when they grabbed Peter. He shuddered at the thought.

"What about the possibility of the mole, Nick, like we talked about?"

"Do you really think the Chief would do that?"

He thought about Chief Rienhardt. The three of them had all started within a year of one another. While he didn't really have anything against the chief, he had never liked him. Probably because it was obvious from the start that he was a political animal. Unlike the eager, fresh faced Nick and John, he was never one of those guys that liked to really get in and do what needed to be done. He was always the one to say, "Look guys, let's think this over. Maybe we should call a supervisor and run it by them first."

In police work, one didn't always have that luxury. That took time and on some occasions, time was not a luxury they could afford. If you wanted to get the bad guys, oftentimes you had to act right then and there. But that meant that they might be second guessed by the Monday morning quarterbacks who sat in their nice, comfortable, air conditioned offices, with all the time in the world to think things through. Which meant that they could decide that you acted inappropriately. That was something Officer Rienhardt dreaded.

Then there was the sickening relationship between the future chief and the Chief at the time. Officer Rienhardt found that the Chief was in need of a hunting dog. Paradoxically enough, Officer Rienhardt just *happened* to have an uncle that, would you believe it, just *happened* to have a litter of puppies of that same breed. He gave one to the Chief as a gift. Then, of course, there were the trips with the Chief to seminars all over the country. Officer Rienhardt paid for his way with his own money and used vacation time so that he could attend these meeting with the Chief.

This led to dinners and meetings with councilmen, Mayors, and other political people. At the time, everyone else at the department had laughed at Officer Rienhardt and shook their heads. But it paid off and now he was Chief. So who had the last laugh?

But John never thought that Rienhardt was a bad guy, just not the type of person he liked to hang with. The Chief had spent a lot of time on his knees to get where he was today. John didn't think it was likely that he would throw it all away just for money. Money wasn't the attraction for men like Rienhardt. Power and recognition was their aphrodisiac. So, he guessed, it all boiled down to who else would be involved once the Chief knew. That, and as he knew all too well, the Chief liked to do things by the book, so that none of the proverbial crap could come back on him if it did hit the fan.

He turned his attention back to Nick. "Okay, I doubt the Chief would be part of this, but what about who he's going to tell? You know how he is about being by the book."

"Yeah I know. I've been thinking about it. I think that if I'm straight with him about who this group is, their history and our fears of infiltration, I can convince him to let me run the investigation. I tell who I think should know. That would be perfect for him. If we get Susan and Peter back alive and well, he will have had the foresight of handling such a delicate manner so well. He can, and we know he will, take the credit.

If things go sour, he can blame me and you. It's a win/win proposition for him. Bottom line is, he's not a stupid man and I think he'll realize that as soon as this group figures out the police are involved, Susan and Peter will disappear forever. He's not going to want that to come back at him."

John sighed heavily. "Okay, do it. We could use some help. I have a hunch this little plan of theirs is becoming unraveled and they know it. We may not have much time. Information is key. We've got to find Harris, fast."

"You sound tired John. How's your head?"

"It feels alright. But I'm exhausted. The head's probably part of it."

"Why don't you go back to bed? Until we pop some more info for you, there's not much to do. You know how these things go. Once things start happening, they go fast and who knows how much sleep you're going to get then."

John yawned and said, "If you insist, I guess I will. I'll talk to you later."

"Hey," said Nick suddenly, "I almost forgot. The gun you had Hillbilly bring me had the serial numbers filed off, so we had to raise them with chemicals. Turns out the gun was stolen last month in a burglary."

John thought for a moment. Filing serial numbers off from stolen items was a common practice and in a lot of cases, a futile one. He had learned early in his career that when a serial number is stamped into a metal object, such as a gun, an engine block, etc., it forces the metal to compact downward. The serial number that is seen on the surface is merely a representation of what really goes deep down into the metal. Filing the surface metal off makes the number unreadable to the naked eye. But by adding chemicals to the metal, often, the number miraculously reappears. Turning his attention back to Nick, he asked, "Where was the burglary?"

"From an apartment in one of the other building's in Susan's complex," Nick replied.

"That's convenient. So I'm betting mystery boy stole it himself. I'm starting to feel he's an amateur. He doesn't seem as buttoned down as the rest of the characters from Coeptus Guild."

Nick rejoined, "Not too much of an amateur. He knew where to have the gun fitted with a silencer. But you're right, he does seem to be the odd man out from the rest of the group."

"Which would explain why he's dead," said John. "Could be that taking me out wasn't part of the plan or at least a part that he was supposed to be part of." He breathed a quiet, short, sarcastic laugh. "You try to take a little initiative and look what happens. Typical, just typical."

"Yeah, the corporate world is just a killer, isn't it? Anyway, get to bed. I'll call you as soon as I get anything. I'm going to call the Chief now. Wish me luck."

"You know what they say about that," said John in reference to calling the Chief.

"Better you than me," they both said together and laughed. It was an old joke between them.

"Later."

"Later," and they hung up. John sat by the dying fire a while, thinking. Then he got up and returned to the bedroom. He stood there looking down at Emily's still form, hidden beneath the covers. *This could get habit forming*, he thought. It had been a long time since he'd felt this kind of attraction. He remained in a quiet reverie for several minutes before mentally shaking himself out of it. This was too quick and there was too much going on right now. Get this case concluded and spend more time with her. Then he could get a better feel for what was going on between them. Tonight could be nothing more than two people thrown together in a stressful situation. Like cruise ship lovers who fall in love in unusual circumstances only to find, months later, that they really don't have anything in common and really don't love each other. He'd read somewhere that it wasn't unusual for two people to become infatuated with one another on vacations. Complete strangers, sometimes coworkers working together at an exotic locale, suddenly find themselves irresistibly attracted to one another. However, statistics showed that once they returned home, the attraction usually fizzled in about three months. It had happened to him once and he knew better than to trust his feelings right now.

He sighed, took off his bathrobe and climbed into bed. Still, for the time being, it was a pleasant repose. He turned on his side and snuggled up next to Emily and in a very short time, returned to dreamland once again.

CHAPTER
13

John awoke to the smell of cooking and bright sunshine. He looked at the clock and saw that the sun had been up for some time. It was streaming through the uncovered window and was making the room uncomfortably warm. He pushed the covers off from him. Weather wise, it was a drastically different day. Spring was in the air. The sound of chirping birds and a far off mournful cooing of a dove made him feel very relaxed. He laid there and listened to Emily moving about the kitchen. The opening and closing of drawers told him she was obviously looking for something. Something in the frying pan was sizzling. He sniffed the air. It smelled like pancakes, sausages, and coffee.

After a moment, he roused himself out of bed and put on his robe. He entered the kitchen in time to see Emily bent over, looking for something in a lower cabinet. She was wearing one of his dress shirts and her back was to him. He couldn't help but just stand there, admiring the view.

She stood up, turned, and jumped as she saw him. "Oh!" she exclaimed. Her startled expression quickly turned to a smile as she realized what he had been doing. "Enjoying yourself?" she asked in a husky voice.

He smiled in return. "As a matter of fact, I was. I don't know what you were looking for, but perhaps whatever it is, really is in there. I think you should look again."

She walked over and took him in her arms. "I was looking for a tray. I was going to serve you breakfast in bed."

He put his arms around her and looked around. He noticed his waffle maker standing open on the counter and a big plate of waffles beside it. The sausages sat next to that on an ornamental plate that she had found. He also noticed a pile of silverware, cloth napkins, and two large cups of steaming hot coffee.

"Busy girl. There's a serving tray in the pantry. Not that I have any objections to spending time in bed with you, but now that I'm up, why don't we eat breakfast in the sun room?"

"Okay." She stepped away and began carrying the stuff into the sun room without further ado. He helped and soon they were seated and enjoying their breakfast. Both were facing the lake. "This is beautiful," she almost whispered. "What a wonderful way to start the day."

They talked about the lake and the house as John silently contemplated how to bring her back to reality. She was in such a good mood, as was he. He didn't want to spoil it, but the fact of the matter was they had deadly serious issues to discuss and they really didn't have the luxury of time to sit here in their own little aura, pretending that everything was good in the world. Hopefully, there would be time for this later.

After a while, they stopped talking and ate in silence. He decided now was as good a time as ever. "I don't know if you heard, but my cell phone rang last night." She looked up at him and shook her head. The pleasant, relaxed glow on her face vanished and he felt like an ingrate for having been responsible for it. After all, she had made him this beautiful breakfast and this was how he repaid her.

He forged ahead. "It was a call from a friend of mine on the police department. They found a body in the river."

She looked puzzled. "Why would they tell you? You're not with the department anymore?"

He debated telling her everything, but decided against it. The less she knew, the less the chance that Coeptus Guild would decide that she knew too much and take her out. He had to be careful here. "He does that sometimes," he replied. "We're still friends and sometimes he calls just to get my input. The thing is, the man he described... well, I'm pretty sure he's the mystery boyfriend of Susan's."

Her puzzled expression turned to one of shock, then concern, then finally settled on one of sorrow. Tears welled up in her eyes and she turned her gaze to the lake. She pushed her chair back, stood, walked to the window and with her arms folded, stared out, her back to him. He didn't know what to say. Her reaction surprised him. He knew this would take the gaiety out of the occasion, but he hadn't expected this. "Are you okay?" he asked.

For a moment, she didn't answer. Then, without turning to face him she said, "Like I said yesterday, I just wasn't expecting all this violence."

He got up, walked up behind her and put his arms around her. They stood there for a while and then he turned her around and was once again surprised. She looked scared. Really, really scared. "Wow." he said. "Look, like I said, it's going to be alright. But I think that you should lay low for a while. Do you have somewhere you can go? I don't think you should go back to work or back to your place."

She shook her head with a look of growing determination. "No. I want to see this through. I love Peter and I don't want to see anything happen to him or to Susan. I want to help you. I know I can. What are you going to do next?"

He looked at her, amazed at the resolve that was settling in even as he watched. This was one special lady. It would be nice to have her around, but things were getting nasty. He shook his head. "It's not a good idea. I'm kind of starting to like you and I don't like the thought of what might happen to you if they decide you're in the way."

She opened her mouth to protest when they heard his cell phone ring. He walked into the kitchen and picked it up from the counter where he had left it last night. He looked at the screen and saw that it was Nick. He looked at Emily and said, "I've got to take this. I'll be right back." He walked into his office, closed the doors and made the connection.

"Yeah Nick."

"How are you feeling this morning John?"

"I was feeling pretty good until a few minutes ago."

"You mean even before I called? What's up?"

"Emily's here and I was just telling her to lay low. She

doesn't like the idea."

Nick replied in a conspiratorial whisper, "She's there already? Or is there something you're not telling me John? Ex-partner, current *old* buddy of mine."

"Well, she's been here all night and yes we slept in the same bed and the rest of the information is on a need to know basis and even though you're my loyal ex-partner and my current *old* buddy, you don't need to know."

"Humph, fine, be that way," replied Nick. "On a more serious note, I talked to the Chief last night."

"Yeah, and how'd it go?"

"It took a while, but we're all on the same page now. I made him agree not to tell a soul, not even the Deputy Chief. I haven't told anyone yet, but I've got wheels in motion. If anyone asks, the information is for the Chief. That pretty much puts a stop to any further questions.

"Okay, first, your shooter is/was Richard A. Clemmons. He was forty-five years old and lived in town here. He's had several priors for theft, fraud, shoplifting, and burglary. The shoplifting and burglary were all when he was a kid. The last fraud and theft arrest was about five years ago. I talked to some of the detectives who knew him. Apparently, he was a real piece of work. Smooth talking ladies man. All the women loved him, until that is, they noticed money suddenly disappearing from their bank accounts. Did I mention that none of his girlfriends were poor?

"Anyway, the gun from the apartment had been wiped fairly clean, but we found a partial fingerprint on what would have been the top of the cylinder before it was fired.

So he cleaned it, but didn't open up the cylinder, so the top of the gun protected it. Amateur! The print was Clemmons's."

John interrupted, "Phone records?" He was beginning to get excited. Clemmons must have called someone and even though he'd been in the system all his life, he was obviously mistake prone and John would bet that he called someone from his cell phone who was connected to Coeptus Guild.

Nick continued, "No land phone, but his cell phone made several calls from the Johnsonville area in the past couple of weeks."

Johnsonville, was located several hours north in a wooded resort area. It was a favored spot in the summer for camping and fishing. In the winter it was the place to go for snowmobilers. It would be a perfect place to rent a cabin in the woods and stash someone. In some of those areas, even if Susan did manage to get outside by herself, she could scream her head off and chances were good that no one would hear her. If things went sour and they had to quickly dispose of a body, chances were equally as good that it wouldn't be discovered until hunting season in the fall. That's assuming they didn't bury the body. If they did that, by the time a hunter walked near the grave in the fall, leaves and other falling debris would obscure it from all but the most discerning eyes.

Nick went on to say that they were in the process of tracing all of the calls made from the cell phone. But there were several that they were having trouble with. They were thinking that the numbers were most likely from and to disposable phones, phones that could be bought with a set number of minutes on them. They were cheap and once one were finished with it, one could drop it in a trash can and forget it. They were designed by a toy designer from New Jersey who had no prior experience in cell phones. They were about the thickness of three credit cards and were the preferred communications device of many low life's. There are no contracts to sign or credit checks performed. Walk in, plop down ten bucks, and walk out. They were nearly impossible to track and were law enforcement agency's worst nightmare. A recent upsurge in orders from the middle east had Federal agents scurrying.

"One more thing," said Nick. "It's probably nothing, but there weren't many calls yesterday on his cell phone. So I noticed that he received a phone call from one of the unknown numbers yesterday, around twenty minutes before you were attacked. After the attack, there were a flurry of calls to and from his cell phone. The last call was to his phone about an hour before you went to Susan's office."

"That would be the one calling him to a meeting. The last meeting of his life, but I'm sure he didn't know that," stated John. "So if Harris was the trigger man, he met with Clemmons, shot him, dumped him in the river and went directly to Susan's office to clean it out. Like I said before, busy man."

"It all fits," Nick replied.

"Okay," said John. "What do you think of this picture? Coeptus Guild hires Clemmons to get close to Susan and keep track of her progress on her program. When the time is right, they come in and snatch her. She was basically a loner with her only real contacts being her mother and Clemmons. Contact with her mother was spotty so they think they have plenty of time to work on her and convince her she really should hand over her code to them.

"But they didn't plan on me being there. Even after my scuffle with them, they didn't know for sure who I was. It could have been that I was merely a good Samaritan who happened by and tried to do my good deed for the day.

"In any case, they somehow figured out that I didn't just happen by and now I pose a possible threat. Now they have to change gears. Obviously Susan wasn't cooperating. So to speed things up, they grab Peter Browning. Then, somebody makes the decision to take me out in hopes of slowing things down.

"That, fortunately for me, failed. Now they go into over-drive to clean things up and get back on track. They get rid of the one who botched the hit on me. Then they clean out Sue's office. They should be feeling pretty good and will now, hopefully, take a breather, thinking things are, at least temporarily, back in control. What do you think?"

"Hmm," said Nick thoughtfully. "Not bad, with the exception of one glaring fly in the ointment."

"What's that?"

"Well, most of what you say fits. But the problem I've had with this almost from the start has been this, how did they know so quickly who you are and how much of a threat you really were?"

John contemplated this for a while before saying, "Peter

Browning? Maybe they didn't kidnap him. Maybe he's been in on it from the start and decided to take a powder to wait and see how things turn out. If it goes sour, he's gone. If Susan complies, he comes back with some excuse or goes with the story that they kidnapped him as well."

"What about hiring you?"

"Window dressing. A contingency plan in case anything went wrong. He could use me as proof that he always had his daughter's best interest at heart."

"I don't know," Nick replied. "Why hire you and turn you loose the day before the kidnapping?"

"Good point," said John. "But he didn't know I was going to run out there the very night I received the information. He probably thought I wouldn't start any surveillance for at least a day or two." He thought for a moment. "The only other way I can think of is a possible mole at your department. Maybe someone saw me come in and put two and two together."

"I know you don't come in here often, but that would still be a pretty heads up move on the mole's part."

"Just a guess. I don't know what else to think. I think I'm going to head up to Johnsonville and take a look around. Who knows, maybe I'll see Harris or his car. Can you give me his plate number and vehicle description?"

Nick gave him the information. "Once again, be careful and make sure you have your gun with you," cautioned Nick. "I can't believe I even have to say this. When are you going to learn to dress yourself? Daddy can't always be there you know."

John laughed. "Listen Daddy, why don't you go and fool around with Mommy for a while and let Junior do his thing?"

"Well, since you put it that way, I believe I will. Later dude," and Nick hung up.

John laughed and walked back out into the kitchen. Emily was there and much to John's disappointment, fully dressed. Just as well, the mood was kind of gone anyway. She looked at him and said in a sharp, serious tone, "So now what?"

"Now, I'm going to take a little trip, probably overnight." he replied.

"Where?"

He thought for a moment and replied, "The less you know, the better it is for you, getting back to where we left off."

"I told you, I want to be involved." Tears were once again filling her eyes. "I'll go nuts if I have to just sit and wait. What am I going to do? Watch TV? Read a book? I'll go crazy. Besides, if you're so concerned about my safety, wouldn't I be safest with you. I know I feel safe when I'm with you."

John was torn. He did like spending time with her. He felt good when he was with her and it was nice having someone to bounce ideas off from. But god, what if he got into some real shit? If there was a brawl or even a real shootout, he'd be more worried about her than himself, and that was not a good thing.

She decided for him when she walked up and gave him a

long, sensuous kiss. Then she put her arms around him, put her head on his shoulder and hugged him much tighter than he would of thought possible from a girl that petite. "Please," she whimpered.

That was it. The last of his resolve fell away like ice cream melting on a hot day. He held her for a while, having already made up his mind but enjoying the moment. "Alright." he said finally, without breaking the embrace.

"Thank you," she said quietly.

After a few minutes he broke away and said, "What do you need for an overnight trip?"

She wiped the tears away. "I just need to stop by my place for a moment. It won't take long."

"Okay. I'm going to throw some things together and we'll go."

He walked into the bedroom, got dressed and had his small duffle bag ready in about three minutes. He was used to packing. Then he went to his gun case. This time he was taking the .45. The gun was heavy, but reassuring.

He'd been told once that he had small hands and the gun was too big for him. Some even argued that the .45 was too much gun in a gunfight. The recoil, they said, prevented one from staying on target when firing rapidly. But when John became a detective and started wearing the gun regularly, department regulations required him to qualify with the weapon on a combat course.

He found that he and the gun fit like a hand and glove. He'd always qualified with high marks. But when he began using the .45, his marks went to one of the highest in the department. Most people think that a shooting rating of "Expert," was the highest. It is not. "Combat Master," was the highest rating and John became one of only three in the entire department. He loved the gun.

He also decided to take the Walther, as well as a couple of boxes of ammunition. *Have no fear Nick*, he thought. *This time I'm fully prepared.* He put the .45 into a belt clip and wore the Walther in a shoulder holster underneath his shirt.

He grabbed his bag and returned to the kitchen. He found Emily in the sun room staring out at the lake. "Ready?" he asked.

"Yep." she replied and stood up.

As they walked out onto the driveway, Emily moved to the passenger side of the truck. "Nope." he said. "I've had too many encounters with them while driving that vehicle. We're taking the Audi."

He put the truck into the garage and started up the low slung, gleaming black Audi TT. It started instantly with a satisfying roar. He pulled it out of the garage and waited while she got in. She sank into the passenger seat and looked around. "This is nice." she commented before putting her seat belt on.

He pulled onto the road and headed in the direction of Emily's condo. When they got in the area, she directed him to her unit and got out. He got out too and she looked at him. "There's no need for you to come in. I'll only be a minute."

"Are you kidding? We're going to be together like glue. How do I know that you don't have a surprise in your closet like the one I found in Susan's?"

Emily smiled. "Okay, be my guest Mr. Knight in Shining Armor," and proceeded to unlock her front door.

Once inside he gently grabbed her arm and said quietly, "If you don't mind, I'm going to take a quick look around. Don't mean to be nosey, but I want to be on the safe side here."

She stood where she was directed and with a bemused look on her face, she held her left hand out in a gesture saying, 'It's all yours.' John moved his jacket to the side and put his hand on the .45. He used his thumb to flip off the safety. The gun was in what is known as a, "Cocked and locked," position, a condition that was ready to fire without have to jack the slide back.

He moved quickly and quietly through the condo. His movements were smooth and practiced, honed through years of performing this very same task countless numbers of times in countless numbers of buildings.

When he was satisfied they were alone, he flipped the safety back on and returned to the front door. "All clear," he stated. "Get your stuff quickly and let's get out of here. I don't trust these guys. They have an uncanny knack of showing up where they're not wanted."

She nodded silently and quickly disappeared into the bedroom. John moved to the window overlooking the parking lot and spent the entire time surveying the area. Emily came out of the bedroom carrying a small bag slung over her shoulder. It looked heavy.

"What, do you have an oven in there?" he laughed, "Or

thirty pairs of shoes. It's just for one night."

"I'm a woman and women need things. We're not like you men who can throw a pair of underwear and socks into a bag and say, 'I'm ready.'"

John's eyes grew wide in amusement as he returned, "Hey! I'll have you know, I took a *couple* of pairs of socks and underwear. I even brought extra shirts and pants."

She laughed. "Oh no. Now you're ready to be gone for a couple of weeks!" She hit him on the shoulder as she went past him and opened her front door. "You ready?"

They had just returned to the car when John's cell phone rang once again. He made the connection and found that Dana Pittman was the caller. "I haven't heard anything from you or Peter and I was just wondering what is going on." She sounded worn out and her voice was full of concern. He could almost picture her worried face and he instantly regretted not calling her earlier. John also felt a bit guilty at having had such a pleasurable night. He knew just how upset Dana must have been to make this call. The responsibility to call was really his.

"I'm sorry I haven't called," he said. "Things have been kind of popping, but I don't have anything concrete. I'm heading toward Johnsonville as we speak. I don't know if Sue is there, but I have reason to believe that at least one of the people responsible for her kidnapping has spent a lot of time there the last two weeks." He didn't feel it was necessary to add that the particular person in question was now lying cold and stiff in a morgue drawer.

"Do you think she's there?" Dana asked tentatively, like

she was afraid of the answer.

"I don't know. But I think that it's a good possibility. I don't want to get your hopes up. It's really too soon to tell. Give me some time to check it out and I'll get back to you."

"What about Peter?" she asked. "I've been leaving him messages and trying to get hold of him, but I haven't been able to. He's not my husband anymore and I really don't think there are any remnants of love left for him, but that doesn't mean I want anything to happen to him."

That would change if she knew his and Nick's suspicions about his possible involvement, he thought. But to her he said, "I'll be frank with you. I think his disappearance is definitely linked to Susan's abduction. However, at this point, I just don't have anything definitive." John hadn't really lied to her. He believed that one had to develop a bond of trust with the people one dealt with in this business. That included victims, witnesses, snitches, coworkers, and even suspects. Part of being a successful interrogator involved making the suspect believe what the interrogator was telling them. Once the suspect catches the interrogator in a bald faced lie, that interrogator is effectively finished with that suspect. That didn't mean that the truth couldn't be skirted, even stretched a little, a "white lie," as his mother used to say. In this case, if Dana caught him in one lie, she would then question everything he told her and that could definitely work against him.

He heard a man talking in the background. She said something to the man he couldn't quite make out before she spoke into the phone again. "Okay. I have to go now. But please keep me informed." Dana said shakily. He promised he would and hung up.

"Dana I take it?" Emily asked.

"Yeah, poor woman. I think this is making her realize that she still cares for Peter more than she knew."

"So we're going to Johnsonville, huh?"

"Well, you heard my side of the conversation. Phone records from Sue's boyfriend indicate that he spent a lot of time there over the past couple of weeks. If you think about it, it would be the perfect place to stash a kidnap victim. It's quiet, out of the way and the heavy tourist industry prevents any strangers in town from standing out. You could have a bevy of kidnap victims up there and no one would be the wiser."

"Phone records, huh?" she stated a little flatly. "You do have your sources don't you? I thought that was supposed to be my forte," she added mournfully and with a touch of defensiveness.

She gave him a hang dog, disappointed look, accented with a pouty lower lip. He laughed. "Aw give me a break. When have you been by your computer since I picked you up yesterday? Not only that, but you know my concern about your involvement in this case. I appreciate the offer and I would like for you to help me in the future. But right now, I felt it best to go elsewhere."

She looked at him with obviously feigned anger. "Fine. Just fine. Now if you don't mind I would like to be alone with my thoughts for a while and enjoy the scenery."

With that, she turned and looked out her side of the car. She kept her word and didn't speak again for the remainder of the trip.

CHAPTER

14

They arrived at Johnsonville at dusk. The expressway had taken them to within a couple of hours of the town. Then a wide, nicely paved two lane road took them to within another hour. After that, the road became narrow as it wound its way up and down hills, around sharp bends and over small bridges. Many times, the advised speed limit dropped to fifteen miles per hour. Though slow going and at times even a bit tedious, the road was quite scenic as it passed along the streams and the numerous lakes. Emily found that the thick stands of trees on either side of the road, would suddenly gave way to a peaceful lake or a calm meadow. Only an occasional driveway would break the otherwise natural setting and, she noted, she hadn't seen a gas station since they got off the expressway.

All in all, it was not considered an easy place to get to and more importantly for out-of-towners trying to get there for a weekend, it took time. Because of the heavy tourist traffic, there had been many calls to improve the road, to widen it and in some places, straighten it out. But these calls came mainly from people trying to get there, not the ones who actually lived there. The souls who resided in and around Johnsonville year round, were perfectly happy with their isolationism and the slow moving pace it produced. For many, it was why they lived there in the first place.

The lumber industry that had created the town had been replaced by the dollars of the city dwellers, eager to recreate the lifestyle of the locals, if only for a week or two. It was true the vacationers accounted for the bulk of the money that was made in the area. But the residents had seen the influx of tourists continue unabated for almost a hundred years so why, they asked, should they alter their own lifestyle when in the end, it really didn't seem to deter the backpackers, skiers, hunters, and fishermen anyway? So every time a vote to improve the roads came up, they voted it down and life continued pretty much the same.

John didn't mind the drive up. As a matter of fact, he loved it. Not only did he love the area, but it gave him a chance to put the Audi through its paces. The car was built to handle the curves and the hills and he thoroughly enjoyed pushing the little two seater to its limit. He hadn't even noticed that though Emily hadn't said a word, her often white knuckles evidenced the fact that he drove considerably above the *advised* speed limit on numerous occasions, especially the curves.

"You hungry?" he asked Emily as they stopped at the first man made light they had seen in two hours.

"Yes, and I could use a drink." she said looking at him with a face John didn't quite understand. She could see the confusion on his face and gave a short, quiet laugh. "I didn't realize I would be driving up here with Jeff Gordon, the race car driver."

It finally dawned on him that she had been more than a little skittish during the drive. "Sorry, I didn't realize that I was making you nervous."

"You didn't realize it because you didn't even know that I existed. When I wasn't holding on for dear life, I was watching you. You were completely in another world, smiling from ear to ear. I think I could have opened the door, jumped out and you wouldn't have known it and wouldn't have cared if you did."

He grinned sheepishly, "That's not true. I definitely would have cared. Your sudden departure would have upset the delicate weight ratio of the car and if you left the car door open, well, that would have destroyed the finely tuned aerodynamics and quite possibly ruined my door."

She laughed and playfully backhanded him on his shoulder. "Do you know of a place to eat around here?" she asked.

"As a matter of fact I do." Five minutes later they pulled into the parking lot of a small restaurant nestled amongst towering pines. The building itself had obviously started life as a single family home. A small stream ran along the back of the establishment and several picnic tables sat beside it. The atmosphere was more like that of the single family home it had once been, than that of an eatery open to the public. He parked and they got out.

"This is different," said Emily. "I'm surprised the parking lot is paved."

"They only paved it to keep down the dust. If the wind is right and you're eating at one of those picnic tables, someone pulling into the parking lot would send a plume of dust onto you and your food."

"This place is definitely off the beaten path and you seem to know a lot about it. You must have been here before."

"Once or twice." he remarked as he opened the front door for her. They walked into what would have been the living room. Walls had been removed so the area also absorbed the dining room and two long gone bedrooms. The dining room had a large picture window that overlooked the stream in the back. Where the master bedroom had probably been, sat a small bar. The tables were covered with red and white checkered table cloths. Emily was mildly surprised that the place appeared very neat and very clean and she instantly felt comfortable and welcomed. A portly woman in her mid-sixties approached them wearing an apron. Her graying hair had been done up in a bun and her cheerful round face gave the appearance, at least to Emily, of a perfect Mrs. Santa Claus.

"John!" she exclaimed as she walked up and laughingly threw her arms around him. "How the hell are you? Where have you been?"

A door suddenly burst open from the back and a very tall, thin, elderly gentleman walked out wearing an apron and a huge smile on his face. "John?" he said as he quickly moved toward them.

"I've been busy Emma," he told the woman. He looked up at the approaching man and said, "Hi Dwight. How's it going?"

Dwight walked up to him and he too put his arms around John. The three of them stood there like long lost relatives, arms clasped, patting each other on the back. After a moment, they disentangled themselves. Dwight and Emma looked at Emily. "Who's this?" Dwight asked.

"Emily," said John. "I would like you to meet Dwight and Emma Johnson. They are the owners of this fine establishment."

"Nice to meet you," Emily responded, a little taken aback at this turn of events.

They exchanged greetings with Emily and Emma showed them to a table. Emily sat down. Dwight tagged along. "Where's Mary Kate?" he asked.

"She's with her mom, Dwight."

"Bet you miss her," Emma chimed in. She looked at Emily. "Those two are inseparable and she's such a charming little creature, don't you think?"

Emily smiled tentatively, "I don't know. I've never met her."

Emma was nonplussed. She laughed heartily and said, "Then you're in for a real treat! To know her is to love her," and laughed again. "What can I get you?"

"Do you have wine?" she asked, a little uncomfortably. They seemed like very nice people and she didn't want to offend them. But the place was quite small and she couldn't imagine that they had a very large stock of assorted liquors.

Emma laughed again. "Don't be shy honey. Of course we do. Red or white?"

Emily decided to let well enough alone and politely responded, "Red please."

Emma and Emily both turned to look at John and Dwight. They were standing next to the table and had already descended into a deep discussion about ice fishing. Emily wondered who these people were and how did they know John so well? Emma interrupted them by placing a hand on John's arm with a smile and saying, "I'm assuming you want your usual, Bass Ale?"

"Is there any other beer that's fit for human consumption?" John laughed.

Emma looked back at Emily and said, "We keep it in stock just for John. We do sell a little of it to others, but most of the people that know about this place usually just want the normal beers." She looked back a Dwight and John. "Don't you two go and ignore this pretty lady here." To John she said, "About time I saw you with a woman. Now don't you go and blow it. You hear? As a matter of fact, Dwight, you have work to do. Leave these people alone. You can talk to John later."

John laughed, "I won't blow it. Don't you worry now Emma." With that, Dwight and Emma walked away.

John sat down and Emily said, "I think you have some explaining to do. 'Once or twice.' I believe you said when I asked if you've been here before." John looked at her for some time, without saying anything. Emily realized that he must be struggling with what he wanted to say. Finally, with a somber look that surprised her, he started to answer.

"Since you've done such research on me, I'm kind of surprised you don't already know about it." He slowly let out a long breath. "I've been coming up here for years for the hunting, fishing and snowmobiling," John slowly started to explain, "though not regularly until my second divorce. I decided I needed to get away for a while and use some accumulated sick days and vacation time to come up for a few weeks. I started to get to know the locals and soon found out about this place.

The night before I was scheduled to leave, I decided to come in here for dinner. I was renting a cabin just upstream and had elected to use my boat rather than a car. I was the only customer and I was seated in the corner over there when two men came in. There were no cars in the parking lot other than Dwight and Emma's truck and they obviously didn't see me when they entered.

When Emma approached them, one of them pulled a gun and the other grabbed her. It was a robbery. Idiots! This place does a pretty good business, but nowhere near good enough for something like that.

They called for Dwight to come out of the back. They didn't know his name but they knew he was back there. When he came out, they ordered him to empty the cash register. They got pissed when they saw how little was in there and started to pistol whip them both.

I was armed. I was still an active cop back then and had learned that you never knew when or where you would meet someone you had arrested and not all of them were happy about it. I had an off duty incident once in a hardware store and after that, I rarely went out without a gun.

Anyway, though I was armed, I hadn't taken any action because they had Emma as a hostage and because in most cases, robbers will just take the money and leave, so it wasn't worth interfering and having civilians shot. But when they started to pistol whip them, that took it to a whole new level.

I wanted to wait until I had a clear shot. Unfortunately, that didn't come until they had beaten them to the floor and then stood above them while they started to kick them. At that point I stood, pointed my weapon at them and identified myself as a police officer.

I had them dead to rights. To this day I don't know why they just didn't give up. I suppose because there were two of them, they felt they still had the upper hand. So they both raised their guns to shoot me. I shot the one that moved first. He was dead before he hit the floor. The second got off two shots before I fired at him. I missed and he got off a third before I fired again and hit him. It wasn't a killing or even a disabling hit, so he fired again. The next time I hit him right in the forehead. End of story.

What I didn't know, was that there was a third guy. He was the driver. He heard the shots and came flying through the door. I had already begun to move toward the shooters and the Johnsons, all lying on the floor. When the third guy burst through the door, my back was to him.

He fired three rapid shots and hit me once in the leg. I went down and returned fire, striking him twice. He lived for two days, then he was gone too."

It turned out that the three were wanted for killing a police officer downstate. They were hiding up here and staying in a cabin they had broken into, not far from this place. They were desperately low on cash and had been drinking, not enough to be considered drunk, but enough that it gave them some 'liquid courage.' They were driving into town to take a 'loan,' when they saw this restaurant. They came in, had a drink and left. Came back a few minutes later and hit the place. I had arrived in the meantime by boat and they didn't know I was here. I don't really regret what I did, they were plain mean people, I would just have preferred it hadn't happened at all, especially here."

Emily sat, transfixed by the tale. When he was finished, she waited a moment and said, "I asked you if you had ever shot anyone and you avoided the question. Now I know why. Have there been others?"

He gave her a rueful grin. "Like I said, the vast majority of policemen never fire their gun in anger, I'm not a good example."

"You still haven't answered the question."

He looked at her with a pained expression on his face. He suddenly shifted his gaze and Emily heard Emma's cheerful voice over her shoulder. "Here you go." She placed the drinks on the table in front of them. Emily looked at John and saw that he was looking at Emma, grinning from ear to ear. Not a trace of the agonizing look that she had just seen remained.

"Now what do you two want for dinner?" queried Emma.

"I'll have one of your great three quarter pound burgers,"

John happily replied.

"I haven't even looked at the menu," Emily responded. "But I know I don't want a hamburger and certainly not a three quarter pound one. What do you suggest?"

"Do you like chicken?" said John "Dwight's chicken is to die for."

"That would be fine."

Emma walked away and Emily attempted to return to their previous conversation. "You were saying?" she asked.

"I was saying that the food is great here. You're gonna love the chicken, really."

It was obvious that she would get no more from John on the subject, at least for the time being. She decided to switch gears. "What are you planning to do up here?"

"Well, there are a lot of tourists, but not that many places for them to go in town. If Harris and his cronies are here and they stay at the cabin, there's not much chance of finding them. However, if we're lucky, they might come into town for groceries or something else."

"What if they don't come into town?"

"Then we fall back to plan B."

"What's plan B?" she asked, her eyebrows furrowed in a confused stare.

He grinned. "Still working on that. Let me get back to you." Emily's look went to one of complete exasperation with a hint of anger and he could see that she didn't appreciate his humor. He continued in a more serious tone. "Okay, look, I know quite a few people up here. I can make some discreet inquiries to ask if anyone has seen a black Mercedes tooling around. Because it's a tourist area, I'm not sure how far that will get me, but you never know. I have to be careful because this is a pretty small town and because of the incident with the Johnson's, if I start asking a lot of questions, it's going to get around."

John looked up as Emma returned with their food. "Here you go. Would either of you like something else to drink?"

"I'm fine," Emily replied. "It smells delicious!"

"I'm good, too," John added. "Emma, I'd like to ask you something and I would appreciate it if we could keep this to ourselves."

Emma's smile wavered slightly as she responded. "Sure John. You know Dwight and I will help you in any way we can. I take it this isn't a social trip then? Damn! I was hoping you were finally introducing us to a significant other."

John grinned slightly and looked at Emily with more than a bit of embarrassment. "Well, that remains to be seen. But as of right now, I'm looking for a man driving a black Mercedes. He's in his thirties and probably in good shape." He reached for his cell phone and said, "Here, let me show you a picture of him."

He pulled up the picture Nick had sent him and showed it to her. She shook her head. "Nope, I haven't seen him or the car." She turned toward the back of the restaurant. "Dwight!" she yelled.

A moment later Dwight came through the doors in the back and was in the processes of drying his hands with a white towel. "What's up?" he asked as he approached them.

"John wants to know if you've seen this guy," she said as

she took the phone from John and gave it to Dwight.

He studied it a moment and replied, "Yeah. As a matter of fact I have."

John's eyes opened wide in astonishment. He hadn't really had much hope of anyone recognizing Harris. He tried to hide his excitement when he asked, "Where did you see him and when?"

"Last week. Some woman backed into his car in the parking lot at the Town Center grocery store. I was just coming out of the store when it happened. She just backed up without seeing him. She was attempting to give him her information as I was walking by, but he didn't want it. Just kept saying it was an accident and he understood. She popped him pretty good too, so I was pretty surprised at his reaction. I didn't recognize her. I think she was a tourist."

"Where did she hit the car?" John asked.

"Left front. Bent the bumper and took out the headlight. It was a damn shame because it was an absolutely beautiful black Mercedes."

That answered John's next question. It was the Mercedes. "Have you seen him since then?"

"I saw him stopped at a light about ten o'clock yesterday."

"Was he with anyone?"

"Yeah, there was a guy in the front seat. He was younger and not as big. Somebody was sitting in the back too, but the car's windows had a heavy tint, so I couldn't tell anything else."

This was more information than he could have hoped

for. He was betting that the smaller man in the front seat was probably Harris's accomplice from the night he took Sue. Who was in the back seat? Sue? Probably not. Why bring her into town in broad daylight and take a chance on something happening?

Pete? That would depend on the circumstances. If Pete was involved, then it could very well have been him. If Pete wasn't involved and was another kidnap victim like Sue, why take a chance and bring him into town in broad daylight?

He suddenly had another thought. It may have been Sue's boyfriend, Richard Clemmons. Dwight may have been witness to Clemmons's last car ride. He quickly worked out a timetable. He shook his head. No, it didn't fit. Scratch Clemmons. Harris had to have left town right around then in order to get back to the city in time to bump off Clemmons and clean out Sue's office. Unless he took both of the other passengers with him, that meant he had to drop them off and that meant wherever they were staying had to be very close to town.

He looked at Dwight again. "What direction were they heading?"

"South, out of town."

The main road coming into the area ran east and west. That tended to support a theory that Harris dropped his passengers off before leaving. So wherever they were staying was most likely south of town and close. He thought about what cabins were down there. He was mostly familiar with cabins to the northeast, since that was where he usually stayed. He had only been down to the south on a few occasions while fishing with local friends.

He began working out a timetable again. The cabin had to be located within ten minutes of town. Fifteen at the outside. Otherwise Harris's tight schedule would not have allowed him to drop his passengers off and still make it to the city on time. This reduced the search area considerably. Still, John knew that it would take several days to search the cabins within that zone. Not an option.

His thoughts were interrupted by Dwight. "Care to fill us in on what's going on?"

John looked at him and shook his head. "No, sorry but I don't think it's a good idea. This is some pretty serious crap and the less you know, the better Dwight. You know how I feel about you two and I certainly don't want to be responsible for bringing anything bad your way."

Emily watched as the smile fade from Emma's face for the first time since she had met her. "We owe you our lives John. We would do anything for you." She looked sad and concerned at the same time and Emily could see the whirlpool of memories cascading over her like an unexpected waterfall, brutally bringing the events of that day back to the here and now.

"I know that," he softly responded, "and I appreciate it. But all I want from you guys is to live a long, happy, and peaceful life and getting involved in this stuff is not the way to accomplish any of those things."

Emma bent as she leaned over to one side and put one arm around John and quietly said, "We love you like a son and we just want you to know that we're here for you."

Dwight suddenly spoke up in a loud and cheerful voice, "Didn't you hear what he said woman? He said 'be happy,' and that's just what I intend to do so leave them alone so they can eat their dinner in peace. By the way, do you have a place to stay yet?"

"I was thinking of staying at The Lodge." John replied.

"What? Did you suddenly get independently wealthy?" Dwight saw Emily's confused look and said, "The Lodge is the nicest place in town. They have a cool swimming pool that's indoor and outdoor. They have a glass partition that goes a few inches underwater. You can get from one side to the other by swimming underneath it. It's a pretty neat place… and pretty damn expensive." He turned back to John and threw a set of keys at him. "Unless you have your heart set on spending a lot of money, or you want to impress Emily here, use our cabin. Nobody's renting it at the moment." He looked at his wife and said, "Come on Emma, before he tries to turn us down." They both quickly left the room.

John caught the keys in one hand. "Thanks. I appreciate it." he yelled after them. Dwight waved a hand back at them as he and Emma went through the double doors.

"Nice people," said Emily.

"The best there is." John replied and he and Emily started talking about the Johnson's and the area as they ate their dinner. She wanted to know more about how John was going to handle this. But after her previous rebuff, she decided to let well enough alone. He would tell her in his own time.

They finished eating and Emma came out to ask them if

they wanted anything else. Neither of them did. Emily, in fact, was as full as she had been in a long time. The food, the atmosphere, the company and the wine had been so good. She had temporarily forgotten all of their troubles and it felt simply wonderful.

She watched in amusement as Emma and John good naturedly fought over the check. They finally reached a compromise, said their good byes and she and John left.

The evening was pleasantly cool as they walked back to the car. "Let's put the top down," she said as they were getting in.

"I'd love to, but it's not a good idea." he responded. "We are here on business after all. I want to go through town and take a quick look around. Then I want to spot check the area to the south. If we happen to see them, they will easily recognize us if we have the top down. So forget the top for now."

She had the look of someone who has just had a bucket of cold water thrown on them. Once again he felt guilty for having caused it. He quickly added, "Once this is over, I promise that we will go anywhere you want, with the top down, up, or sideways." He looked at her and grinned as he backed the car up.

But his attempt at joviality appeared to do little good as she gave him another of her strange looks and returned once again to the position she had held when he pulled into the parking lot earlier, looking out her window, facing away from him. He shook his head in confusion and pulled out of the parking lot.

CHAPTER
15

After leaving the Johnson's restaurant, John headed toward town. It was dusk when they arrived and he began to slowly traverse the main streets, looking for Harris or his car. He did a quick scan of the parking lots that he could see from the road as well. He didn't think the chances were good that he'd find Harris right away. But then again, he hadn't thought that he would have found out the amount of information that he'd garnered already. A stroke of luck that was.

Luck... was it really? It certainly appeared that he had indeed been lucky to have had Dwight as an eye witness but he also knew that was how most investigations went. It was a matter of asking the right questions, of the right people, at the right time. Almost always the answers were out there. Almost always, someone knew something. They saw it. They heard it. They experienced it. Like an Easter egg hunt, it was a matter of looking until each little jewel of information was discovered. Each nugget was a piece of the larger puzzle. Once fitted together, each piece provided a clue to the finished picture.

He remembered being taken to the side by a grizzled, gray haired patrol sergeant when he had been a rookie. He was the responding officer on an armed robbery and he was a bit intimidated. Not by the thought of a shootout. That was every rookie's dream. Besides, the perpetrator was long gone. Rather than feeling excited, he was overwhelmed by scope of the crime and since he was the responding officer, he knew the information that he gathered would be crucial to the case. He found that it was one thing to be taught the proper procedure at the Academy, it was quite another having to do it for the first time.

He had gotten the description of the perpetrator and had already given that out over the radio, when his sergeant arrived. Knowing this was John's first big case, he took him to the side and told him simply. "Remember the five 'W's:' Who, What, Where, When, and Why. Answer those five questions and you can't go too far wrong. Stay calm, use your head, remember your training and don't hesitate to ask for help if you need it. You'll be fine." It was sage advice and it calmed him immediately. Over the years, that discussion came back to him on many occasions. Replaying, like a training video, it always set him on the correct path.

And now John knew that he didn't need too many more pieces of the puzzle to find out where Susan was. Finding Harris or his car would be a big piece, probably the final piece. He briefly debated calling Nick to ask for some air support in the form of a helicopter, but decided against it for two reasons; First and foremost, with Harris's military training, he would probably be leery of helicopters or other low flying craft. The second reason was the need to keep this investigation low key. When it got to the point of bringing in aircraft, the chances of keeping the investigation quiet would pretty much go out the window.

As on the trip up, Emily never said a word. John was confused. He thought they had a really good thing going, so why the silent treatment? She was fine one minute, ice queen the next. He hoped that it was the stress of their current situation and not her habitual behavior. He wasn't sure how long he'd be able to put up with this condition if this was her norm. Perhaps that was the reason for her unmarried, unattached status.

They cruised the town for about two hours before she spoke, so softly that he hardly heard her. "How long are we going to do this?"

He looked at her and saw that she looked exhausted and stressed to the max. The obvious strain on her face just added to his already jumbled feelings. "I'll probably call it a day soon. It's just that confirming was Harris definitely here gave me a real boost and time is of the essence. We don't know if they have any idea how close we are and I have a feeling that once they know, Susan will be in some serious shit."

She looked at him a moment before saying. "I don't mean to complain but I can hardly keep my eyes open If it's going to be much longer, can you please take me to where we're staying and drop me off?"

They were stopped at an intersection on the main street in town and he was looking over at her. Suddenly, in the distance beyond her, he saw a car running parallel to them, about two blocks away. He couldn't tell what make it was, but he saw that the left headlight was cockeyed and pointing toward the center of the road. Could have been nothing more than a misaligned beam, or... it could have been a damaged fender. He quickly looked around to make sure there was no traffic and made a quick right hand turn, accelerating rapidly.

"What's going on?" Emily asked in a high pitched, frightened tone. Her exhausted eyes were now wide open and she didn't look tired any longer.

"There's a car down here with a weird left headlight. Couldn't tell anything else so I want to check it out," he said hurriedly. He was rapidly approaching the street the car had gone down.

"Is it him?"

"Tell you in a minute," and with that he began braking hard as he approached the street the car with the damaged headlight had been traveling on. He slowed to almost a stop before poking the nose of the little car far enough into the intersection to see down the street to his left. He was just in time to see the car make a left turn three blocks down. It looked like a Mercedes!

John made a left and zoomed down one street before he made another left as well, mimicking the directions of the Mercedes, but two blocks down. He spurted back toward the main street. As before, he applied the brakes hard and approached the intersection slowly. Nothing attracted attention more than a vehicle that screamed up to an intersection, only to apply squealing brakes at the last second. Even the most casual drivers would take notice of such an action. For someone who was constantly on the lookout for cars that might be following them, it would be a huge, flashing neon sign saying, "Hey look at me!" That was something John wanted to avoid at all costs.

The car in question turned right, onto the main street. The businesses on the corner provided enough light that he could now clearly see that the car was a black Mercedes Benz. He waited for the car to get further down the street before he too, pulled out onto the main street and began following it.

The Mercedes had John's rapt attention. He jumped as he heard Emily ask, "How do we know that's him?"

He was in full pursuit mode now and her question annoyed him, breaking his concentration. "We don't know for sure, but it's a black Mercedes with a bum headlight. What are the odds in a town this small?" he said quickly and harshly, without taking his eyes off his quarry.

The big Mercedes proceeded down the street for approximately half a mile before suddenly turning left onto another side street. Something about the maneuver sent alarm bells ringing within John's head. He'd spent a lot of years following people, his entire adult life in fact. He thought about the side street the Mercedes had been on when he had first seen it and the unexpected quickness of this last turn. He decided that his target was looking for a tail!

This was not an unusual event and it certainly did not necessarily mean he had been detected. It was really quite a reasonable precaution that anyone in Harris's position would take. Truth be told, Harris would be extraordinarily negligent if he had not done so and nothing in Harris's background suggested such incompetence. It had turned into a game of wits and now the question was whether John could outwit his opponent. He had to. Lives depended on it, for if he was caught... well it would be safe to say that Susan's stock in life would suddenly take a dramatic downturn.

He suddenly remembered that it wasn't just her life at stake here. If Coeptus Guild succeeded in getting her program, the lives of *millions* would be affected. And not just financially. The possible overthrow of governments would mean lives would be lost, in numbers too horrible to imagine. As the cliché goes, "Failure is not an option." With this grim thought in mind, John concentrated on his efforts even harder.

He quickly checked to see if there was another street he could go down that would run parallel to the street Harris had gone down. He was far enough behind Harris that there were four streets open to John. He took the first one and doused his headlights soon after he made the turn. There were enough street lights that he could safely proceed. As he approached each intersection, he looked to see if he could see the Mercedes.

The first block, nothing. The second block, still nothing. He picked up speed and as he entered the third intersection, he saw the Mercedes turning left, *toward him*. Harris was doubling back! He hoped he was far enough away that Harris had not seen John's unlit Audi passing through the intersection. Most likely Harris was looking where he was going as he made his turn and looking for what was behind him, therefore unlikely that he would picked John out.

John sped two more blocks before quickly pulling to the side and putting the car in neutral. He took his foot off the brake and told Emily, "If he comes down here I want you to put your arms around me and kiss like you've never kissed before."

In spite of her fear, she smiled. This was a world far from her computers and monitors and endless lines of computer code. She felt a mixture of deep rooted angst and at the same time a sense of primeval sexual arousal. "You think that's the only way to throw him off do you?" she asked in a husky, sensuous voice.

John looked at her in dismay. She had gone from Ice Princess, to this. Go figure. He didn't answer her as he returned his attention and his gaze back to his rearview mirror. Harris had plenty of time to pass the intersection and he hadn't. John quickly put the car into gear and performed a u-turn. He passed the intersection Harris should have gone through and saw no sign of him. John turned his own lights back on as he accelerated back toward the main road. Emily watched as the speedometer approached ninety.

John reached the street just in time to see Harris turning back onto the main street and continuing on his original course. Not wanting to take any chances, John continued on across the main street. If Harris was looking for a tail, he'd be watching for any car that turned in his direction from any of the adjacent streets he had just come from.

As soon as John was out of sight of Harris, he quickly turned into a driveway and turned around. He went back to the main street and saw that Harris was continuing in a normal fashion. He pulled out and began following once again.

A few minutes later, Harris wound up approaching the road leading south out of town. He was heading toward the exact area where John had figured Harris was holed up. There had been no further shenanigans. Harris turned on to the road and proceeded south. Upon approaching the road himself, John had once again turned off his headlights. He waited as long as he dared before turning onto the road and began following in Harris's path.

He drove down the barely lit road for some time and didn't turn his lights on until the Mercedes had disappeared over a hill. There were few houses here and the road had a posted rural speed limit. Harris was doing about eighty and John was following with no lights! Emily had just about reached her breaking point when, much to her relief, he switched the headlights back on.

John was beginning to relax, but quickly stopped himself. He knew that this would be an excellent time to make a mistake. It appeared the worst was over and now it was just a matter of following the target to his destination. It was now, when the adrenaline was leaving, replaced by a relaxed euphoria that comes from a job well done, that mistakes happened. There comes a time when, in most cases, the pursuer has just successfully followed a car through a particularly difficult situation. Then, it appears, the worst is over and it is just a matter of following the vehicle to the final location, no snags in sight. That couldn't be more wrong.

He had known a seasoned investigator that had once lost a bus during this time period. Everyone had a good yuck over that one. But those with experience, laughed a knowing laugh and prayed that it never happened to them. The first rule of tailing was that one never relaxed, even if it was a bus or a little old lady tooling around in her twenty year old car, until the pursuit was at an end. Until that time, *anything* could happen.

About five minutes out of town, Harris suddenly darted down another street. Though he wasn't too familiar with the area, it appeared to be another small subdivision off from the road leading into town. John made a quick decision and pulled to the side of the road. He stopped, doused his lights once again and waited.

"Aren't you going to follow him?" Emily asked tentatively. In his current operating mode, she wasn't sure if he would snap at her again.

Instead, he replied calmly. "I think we're very close and he's probably being very cautious right now. I'm taking a chance here. This looks like a small subdivision, probably only two or three streets in the middle of nowhere. I'm betting that the only way out of that area is this road, which means he has to return to it. I'd put money that Harris has familiarized himself with the few houses and the related cars that belong there. It's the perfect place to ferret out a tail. If I go in there, I'm liable to go around a corner and find him sitting on the side of the road, waiting to see who comes around the corner after him.

The trouble with taking chances like this, is that it can come back to bite you. I could be completely wrong and right now Harris might be two miles away and for all intents and purposes, long gone. If that's the case, at least we're a little closer and we can narrow our search pattern for tomorrow."

Emily nodded, but said nothing. A minute went by. Two minutes. Three. Emily was beginning to squirm. Another minute and then another. Finally she could see headlights coming out of the subdivision, on a road further to the south from where Harris had gone in. Was it him? The car behind the beams stopped at the intersection and she could tell from the misaligned headlight that it was Harris. He turned left and continued south. John had been right.

John pulled out and once again began following. As before, he didn't turn on his lights until Harris went out of view. A few minutes later, Harris once again turned off the road. But this time he did so in a normal fashion. John approached the turn off point and they could see that it was a small road or a very long driveway. No house was in sight.

As they passed, neither John, nor Emily could see any sign of the Mercedes. John drove on without slowing down. He continued until he was out of sight. He then pulled onto another road and he continued down this road until he came to a grove of trees. Then he turned around and headed back the way he had come, but stopped by the edge of the trees.

"Now what are you doing?" Emily asked.

"Once again I'm taking a chance and I'm being cautious. I'm trying to anticipate Harris, asking myself what I would do in this situation. That road is barely one car width wide and heavily wooded, most likely a driveway. The prudent thing for him to do would be to turn on to the road, turn off his lights, wait a minute or so and see if anyone passes by. If someone does, wait another minute, then back out on to the main road and follow in the direction of the car that just passed. If the passing car has turned around and is coming back toward the direction of the driveway, it's probably a tail. If not, he's good to go and he can drive to his destination.

We're sitting here now while we wait to see if he does follow us. If he does, we drive off out of the area, like nothing has happened and we hang it up for the night. There is also the possibility that he pulled into the driveway as another check to see if anyone was following and is long gone, but I don't think that's the case. Keep in mind that it's difficult to remain vigilant every day, day after day, time after time. You start to relax, cut corners."

They waited in silence for several minutes. "I think we're safe." he said finally.

"Now what?" Emily asked.

"Now I'm going to take a little walk and see if I can get an exact location on their cabin, maybe see if I can spot Susan or Peter."

"Shouldn't we call the police now?" she queried.

Without saying a word, he reached for his cell phone, opened it and showed it to her. Small words on the screen told them there was no service. "Besides," he added, "Until I get an actual visual confirmation, we're not calling anybody. We need to know the lay of the land, exactly what's going on, before taking any action and unless I actually see them tonight, this is strictly a re-con mission." He reached for his door handle. "I'll be right back."

He got out, walked to the trunk and opened it. He spent a couple of minutes putting on some leather boots and a black wool sweater. Then he collected several clips of ammunition for his .45 and put them into his coat pockets. He also retrieved a penlight and a small, but powerful set of binoculars that were equipped with night vision. He surveyed the trunk and did a mental check. He was as ready as he was going to get.

He walked back to the car and got in. "Now here's how this is going to work." he told Emily. "I want you to drive up near the entrance to the driveway. We can go slow, but I want you to do it with no lights, think you can do that?" She nodded and he continued. "Okay, when it's time to pull over, I don't want you to use the brake pedal. Instead, I want you to use the emergency brake to stop the car. That will take a lot longer to stop, but there will be no brake lights for anyone to see. Got this so far?"

"Yeah." she responded.

"Any problems with it?"

"No." she responded again.

"Good. Now when we get there I'm going to get out and walk down the driveway. You stay where you are unless you hear gunshots. If that happens, I want you to drive like hell until you get into cell phone range and call the cops. Otherwise, stay here until I return. If I'm not back in two hours, leave. Come back in two more hours. If I'm still not back, call Nick Giovanni at our police department. He's a friend. Talk to no one but him. Okay?" She nodded in affirmation. "Alright, let's switch."

The both got out of the car and switched positions. When they got back in Emily put the car in gear and got off to a jerking start. "I forgot to ask if you can drive a stick shift."

"I had a boyfriend that had a stick, but that was years ago and I haven't driven one since. Don't worry, I'll get it," she said in response.

She pulled back onto the main road and proceeded in the direction of the driveway. As they got closer John said firmly, "Start applying your parking brake now. You're not used to it and like I said, it takes a lot longer to stop the car with it."

She started to do so as he was speaking. The car's speed began to slowly drop. As they approached the entrance, he continued, "Go about fifty feet past the entrance. Keep watching for headlights coming out of the driveway, indicating that someone is leaving. If that's the case, I want you to leave. By parking on the other side of the driveway, they won't be as apt to see your lights when you turn them on, which I don't want you to do until you're on the roadway proper. If that happens, come by every half hour and be watching for me, I'll be walking back toward the road where we made our switch. Ready?"

She nodded. They were stopped on the side of the road. "Be careful." she cautioned.

"Always." he grinned. Then he got out and quietly shut

the door. He walked back to the entrance and began to move down the driveway, but far to one side. He didn't like being out in the open like this, but the only other alternative was to walk in the woods. He didn't want to do that because walking in the woods, especially at night, would be noisy. The crunching sound of snapped twigs and fallen leaves was incredibly loud in the otherwise still surroundings and there wasn't enough snow left on the ground to muffle the noise.

He walked only a short distance before he saw an odd shape sticking out from the trunk of a tree. There appeared to be some sort of line dangling from it. He took out his binoculars and switched them to night vision mode. Whatever it was, was box shaped and appeared man made . He put away his binoculars and retrieved a pen light. He covered the lens of the light with his hand so that the already small beam of light was now nothing more than a pinprick. He carefully checked for anything in his path that might make a noise as he stepped off the driveway and cautiously approached the protruding box.

When he got to it, he was dismayed with what he found. It was obviously a camera, most likely equipped with night vision. He followed the line and found that it led up to the driveway, where it crossed, hidden beneath a thin layer of dirt and gravel. This made him feel a little better, but not much.

What he had found, was an alarm system. The line going across the driveway was obviously pressure sensitive. A vehicle passing over it would trigger the camera on the tree. It was most likely a video camera and a short piece of wire coming out of the top of the box told him that it had a wireless connection that was hooked up to some sort of monitoring device.

The good news was that he had not driven over the line and the presence of the system pretty much confirmed that Harris was here. The bad news was that he didn't know if it was a passive/active device. If there were more cameras in the woods like this, they were most assuredly hooked up to at least one monitor, maybe more. In a passive system, the camera remained off until triggered by the pressure switch. In an active system, the camera was always on, constantly feeding video back to the monitor. In a passive/active system, this remained true, but with a caveat. If hooked up to some sort of alarm system, it would either trigger an audible alarm and/or, if there were multiple cameras feeding the monitor, the feed would switch immediately to the camera with the tripped alarm.

John didn't know if this was the case. If it was an active system, he could only hope that there were other cameras and no one noticed him. He briefly considered pulling out and trying again later, but decided against it. He had to gather some intelligence so he could proceed as soon as possible. Time was precious at this point. But now he would have to go slowly and as carefully as he could.

He weighed his possibilities. He was lucky in one sense, if that had been a motion detector instead of a pressure switch, they would have had him dead to rights. However, John also knew that there were practical drawbacks to motion sensors of any type in these conditions. The chief problem being that of wildlife. A deer could easily pass for a human with a motion or heat detector. But a deer couldn't pass for a car, as in the case of the pressure line going across the driveway. That made sense this far away, but closer in, it may be entirely an different situation. Ground sensors were another matter, he prayed there were none. Regardless, he would have to proceed judiciously.

He decided that the woods were a better option at this point and began to carefully parallel the driveway, heading toward what he assumed would be the house. He found one more pressure switch before coming to a clearing. He figured that he had already gone approximately a quarter mile. This was taking a lot more time than he had thought it would. Instead of walking straight across the open area, he steered himself around the edge of it until he was back in the vicinity of the driveway.

He had walked a short distance further down the edge of the driveway before seeing two things. The first, were lights coming from a house. The second, was another tree with a camera, but this one was different. He approached it, watchful for other alarms or at this point, human guards.

He found this camera was hooked up to an infrared beam. The beam was set high enough that no deer was likely to trigger it, a human certainly would. If John had been walking down the driveway, he would have entered the beams effective area. By traveling some distance off the driveway, he had avoided triggering it.

After inspecting the box, he remained still in that position for several minutes. He carefully scanned the entire area visible from his position, trying to find anymore devices. He could see none, nor did he see any outside human activity.

After he was as certain as he could be that there was nothing else in this immediate area that would alert the occupants of the house to his presence, he moved slowly forward. When he got to the edge of the woods near the building, he hunkered down and took stock of the situation before him.

The house was a one story log home with a large front porch. An oversized, detached garage sat in front of the home but off to one side, approximately one hundred feet away. The garage was large enough to accommodate at least three cars and a lot of toys such as snowmobiles, boats, and other recreational wilderness items. He could not see the Mercedes and he assumed it must be inside the garage.

Several lights were on within the home, but the shades were drawn and he could see no figures. He picked his way around to the back of the house, always vigilant for guards or other devices. He found none and curiously, this was disconcerting to him. What bothered John was that it was not likely that Harris had done such a thorough job of securing the driveway but had neglected the other ways of approaching the area.

After reaching the woods at the back of the dwelling, he sat for a while and surveyed the area, looking for any indication that he had been discovered. He dared not approach any closer. Much to his relief, he appeared to be in the clear and so he went back to studying the house.

He immediately noticed that two of the windows had

grates over them. His heart leapt! These grates were common in inner-city areas where crime was a problem. The bars prevented any intruders from easily gaining access into the residence. Unfortunately, as was the case for some fire victims, they were equally as good at preventing anyone from getting out of the home.

In his own mind, this confirmed that Susan had at least been here. There seemed to be no other logical explanation as to why only two of the windows would be covered. If the purpose was to prevent a burglary, what good would it do to only cover two windows? Still, that did not mean she remained here, especially in light of the fact that things had not gone according to plan. Since Sue's boyfriend, Clemmons, had made calls from this area, it was safe to assume he knew of this place. If Harris thought that Clemmons had been compromised, he could very well have moved her. But if that was the case, then why was he still coming here?

After several minutes, John decided to move over to the garage. He peered in one of the windows that were further from the house. He risked a quick search of the interior with his pen light. There was the Mercedes! Next to it sat a Jeep CJ5. Clemmons's? How did that get here? He rethought his original timeline. No, it still didn't fit that Clemmons was killed up here. He simply didn't have the time to make it to Johnsonville after his run in with John.

He finally decided the reason for the Jeep being here was the least of his worries right now and it was time 'to get out of Dodge.' He'd been on this little impromptu excursion long enough and he didn't know how much longer his luck would hold. Better to get out with what he had, map out a strategy and return when he was properly equipped and better prepared.

He retraced his route and was back to the road much faster than it had taken him to get in. By now he was pretty sure there were no outside guards and he was fairly confident that he'd discovered all of the devices near the driveway, otherwise, he reasoned, he would have already been discovered.

The Audi still sat on the side of the road, exactly where it had been when he left. He walked up to the passenger door and tried to open it, but it was locked. Emily exclaimed, "Oh!" She had her cell phone up to her ear and was obviously taken aback by his presence. She unlocked the door and as he was getting in said to him, "I was watching for you, but I didn't see you until you tried the door."

"Go," he said simply, "and remember, no lights."

She pulled out on to the road and a short time later asked, "Is it okay to turn on the lights now?"

He had been looking back, making sure that no one was following them. "Yeah," he replied. "Who were you on the phone with? I can't believe you got a signal out here."

"I didn't," she answered a bit defensively. "I was trying to get hold of my mother. I call her pretty often and I haven't for a while. I was bored and I wanted to see if I could get through. I didn't dare leave for fear you would come back and find me gone, though I was about to leave anyway since you said to go if you weren't back in two hours."

John quickly looked at the dashboard clock and was

shocked to find that he'd been gone over two hours! It seemed like twenty or thirty minutes, certainly no more than an hour. He also realized that he was exhausted.

"What did you find?" Emily asked. "Are they there?"

"I don't know for sure if Susan or Peter are there, but Harris's car is in the garage, along with the Jeep that belonged to Sue's boyfriend.

She gasped. "Really? What would his Jeep be doing here?"

"I'm not sure. They probably wanted it to disappear for a while. They had no way of knowing his body would be discovered so quickly. That also means that someone other than Harris had to drive it up here." He didn't add that if Peter was involved, *he* could easily have been the one to drive the Jeep to Johnsonville. His cell phone suddenly beeped several times, announcing to both of them that they were back in cell phone range. It seemed unnaturally loud in the quiet confines of the small car.

He picked it up and saw he had two voice mail messages. He dialed the phone center and listened. The first was from his daughter, who sounded very disappointed and upset that he hadn't answered. It was time for their evening goodnight call ritual. Oops! Too late to call her back now.

The second message was from Jenny, the dispatcher from his old police department. She was talking in a whisper and sounded frantic. It wasn't like her to sound like this. She'd been handling emergency calls for years and nothing much shook her anymore. Her tone made him sit up and listen intently, his face furrowed with concern and at least a little confusion.

"Where the hell are you?" she demanded. "I need to talk to you, ASAP. The Deputy Chief's..." The phone went quiet for a moment, then he heard her voice again, but she obviously wasn't talking into the phone anymore. "No, I'm just having a smoke break." He heard a man's voice in the background, then from Jenny, "Can't it wait until I'm done with my cigarette?" and suddenly the connection broke.

He looked at his watch. He could try to call her back at the station now, but judging from when he last saw her working, her shift was probably over. He looked at the caller ID on his phone, her number was blocked and he didn't know her home number. He considered calling Nick, but decided against it because he was sure Nick was home in bed. He knew between Clemmons's body last night and the rape/homicide from the night before, Nick wouldn't have gotten too much sleep lately. Oh well. He was sure Jenny would call back when she got a chance. He was curious about the way she sounded.

He turned his attention back to Emily and guided her to the Johnson's log cabin. As was everything else in the area, it was secluded and nestled deep in the forest. It sat on one of the many small lakes and appeared to be quiet, old, which in fact it was. It had been built by a trapper around the turn of the century, but had undergone many renovations over the years. It was now equipped with all the modern conveniences. All, except that is, air conditioning, which generally wasn't needed up here anyway.

They walked through the front door and into the main

room of the cabin, that was dominated by a massive stone fireplace. There was a small compartment to either side, each equipped with a cast iron door. The trapper spared no expense when he built the fireplace. The compartments were ovens that took their energy from the heat that radiated through the stones of the fireplace. Stone slits made by pieces of slate at the top of the fireplace, opened into chambers built behind the face of the structure. These gathered the hot air from the fireplace as well and directed it through the vents and into the room by convection power for further efficiency. All in all, a masterpiece in turn of the century engineering.

They took their bags to the bedroom and Emily announced, "I'm going to take a shower. How about you?" There was a tired, but mischievous look in her eyes.

"I am pretty rank myself. It's not the end of the week yet, but I suppose I could take one now, if properly persuaded."

With that, she began disrobing, never taking her eyes off from his. When she was finished, he stood there in awe, taking in all of her feminine beauty. To John, at that moment, Michelangelo himself could not have sculptured a more perfect specimen. At last he said, "Consider me persuaded," and with that he took her hand and led her to the bathroom.

CHAPTER

16

The woman stared, mesmerized by the dazzling light show provided by the screen saver on the computer monitor in front of her. She was tired, upset, angry, confused, mentally drained, and truth be told, more than a little scared. Her normally beautiful face was etched with lines of worry and sadness. But in spite of all this, there were the twinges of a smile at the corners of her lips. She was looking at the bright lights of the screen-saver without really seeing them. Her mind was elsewhere, far, far from this small, moldy smelling room in which she now sat.

She was thinking of happier times. When her father would throw her up in the air and catch her screaming, laughing form only at the last possible moment. How they would laugh together. She remembered piggy back rides and fishing trips. She remembered ice skating and birthday parties, which her father always insured were to her liking and always went off without a hitch. She had to admit, he was a good father. The best and she couldn't have imagined how he could have been any better. She had loved him with all her heart. But then, she learned, he had faults. He wasn't the perfect man she had thought him to be. He was just a man and in her eyes, he had betrayed her. Now, years later and obviously in deep trouble, she found herself thinking of him and quite possibly, his fate. Because, apparently, she held his life in her hands. She had a decision to make.

Susan Melissa Browning sat in the room and stalwartly held back the tears that threatened to well up in her eyes once more. Her middle name belonged to her grandmother, whom she had always admired and looked up to. Her grandmother was another in a long line of steely-spined women. Like Melissa and her daughter, Dana, Susan had a strong mind that she could bend to her iron will as staunchly as her father could. It took strong men to stand toe to toe with such women. Which was why her mother, Dana, had first fallen in love with her father. She was way more like her parents than she really liked to admit. It was this unwavering determination that made her so good at plowing through line after line of computer code. Couple that with her mother's fierce desire to do good, be good, and it was most likely pre-ordained that she would become such an activist extraordinaire.

For truly, she meant only good by this creation. As with so many inventions, the original purposes of their creators were warped by diabolical men intent on using them to fulfill their own desires. The history of mankind is littered with such inventions gone awry. In more recent times, Richard Gatling, the inventor of the fierce Civil War era Gatling machine gun, had not invented it to improve the efficiency of warfare. Rather, he wanted a gun so terrifying that no man would choose to face it and would instead meet at the peace table. But nobody stayed home. Armies across the world eagerly snapped up every Gatling they could get their hands on and wars became bloodier than ever.

Almost exactly like Richard Gatling, the inventors of the Atomic Bomb, did so out of an aspiration to promote peace, to save lives by compelling the Japanese to the bargaining table, not to show men how to wipe out the entire planet. But though peace was obtained for a short time, the world became a far more terrifying place in the end.

Now, like the countless inventions before it, her crowning achievement was about to be warped into something for which she had never intended. She wanted it to be used to *protect* the world community from malicious hackers and now these people obviously wanted it to *attack* that very same community. In retrospect, she'd been a fool really, possessing a naiveté that the world at large may now have to pay for.

Her work was set up in two stages. The first was the hacking part in which thousands of tiny "bots," were sent out to search for information. "Bots," short for robots, were a programmed version of the physical kind that everyone knows about, a sort of mindless, mini program that would do it's master's bidding. In this case, obtain information and relay that back. She created this as the ultimate hack, thinking that if she could find a way to stop *this* program, she could stop anything. Fortunately, she hadn't completed the first stage yet, the stage that contained the ultimate hack. Almost though. They had sprung their trap too soon. Had they waited, maybe even only a week, she would have been finished and they would have found it on her laptop. It would have taken them a while to crack the encryption she had placed on it, but probably not as long as they surmised.

That was what had saved Susan. They thought that she, of all people, would have had a top flight encryption program on it that may never be broken. They assumed they needed her to unlock it. Little did they know that she had only a rudimentary lock. She had started the program more as an after work lark, meant only to stave off bouts of loneliness, only a couple of steps above playing a video game. But then she became more and more entranced by it. It sucked her in and before she realized it, it had become her full time obsession. She wasn't scared by it and she didn't really think anyone would care about it. Certainly not enough to steal it. She talked about it openly to anyone who wanted to listen, and there weren't many of those. That naiveté again.

It had taken up all her time, until that is, she met Richard Clemmons. She had bumped into him at the health club and was immediately attracted to him from the start. However, as beguiled as she may have been, the bitter lessons she had learned from her past love life, limited though it was, as well as her father's actions, outweighed any immediate desires to become involved. For she had learned that there were many men out there just like her father, more than willing to hop into the bed of a beautiful woman, consequences be damned. Worse yet, as soon as they found yet another beautiful woman, they would hop into that bed too and so it went.

So it wasn't a question of being swept off her feet and acting impulsively. Rather it was a persistence on his part that lasted long after most suitors would have surrendered. He started showing up whenever she worked out. He always seemed to know the right thing to say. He invariably made her laugh and brightened her day. Clemmons began to ask her to play racquet ball and to rock climb with him at the health club facilities. And eventually, she began to consent. Finally, one day, he asked her to go to a Jimmy Buffet concert with him. He said he had a date, but she cancelled at the last minute and now he was stuck with an extra ticket. She absolutely loved Jimmy Buffet. Bulls-eye! She agreed.

So it went. The next thing she knew, he was coming over to her apartment every day, and leaving less often at night. She liked having him around because, unlike most people, he always seemed so interested in her work. She could talk about it for hours and he never seemed to get bored. Again, the naiveté.

All was heavenly bliss, for a while. But then things slowly began to change. It seemed that he wanted to go out with her less and less. Instead, he wanted to talk about her work, to the point that even *she* was getting sick of it. She was already beginning to feel uneasy about their relationship when one day, he announced that he wanted to be her manager and sell her new program. She steadfastly refused. He persisted and she began to get angry.

The final straw came when she had wanted to go out for dinner and catch a movie that she had been waiting to see for some time. To her utter disbelief, he wanted her to stay at home and work on the program. They had a horrendous fight and at the end, in spite of his pleas for forgiveness, she showed him the door. She refused his calls and hadn't talked to him or seen him since that night. That was two months ago.

Sue reverted to the same humdrum existence that she had led before meeting him, more convinced than ever that men weren't worth the bother and that unfortunately, her grandmother's heredity would end with her. She poured herself into her work and was very nearly done when they had taken her.

She had been at home, cleaning up a late night dinner and watching the news, when she heard her front door open. She felt certain that she was mistaken. Maintenance always called, or at least knocked before entering. She had given her key to no one.

She came around the kitchen corner in time to see two figures rushing at her. Instead of trying to run away, she stood stock still in shock and disbelief in what she was seeing. By the time she snapped out of it, they were on her. The bigger man grabbed her and threw her face first into the wall, making the thump that John had heard from just outside her window. A damp cloth came over her mouth and nose just as she was beginning to struggle, but by then, it was far too late. She made a feeble attempt to cry out as darkness over took her and she knew no more.

She woke up on the bed, here, in this room. The room was in total darkness and she could see nothing. Disoriented, but fearing the worst, she immediately checked her clothing and found, much to her relief, that they did not appear to have been disturbed. She got up, felt around the room, found the windows and pulled the drapes open. The windows were boarded shut and there was absolutely no light coming in from the outside. She continued to bump her way around the room until she found a light switch. She flicked it on and was rewarded with a blinding light from a small table lamp by the bed.

She tried the door, locked. She got down on her hands and knees to look under it, nothing, no light whatsoever. She stood up and began to inspect her surroundings. The room appeared to be a master bedroom. It was equipped with the normal bedroom furniture with the exception of small, "L" shaped desk in one corner. A rather expensive computer sat on it. She also realized about that time, that there were no clocks in her small quarters.

The room had a normal sized closet and its own private bath. She opened the medicine cabinet in the bathroom and as expected, found nothing. A further search revealed a washcloth, towels, soap, and various other sundries under the cabinet. No razor blades or shaver, she wryly noted. She moved back to the bedroom and checked the dresser where she found underwear, several pairs of slacks and shirts, all new and she realized in growing horror, all in her size.

She was just finishing her inspection when she heard the door opening. She spun around to face the door and watched as a nicely dressed, small, wiry man in his late fifties entered the room. "Good evening Ms. Browning." he said in a pleasantly soft but oddly gravelly voice. "I hope my men didn't cause you too much discomfort. I would really like us to be friends."

"You've got to be kidding!" replied a stunned Susan. She was struck by the thought that the man was acting as though this were nothing more than a casual business meeting, not a kidnapping and probably more. She apparently hadn't been raped. Intuitively, she could think of only one other reason her kidnappers would have gone to such lengths... her program.

The wiry man continued, "Susan, may I call you Sue? Please, call me Carl. You and I have something in common: a love for computers. They really are wonderful things and you understand them far better most, better than even I. I know that this has been rather unorthodox to this point. I am very sorry about that, but it couldn't be helped. I tried other means to persuade you to work with me, but apparently you were not inclined to do so."

Sue felt her knees trembling beneath her. She was afraid they would give out at any moment, so she walked over to the bed and sat down in complete disbelief. She felt disoriented and faint. This was too much like watching an episode of the Twilight Zone.

"I... who are you." she stammered.

"I told you. My name is Carl and I would like us to become friends and I would like to help you manage your new program. I think you will find me very accommodating and very, very generous. There really is no need to be so upset Sue. You will soon be back in your apartment, at least for a while. I say, 'a while,' because you are about to make more money than you ever imagined. You will soon want to move out of that quaint little place and into something, shall we say, a little more spacious. Everything is going to turn out quite peachy."

Susan sat there, her head looking around the room without seeing, listening and desperately trying to pull herself together. Peachy? What the hell kind of thing was that to say? That's something you would say about a newly decorated room or maybe a new car. *Peachy*? Here, at a time this? She shook her head. It was all too much, too surreal.

He said that he'd tried to work with her before. What was he talking about? No one had tried working with her since she started her own business. She looked back at him. "You said you tried to work with me before. No one has tried to work with me. What the hell are you talking about?" Her voice was getting stronger and her head was spinning a little less.

"I had an acquaintance try to convince you to work with me. He apparently was not adept enough in these matters. It was an uncommon error on my part and I do apologize." He smiled, A squirmy little smile that did nothing to alleviate Susan's growing dread. "You should feel flattered Sue. I do not usually apologize and now I have done so twice since I entered the room.

"I can see that you may need some time to get your bearings and sort this all out. Unfortunately, until we have come to some sort of agreement, you will have to remain here. Sue, let me say one more thing and then I will leave you alone for a while. All I want is the key to unlock your program and the right to use it however I see fit. Oh, and one more thing that is very important. I do not want the program released to anyone else. For that, I am willing to pay you quite a large sum of money. With royalty checks to follow on a regular basis of course.

"Now, are you hungry? If you want something immediately, I am afraid that our capabilities in that regard are rather Spartan. But if you are willing to wait a bit, we can get you almost anything."

He was smiling at her, looking completely relaxed and in other circumstances, a most pleasant, gracious host. She wanted to kick that smile right off his face. She thought about what he had said. An "acquaintance." What? Who?

Suddenly, it dawned on her. *Richard*! That lying little bastard. The realization came to her that it had all been a set up. She should have known something was out of whack. He was *too* perfect. That's how they had gotten in. He must have made copies of her keys and given them to Carl and his thugs. The ultimate example, the proof of that naiveté.

She now began to remember their various conversations and arguments about her program, including the final one when he wanted her to stay home and work on it. It all made sense. Richard Clemmons had not been a computer programmer or even a geek. She was so stupid! Who in their right mind, other than a fellow programmer or geek, would sit and listen to her talk about her program for hours? Someone who looked at it as a potential profit center, that's who. Money can make one take an avid interest in all sorts of things.

She looked at Carl and said stonily, "I don't want anything from you but to be released. My parents are going to miss me soon and then you're going to have every agency known to man looking for you and those creeps that took me."

Her tirade seemed to bounce off him like water from a duck. He continued to smile as he replied, "Now, now, Sue, I understand that you are upset and I realize you still do not understand how beneficial this can be for all of us. Give it some more thought and you will come to see what I mean." He waited a moment, then continued, "When you are hungry or want to talk, use the computer in the corner over there. I'm sure you have already found it. On it, you will find an in-house chat program that will allow you to communicate your wishes.

"I do want to tell you that this room is fairly sound proof and if you decide to scream, pound on the walls, etc., you will find it will all be in vain. I assure you, this really is unnecessary. I am sure that in a short amount of time, you will see that working with us is really the only way to go and then we can happily move on together in our new venture."

With that, he walked out of the room. *That was yesterday*, she thought, *or maybe the day before. Damn it*! The computer had no clock program on it and with no light, it was impossible to tell how much time had elapsed. She continued to call in Carl, with vague excuses, in an attempt to see what time it was based on whether he was available and if he had changed his clothes.

But Carl was always available and he always appeared

promptly. He was always wearing the same clothing and always appeared fresh. No clues there.

She also found that Carl was not going to give up easily. For the most part, he kept that stupid smile plastered on his face at all times and always remained calm, collected. Except once. That was when she told him that her program wasn't finished yet.

The smile faded then and he began to ask her a series of questions and he wasn't putting on any pretense of nicety. That was also when she realized that Carl was wired for at least sound, possible video as well. He would periodically hesitate and his stare would become blank, as if he were in deep thought. Eventually, she figured out that what he was really doing was listening. Obviously, someone in another room was hearing their conversation. They would then relay to Carl what question he should ask next. Bunch of creeps. They probably had cameras in her room as well. *Hope you're getting a good show assholes*, she thought.

When a very distraught Carl left, Sue felt like she was finally gaining some measure of control once again. She had gotten him off his game. It made her feel better and she began to feel her self confidence returning at last.

Shortly after that conversation, an unsmiling Carl returned to her room with some shocking and devastating news. "I realize now that you are more adverse to this arrangement than I had thought you would be. Therefore, I have been forced to take steps to provide incentive for you." He stood there a moment and said nothing, letting his words penetrate and stimulate her imagination. After a while, he continued, "I have brought your father here. To persuade you to finish your program. He may even be able to help you."

His words sent Susan reeling. Up to that moment, she had thought she hated her father, didn't care if he lived or died. But upon hearing this news, she felt control once again slipping away. "It doesn't matter. I won't give you the program," she said weakly.

Carl ignored her, turned, opened the door and waved at someone standing out of sight. Her father walked in and Carl stated flatly, "See that she understands the importance of cooperating." With that he left the room, leaving them to themselves.

Neither spoke while each studied the other. To say that Susan was dumbfounded would be a gross understatement. There were no words that could come close to expressing the utter shock and amazement at this turn of events. Her knees suddenly became weak and for a moment, she thought she would faint. Her world, which had already been thrown into complete pandemonium, began to spin about like an out of control asteroid.

Because of his constant vigilance of her, he at least was familiar with how she looked and what was going on in *her* life. She, on the other hand, had not seen him in years and had no idea what had been going on in *his* life. She supposed that her mother would have let her know if any major calamity had befallen him, but other than that, she knew nothing other than he had remarried some years after.

After a while, he spoke in a gravelly voice, choked with

emotion, "So how have you been, Sue?"

"I," she returned hesitantly, "have been fine." Sue found that she was a jumble of emotions. This was the man who had betrayed her and her mother. This was the man that had abandoned them for some, "Floozy." She felt her old anger flare, briefly. But then, it began to melt as rapidly as an ice cube on a hot griddle. The blood began to drain from her head and she felt faint.

Her father saw the paleness come over her and quickly closed the gap between them. It felt so good to hold her in his arms. Old memories flooded back to him, of her as a little girl hugging him hard with those little, spindly arms. The best feeling in the world, that was. Other than hearing that tiny voice saying, "I love you Daddy." Oh how he had missed both. As he had on many occasions, he once again thought of what he had thrown away for a few moments of pleasure.

And now she was a grown woman, with a life and a career of her own, troubles of her own as well. He fervently hoped that maybe, in some small measure, he could make up for his past mistakes and lead her out of this quagmire.

For her part, Susan semi-reluctantly put her arms around him and placed her head on his shoulder. Then, the flood gates opened. All the built up frustrations with her father and the terror of the past two days, overcame her in a prodigious wave of emotion. She held him tighter and began to not just cry, but with great wracking sobs that came from deep within her very soul. She cried for everything. For the lost time with her father, for the destruction of her family, for the loves that were lost due to her inability to trust, and finally, for her, no their, current situation.

All the while, he quietly held her and said nothing. Eventually the tears and the trembling subsided. "It's going to be alright," he said gently. He led her to the bed and together they sat down.

"Sue," he continued, "you need to just hand over the program. Nothing is worth your life and I fear that may be where this is going if you don't cooperate."

He appeared, considering the circumstances, to be very calm. She shook her head. "No. I can't. You don't understand what this would mean. Only now have I pulled my head out of my own little world long enough to realize that the user of the first part of this program will quite literally own the world."

She continued, "Up to now, it's merely been an obsession of mine. A sought after goal that provided a means for me to reach the end point. I wanted to create a program that would put a stop to all the hacking. Computers and the internet are wonderful and invaluable tools that are being exploited by a few. People shouldn't have to have their convenience and their security spoiled. I wanted to stop all that. Though my end goal was noble, I realize now that the first part of the program must be destroyed."

Peter shook his head. "That won't do any good. The genie is out of the bottle now. Even if you destroy it, they know that you can put it back together again. They'll hold you and stop at nothing in order to make you give it to them."

"No Dad, you don't understand. I'm not finished with it yet. I..." She was going to tell him that she was close, very close. But something held her back and instead she finished her sentence by saying, "I don't think I can make it work. I've come this far only to fail and look at the chaos I've caused."

She thought she saw a fleeting look of dismay come across her father's face, but then it was gone so rapidly that she wasn't sure if she had misread him. "You've got to try!" he replied crossly, his voice rising. "These people aren't screwing around. If you don't do this, they're liable to start killing off people that you care about, starting with me. I know you don't care that much about me, but eventually they'll move to your mother and god knows who else. Trust me, if you don't give them want they want, nobody will walk away. Think about the alternative. They are willing to give you millions and you as well as everyone you care about get to live!"

"And how much will *they* make off of this?" she shot back angrily. She couldn't believe her father was even considering this. "And that's not even taking into account security issues. My God! With the information they get, they can topple governments. Christ! They can set up their own government. There's no limit to what they can do before, or even if, they're stopped. I couldn't live with knowing that I had opened Pandora's Box."

That conversation had been, if she had calculated it correctly, earlier today. Her father had left a very distraught man and hadn't returned. She wasn't sure what his motive for defending them really was. Could it be possible that he was actually a part of all this? As much as she had despised her father, she wouldn't have thought that possible.

The other alternative was that he really did have her best interests at heart and he was willing to do anything to save his daughter. The trouble with that line of reasoning was that she herself, was not willing to go that far. She refused to be a party to whatever horrible future that was out there, all because of her.

But as she sat, staring at the dazzling light show on the monitor before her, she wondered if she could live with being the cause of the death of her father and quite possibly her mother. She knew she would have trouble dealing with anything happening to Dana. Her father was another matter. Wasn't it? As much as it pained her to admit it, it had felt good to be held by him once again, secure. She had almost instantly reverted back to happier times and she felt as though Daddy would make everything alright, as he always had.

Then reality had set in and she knew Daddy couldn't fix everything. It also was depressing that she was questioning his motives. What were they? Did they really kidnap him too? She remembered how calm he had been and how fervently he had argued to give them what they wanted. Good guy? Bad Guy?

She didn't know. The more she thought about it, the more confused she became until her head felt like it was consumed by a giant mushroom, crowding out all reasonable thoughts.

And so, as a refuge, her mind began to think back to birthday parties and fishing trips and being tossed in the air and… Stealthily, sleep overtook her.

CHAPTER

17

John Harvard was looking down in disbelief at the bits of bloody cloth that were protruding from the wound in his chest. The red stain on his shirt was rapidly getting larger and in turn, he was getting weaker as it spread. Try as he might, he couldn't seem to catch his breath. He'd been shot in the back and it had been what is known in the industry as a, "through and through." He didn't understand. He had been with friends, people that he had trusted. Who could possibly have done such a thing? He sank to this knees and wondered who it was that had betrayed him. *I've got to find out who*, he thought as he fought to remain conscious. But he was losing the battle and was slowly slipping away...

... Slowly, ever so slowly, he became aware of Emily's soft, rhythmic breathing as she lay nestled in his arms and equally as slowly, he cleared away the last vestiges of sleep. Light was just beginning to creep through the edges of the windows, announcing the start of a new day. *Wow*, he thought. *That was fucked up.*

John never really thought that most dreams had any particular meaning, just the brain cleaning house and making sure everything was right and proper again. But sometimes, he had discovered, the brain's housecleaning dredged up facts that were lodged deep in his subconscious and put them in proper order for him to see. Kind of like grabbing him by the collar and saying, "Listen asshole, you'd better look at this again and you'd better do it fast."

The trouble with this brain cleansing was that it wasn't always easy to understand. Take this latest incarnation for example. Obviously, he had been betrayed by someone he had trusted. But by whom and when? It could have been his brain bringing up long buried feelings of betrayal by one of his past wives or friends, way in the past. Or, it could have to do with something as recent as his current situation. Or, it might mean nothing.

The more he thought about it, the more he was certain that this dream had meaning. He just wasn't sure what had triggered it or how relevant it was. If it was something way in the past, oh well. Probably not really worth wasting anymore brain power. But if it did have something to do with what was happening now, that was a different matter entirely.

He was a big believer in instinct, gut instinct, to be exact. There had been too many times in his life when he had suddenly acted inexplicably, and to his benefit. Stop and draw a gun before entering a room, before even realizing that he had done so. Suddenly deciding to go down a particular road or alleyway. Suddenly deciding that this person was lying, when he had no real reason not believe the individual.

All examples that had stood him in good stead in his adult career. He even remembered times when he had been shocked to find that his gun was even in his hand. It was as though someone had frozen him, put the gun in his hand and then had instantly defrosted him. Upon later contemplation of those times however, he realized that whatever inner force had taken control, it had always been appropriate. It had most likely saved his life or the lives of others.

It was the same with his dreams. Many times he had run into situations where he was confused and unsure of what to do next. Then, he would wake up one morning and straight off, everything was clear. Of course it didn't always work that way. Rarely in fact and way more times than not, the dreams meant nothing at all, just garbage getting tossed out. But he was pretty certain that this one meant something. Something important. Something, he felt, was bothering him, sticking in his craw. Something deep within him that up until now, hadn't been apparent. What? It was too bad he couldn't go to the house keeper of his brain and say, *Hey, could you clarify this for me? Sorry to be so dense, but I'm not really getting it.*

Emily stirred slightly and he looked down at her. She must have felt his movement because her eyes fluttered a moment, then opened. She turned her head slightly and looked up at him. "Good morning," she said softly. "You look wide awake."

He brushed away his dark thoughts and smiled. "I just woke up and was laying here enjoying you next to me," he replied, a little guiltily.

She smiled in return and hugged him tighter. "Me too," she countered and sat up. "I'll be right back." With that she clambered out of bed. He watched her perfect naked form walk to the bathroom and close the door. He shook his head. He could get used to waking up next to that every morning.

John began to think about yesterday and how he was going to handle events today. He looked at his watch. Too early to call Nick yet. He had to bring him up to date, especially about finding Harris. Then he remembered Jenny. He sat up in bed and reached for his phone to call dispatch. Another girl answered and informed him that she was in, but not in the radio room at the moment, could she take a message. Something told him not to leave a message, so he obeyed that inner voice and said no, he would call back.

His thoughts turned back to Harris and the best way to approach the house. He gave a fleeting consideration to calling in reinforcements right then to storm the dwelling. He discarded the idea almost as quickly as he had thought of it. If he was wrong and Sue wasn't there, the gig would be up. His instinct told him she was in that house right now, but was he willing to put her life up as collateral that he was right? No.

He needed to reconnoiter the house and the grounds further. He needed to set up the house for surveillance, to see who came and went, develop a pattern for those inside. How many are there? What weapons are visible? What security do they have, other than what he had already discovered? What food goes in? What garbage comes out? Who visits? The more he thought about it, the more he concluded that to rush in now, before he had more intelligence, would be nothing less than foolhardy. He not only had to try to confirm her presence, but what he was up against.

He also realized that the perfect time of day for approach was rapidly passing. Dawn and dusk were the optimum times for this type of work. The lack of light turned colors into shades of black and gray and it was difficult to spot movement amidst the ever changing shadows as the sun came up or went down. Oh well. Nothing to be done about it now.

If Susan was there and she was still alive, he felt he had the situation pretty well contained. The perfect scenario would be that he put the house under surveillance and when the time was right, call in the troops. The problem was the lack of a cell phone signal. He would have to buy a couple of walkie-talkies today and give one to Emily. Then, he could call her on the radio. In turn, she could drive to an area where she could get a signal and call for help. Not a perfect scenario, but the best one given the resources available to him at the moment.

The door to the bathroom opened and Emily, in all her naked splendor, returned to the bed. She snuggled up against him once more and asked, "Are you hungry? I'm famished."

"I could do with some breakfast," he replied. "We've got a lot to do today and who knows when we'll get another chance to eat."

A dark look crossed her face and while looking off into space, she commented, "I just wish this was over now. I thought that it would be exciting, almost fun. But that was before I realized that so many people would get hurt." She hesitated before continuing. "The worst part is that it looks like there's a good possibility that even more will get hurt before it's over. Is there any chance that maybe we should just wait awhile to see if Sue gives them what they want? That way, nobody else needs to get harmed."

He shook his head and looked down at her. "No, I don't think that would be a good way to go. It sure looks like Peter's involved now and they wouldn't have done that unless things weren't looking good. Remember, they have a lot of experience with this sort of thing so they probably already have a pretty good idea by now of the way this is going. If it's going badly, there may not be much time before they decide to cut their losses and start cleaning up." As before, he didn't let on that though he was sure that Peter was now fully involved, it still remained to be seen if that involvement was voluntary or involuntary.

She had listened without returning his gaze. Now, she faced him with a look of profound sadness. "You are nothing like what I imagined you to be. I looked about as far into you as I could using my hacking skills and I learned a lot. I'm not sure how I missed the shootout thing, except that happened before the use of computers was so common, so it probably never got entered anywhere. Now I realize that seeing all this stuff on a monitor didn't tell me about the real you."

"Don't feel bad," he responded. "Toward the end of the Cold War, a lot of very intelligent people, whose job it was to gather information, decided that with all the satellites, eavesdropping equipment and fancy computer stuff, who needs agents on the ground? So they started yanking them all, smug with the knowledge that we had sophisticated equipment that would even let them know if someone took a dump, or so they thought.

Eventually, they began to realize they were missing stuff. Little things, like the fall of Communism in Russia, the first and the second World Trade Center attacks, weapons of mass destruction or lack thereof, in Iraq and North Korea. You know, little things like that. It's known as HUMINT, short for Human Intelligence. They finally realized that some analyst sitting in a room thousands of miles away can't see a person's face, can't read someone's body language and doesn't know what someone is doing if they're not talking or typing. It's important to see a person's face when they are saying something. What are their eyes doing? Is the vein in their neck throbbing? What's their body language saying? Even a lay person can sometimes tell a person is lying just by looking at them. You don't see that on a computer screen or on a print out. So, don't feel bad if you made the same mistake that dozens of so called professionals made."

Emily rejoined, "Until this started, I never realized that outside of computers, I really had no life. Until, that is, I met you. Now, I want life to get back to normal." Her face brightened a little and she finished by saying, "I have a lot of things that I would like to do to you... I... mean *with* you."

She laughed softly, but he could see her eyes were swollen with emotion. He began to stroke her hair and said gently, "Hey, things are going to turn out okay. I'm pretty sure we know where she is now. There's a good chance that by this time tomorrow, this will all be over."

To his surprise, his words appeared to do little to comfort her. He decided that action was the best medicine at this point. "Come on," he said cheerfully. "He disentangled himself from her, jauntily hopped out of bed and began getting dressed. "If we don't eat soon, I do believe I'm going to start chowing down on the bedposts here."

She shook her head and began to follow him out of bed as she said, "You're unbelievable. Is there anything that can shake that optimistic attitude?"

He shrugged. "I learned a long time ago, there's no sense complaining and no one will listen if you do."

She looked at him with a soft, loving face. "I would."

He stopped dressing and studied her for a moment. "Yes, I think you would."

They finished dressing and a few minutes later, walked to the car. It was a warm spring morning and there wasn't a cloud in the early morning sky. The clean smelling, musty odor of the woods, mixed with the smell of the lake and the cheerful warbling of a variety of birds heralding in the new day, urged John to return to the deck of the cabin that overlooked the lake. There, he could and in the past, had in fact done so, sit for hours reading a book or just contemplating life's twists and turns, amidst the serene embrace of the remote area. But he knew that he could not fulfill those desires today and resisted the tempting allure of the north country.

Instead, he opened the passenger door of his car for Emily. He got into the driver's seat and tranquil stillness of the morning was shattered a moment later by the throaty roar of the Audi coming to life. He drove down the long narrow driveway to the road and pointed the car toward the Johnson's restaurant.

They arrived a few minutes later and were eagerly greeted by Emma and Dwight. "Did you two sleep well?" Emma asked.

"Like a rock," replied John. He looked over at Emily. "I'm sorry. I didn't think to ask you, but I assumed you did as well."

She smiled, nodded and looked him straight in the eyes. With a conspiratorial tone in her voice she answered, "I slept great. The conditions couldn't have been better."

Emma saw the look, picked up on the tone, and began to shake in a great, hearty laugh. With a knowing smile, she asked them what they wanted for breakfast. Realizing that he was probably going to be in the woods all day, John ordered a very large breakfast that caused Emily to stare at him in amusement.

After Emma had left, Emily asked, "How are we going to start?"

John began to explain that he needed to pick up some supplies, including the walkie-talkies, so that he could reconnoiter the area around the house and then put it under surveillance.

Emma returned with their food a few minutes late. John had a sudden thought and took the opportunity to ask the cheery old woman, "Do you think Dwight would let me borrow his radios for a day or two?" Dwight and Emma were still avid hunters. Though their days of extensive walking through the woods were long past, they liked to hunt ducks, geese, turkey, and occasionally, deer. None of these required a lot of walking, but did require hours of sitting quietly. They had a couple of high quality radios equipped with headsets so that if one called the other at an inopportune time, they would not scare off any game. They would be perfect for his current situation.

"I don't see why not," Emma replied. "I'll ask him. You need anything else?"

He contemplated the request and added, "Yeah. How about his ground blanket?" Dwight also had a ground blanket that was insulated, waterproof, and lightweight. The air temperature was suppose to be pretty warm today. But John knew that the ground was still mostly frozen and would act as a heat sink for anyone laying on it for any period of time. This was a problem even in much warmer conditions and a good insulated ground blanket, though it wouldn't stop this from happening completely, would at least slow the effect down to manageable levels.

"We don't have anything planned, so I don't see why it would be a problem. I'll let you know," and with that she turned and walked away.

She returned a few minutes later, carrying the radios and the blanket. "You're in luck my dear. He had them in the back of the truck, so that will save you a trip to our house."

She put them down on the table and he thanked her for

letting him borrow them. Emma collected the plates and stood looking at him before taking them to the back. "I don't like the look on your face John Harvard. I don't know what you're into, but that look tells me it's serious. You just watch yourself," she turned and carried the dishes from the room.

He and Emily left the restaurant and returned to the car. As they pulled onto the road, John said, "I want to stop and pick up a sandwich for my lunch. Do you want anything? This will probably be an all day affair."

"No thank you. I'll be fine," she answered sullenly. The forlorn look on her face told John that this whole incident was taking a toll on her. He considered making another attempt to console her, but decided to leave it alone. Frankly, she was becoming a bit of a distraction with her increasingly morose attitude. It wasn't that he didn't care about her. In fact, he was beginning to care a lot more about her than he would have thought possible in such a short amount of time. But he was basically a very upbeat person and even in the best of circumstances, her constant downbeat outlook would have an adverse affect on him. He could only hope, for the sake of any possible future relationship between them, that this current melancholy mood as of late was because of the extremely unusual turn of events in the past couple of days.

He drove to a local convenient store and Emily waited in the car while he went in. He had just finished paying the clerk when his cell phone rang. "Where the hell have you been?" came the stressed, and unusually shrill voice of Jenny. He had been thinking of giving the radio room another call as he walked the isles, selecting his purchases.

"I've been a little busy with some stuff," he answered. "I tried calling you earlier this morning, but they said you weren't around. What's up?"

Her voice turned low and John thought he detected more than a little trepidation in her normally calm but vivacious voice. A growing dread rapidly grew inside him as he listened. "I was delivering some papers to Deputy Chief Ramsey's secretary yesterday. She wasn't there so I was decided to leave the papers on her desk with a note when I heard Ramsey in his office. He was on the phone and he sounded really pissed. It didn't sound like a conversation that I should be listening to, so I quickly finished my note and was just about to leave when I heard your name."

A chill went down John's spine. No! It couldn't be! He had never liked Ramsey. The man was a mean, incompetent drunk who should have retired years ago. All through his career, he had been given rank and responsibility that he didn't deserve. But his uncle was a prominent local politician so everyone knew what the deal was. John never trusted him and strongly suspected him to be a thief and probably much, much more. He had heard stories, and there were many, of the old days when Ramsey was a patrolman. Stories of backing his patrol car up to the scene of a burglary and loading it with goods before the owner arrived. Stories of beatings. Stories of coerced sex in the back of cars. And one particularly persistent rumor of Ramsey putting a bullet in the back of the head of some unfortunate soul that had crossed him.

At first, John assumed these were the various unfounded ramblings of officers who didn't like Ramsey. He had learned early that a lot of cops were like a bunch of old women with too much idle time on their hands. Nothing to do but spread rumors. Cops constantly talk about other cops. It wasn't necessarily that they intentionally lied about anyone. Instead, it was a classic example of the age old game of whispering to the next person. A group of people would sit around a table. One person would write something down and whisper it, word for word to one person. They in turn, would whisper what they heard to the person sitting next to them and so on until the last person would announce to everyone what they had just been told. Then, the original person would read what he had written. As a game, it was hilarious. It never came out the same and in most cases, not even close. It was also an important lesson in life.

So, even though he didn't personally like Ramsey, John had chalked up most of these stories as nothing more than products of the rumor mill. Then, Ramsey had been given a new, unmarked squad car and John had been assigned Ramsey's old one. Though the car was pretty new, there was an annoying rattling sound coming from under the dashboard. Finally, John couldn't take it anymore and climbed under the dash in an attempt to find out what was causing it.

Like most officers, Ramsey worked odd jobs on his off time to make some extra cash. At this particular point in time, he had been working as a security guard in the warehouse of an auto parts store. When John poked his head under the dashboard of Ramsey's old squad, he found a complete set of very expensive wrenches, brand new of course. He could think of only one reason they would be there and suddenly John began to realize at that point that there was probably a lot of truth to the stories being spread about Ramsey. His feelings of dislike for him had quickly grown into those of utter contempt.

The thought that Ramsey knew of John's current assignment dismayed him, but the more he thought about it, it didn't surprise him. It made perfect sense. It wouldn't take a lot of poking around for someone to discover Ramsey's reputation. Who better for Coeptus Guild to approach for the job of being a mole? His greed and lack of ethics pretty much assured that he would cooperate. That, coupled with his rank made him the perfect man for the job.

He turned his attention back to Jenny and asked with resignation in his voice, "So what did he say?"

"When I first heard him, he was telling whoever he was talking to, that they needed to find out who authorized some procedure having to do with phone records and to do it fast. He also told the person to find out if Captain Giovanni had anything to do with it. That's when I heard your name. He said, 'Harvard and Giovanni are like two peas in a pod. Who else is he going to get to do his dirty work for him? Find out if there's anything mysterious going on in the lab.' He listened for a minute and then said, 'Look asshole, I've got my own investigation going on and I don't give a fuck what you're told. I'm the Deputy Chief around here and I'm also the one responsible for that nice little house you just bought. So unless you want to find yourself on the unemployment line, I want answers and I want them today. Understand dick brain?' Then he slammed the phone down so hard I'd thought it would break."

"Was that it?" John asked with a sigh.

"No. Then he called somebody from his cell phone. I could tell cause I heard it beeping as he pressed the numbers. Somebody picked up and his whole demeanor changed. All of a sudden it was 'yes sir,' 'no sir' and 'I'll get right on it sir." He was talking very quietly and I couldn't hear everything. I got as close to his door as I could and I was scared to death his secretary would come back or he would walk out and see me there. He was saying something about he would fix everything and he would let them know as soon as he found out what you knew. Up until then, I thought I was as scared as I could possibly be. But then I heard him say, 'Don't you worry sir. If that's the case, then Harvard's a dead man. I'll see to it personally. He's a little crazy and everyone knows it. It won't come as too much of a shock if he suddenly disappears.'

"He hung up shortly after that and I was just leaving when he walked out of his door and saw me on my way out. He turned white as a ghost and demanded to know what I was doing there. I told him that I was dropping some papers off and showed him the note I had left. He looked a little better then, but you could tell he wasn't completely convinced.

"I left and went outside to call you. I was just leaving you a message when he came out too and wanted to know what I was doing. I told him I had taken a quick smoke break. I was scared to death John. When I got off work, his car was still in the parking lot. I was afraid to go home, so I spent the night with some friends. I wasn't sure if I should say anything to Captain Giovanni or not."

John's mind was racing. How did Ramsey find out? Who was working for him? Obviously someone at the department, but who? Who was he talking to in such a subservient manner? Almost certainly someone from Coeptus Guild. It sure would be nice to get Ramsey's phone records. And what about Nick? He felt the blood drain out of him. Christ! If Ramsey did something to Nick, there was no spider hole Ramsey could crawl into that would be deep enough, John would find him and make him regret the day he was born.

"You shouldn't have gone to work today," he told her.

"I thought that would confirm his suspicions if I didn't," she replied.

"Good thought for the long run," he commented. "Not so good for the short run, and I have a feeling that the run will be very short now. If this all goes bad, there's going to be some major cleaning going on and now that he knows where you are again, you might be considered part of the trash to be taken out."

"Well he's not here today and what are you talking about? If what goes bad? What in the hell are you involved in? Excuse me, not just *you* anymore. What are *we* involved in?"

"I would tell you Jen, but the less you know at this point, the better. Just make sure that you're never alone. I mean, no smoke breaks by yourself, no running out for lunch by yourself, and have some of your friends pick you up from work. Tell everybody that you're having car trouble and have to leave your car there."

"What about Captain Giovanni?" she quietly responded.

"Stay away from him. I don't want anybody to see you talking to him. You heard Ramsey. He obviously has someone else there working for him. We don't know who so I don't want to take any chances."

"Alright. I'll do what you say. John, please be careful out there."

"I will. You too," he answered and hung up.

He immediately called Nick's personal cell phone line. Nick picked up on the first ring and relief flooded through John upon hearing Nick's voice and he said quickly, "It's me. Where are you?"

The relief was evident in Nicks voice as well as he replied, "I'm glad you called me on my cell and not the department line. I was just picking up the phone to call you. I'm at work. You okay? Things are really popping around here."

"Yeah, I'm fine and I'm glad to know you are too. I already know things are coming to a head down there." He brought Nick up to date, informing him what he had found in Johnsonville and telling him Jenny's story. He ended by asking, "Any ideas how they found out?"

"I'm not sure, but I think Ramsey's mole is probably in the computer room. I know from past experience that they can monitor any computer traffic coming in and out of here. That means everything—emails, record checks, even interoffice Instant Messaging. They can also flag a particular work station or person for closer scrutiny. Judging from what Jenny told you, I would say they had me flagged and were alerted when I ran the check on the phone records. They would have seen what I got back and if they knew what to look for, that would be all they needed to confirm their suspicions. Add that to the fact that I had one of the computer room geeks ask me about the phone records. I asked him how he knew about that and what business was it of his. He told me that it came up during a routine audit and wanted to know why I, the captain in charge of the Crime Lab, would be running them."

John chuckled. "So what did you tell him?"

Nick answered in a slightly angry tone. "That it was none of his business and that I have every right to conduct an investigation on my own and if he didn't like it, take it up with the chief. Even with all this shit to the side, he kind of pissed me off. Imagine, some computer twerp questioning a captain about the right to run a records check. Whatever! The question now is, what do they know about your current activities?"

"Well, worst case scenario, all they could know is that we recovered Clemmons's body and ran his cell phone records. That could be explained by the fact that you have a homicide victim and you want to know who he's been talking to. They most likely don't know that we've been in contact or that you realize that Clemmons is connected with me in any way."

"That's pushing it buddy." Nick retorted. "They know

our relationship and I'd be willing to bet that they've pulled your phone records too. They'll know we've been talking."

"Yeah, but they don't know what we've been talking about. I might have been asking you to go fishing. Nick, it's only been a little over twenty-four hours since you found Clemmons. You may be right, but that would mean they put two and two together awfully fast. If they did, they might know or assume I'm up here, but they can't possibly know how close I am. It's a mighty big area to find someone and it was sheer luck I found them as fast as I did."

"Maybe," Nick answered doubtfully. "What's our next move? I say we call in the Feds and hit that place now."

John rubbed his chin thoughtfully. "No." he said slowly. "No, I don't think that the time is right. I need to know one hundred percent that she's in there. We only get one shot at this. If we're wrong, she's most likely a dead woman."

"If they know you're this close, she's a dead woman. We're damned if we do and we're damned if we don't," replied an exasperated Nick.

John changed subjects. "Do you know where Ramsey is? Jenny says he's not in the office."

"No I don't. After my run in with the geek, I half expected to hear from him with some cockamamie story about cooperation and all that, but I didn't. I know the geek has been talking to some of my people, asking questions that have nothing to do with the computer room. I brought in my guy and told him if anyone asks, to keep his mouth shut, without making it appear that he's keeping it shut of course. But the bottom line is that eventually, with all the lab work we've been doing, it's not going to take a rocket scientist to figure out what we're about. Time's running out, buddy."

"I don't like not knowing where he is, Nick. Watch yourself."

"I will, but I'm not too worried about myself. It's you who needs to watch it. Ramsey's right, you do have a reputation for sticking your nose where it isn't wanted. For most people, finding you dead might be regrettable, but not surprising. However, if the captain in charge of the crime lab turned up dead or missing, that would be an entirely different matter. That would open a whole new can of worms and I don't think Coeptus Guild would appreciate the stink. No, I really don't think I'm in danger. You're the one vulnerable one here and I think you should lay low and let me call in the troops."

"No Nick! Give me time to check this out. Twenty four hours, just give me twenty four hours, then you can call whoever you want. Agreed?" Silence greeted him over the phone. "Nick... agreed?"

"I don't know, buddy," replied his torn friend.

"Twenty four hours Nick. I'll keep you posted when I can. Later." He hung up and moved to the car.

He got in and Emily asked, "What took you so long? The place doesn't look that busy."

"It wasn't. I was getting caught up with my phone calls while I'm still in range." He started the car and looked over his shoulder before backing up. There, about three blocks away, he swore he caught a glimpse of the Mercedes!

He quickly put the car in gear, rapidly backed up and

spun around. He accelerated in the direction of the big car. Emily's shocked and fear laden face spun his way as she grasped the dashboard for support. "What are you doing?" she half screamed.

"I think it's Harris again," he responded.

Having learned her lesson from the previous night, she said nothing further as he sped toward the street where he had seen the car. Nothing! He continued to search the area for a few minutes before coming to the conclusion that he had lost them.

Suddenly, as he replayed the incident in this mind, it dawned on him that Harris had been coming from a parking lot. He returned to the area and found that the Mercedes had left the employee lot of the grocery store. *What was he doing back there*, John wondered.

He was staring at the lot, contemplating the area, when a hunch began to dawn on him. He pulled up to a dumpster and got out of the car. He lifted the lid and looked in. There were crushed boxes, several black plastic bags, and one white plastic bag that looked conspicuously out of place! He looked around and quickly retrieved the white bag. He threw it in his trunk and quickly moved the Audi out of the area.

Now Emily spoke, with a quizzical expression on her face. "What on earth are you doing with a garbage bag?"

John smiled broadly. "Emily my dear, you're about to learn the fine art of garbology."

"Garbology? Never heard of it," she replied as she shook her head in wonderment. Her confusion was only getting worse.

"You'll see." He drove back to the Johnson's cabin, got the bag out of the trunk and took it into the kitchen. He got an empty garage bag from under the sink and sat down with the empty bag next to the full one.

"You can learn a lot from people's garbage. What credit cards they have. Where they bank. Magazines will tell you what their interests are. Now, I don't know for sure that this is Harris's garbage and if it is, I doubt we'll find any credit card receipts, but it might be able to tell us something."

He opened the bag. "Ugh!" exclaimed Emily as the pent up stench from the bag assailed their nostrils.

John grinned. "Admittedly, not one of the most pleasant aspects of our work. Sorry." It soon became evident that there were probably three or four days worth of garbage in the bag. He was about half way through it when he came across a piece of paper with a name and phone number written on it.

His heart skipped a beat when he read the name. Clemmons. It was their bag! He smiled and showed the paper to Emily. She looked at it with a blank expression before standing up and walking to the kitchen window. There she stood, looking out, while John continued to look through the bag.

Toward the bottom, he came across a receipt from the local grocery store. It was dated four days ago. He read through the items and found one that caused him to smile once more.

"Emily." She turned and looked at him. He continued, "This receipt says that they bought a box of tampons. Now they may have a woman working for them, but I'll bet that Sue is the only female there. There are no empty wrappers, which could mean this box was bought just in case, like they didn't know if they would need it or not. This is great news. It doesn't necessarily mean she's there, but it is further evidence that she is."

She said nothing, but watched as he went through the remainder of the bag. Picking up each item, inspecting it and dropping it into the new bag. When he was finished, he tied up the new bag and stood up. "I'm going to get ready. I'll be right back."

He moved into the bedroom and put on long underwear, two pairs of socks, a sweater, jacket and over it all, an expensive, lined camouflage suit. He walked back into the kitchen looking like a warrior ready for battle.

Emily's eyes flew open when she saw him. He looked like a predator, ready to spring into action at a moment's notice. His face was set in a look of grim determination that said, *don't fuck with me*. "Let's go," was all he said.

They walked out to the car, where he opened the trunk. A camouflaged pack sat inside. He placed the ground blanket, a canteen, and a digital camera inside. Then he closed the trunk and handed the keys to her. "You drive," he said and they got into the car.

As they drove, he explained. "I want you to drive me to that grove of trees where we waited last night. I'm going to go in there. You stay and wait for me. It's the opposite side of town and some distance from the road they're on. If they leave, they probably won't go in your direction and if they do, chances are they won't see you sitting down there. If they do, and they stop, tell them you're lost and you were looking at a map to see how to get back to the expressway.

Keep your radio on, but don't call me unless it's an emergency. I'll call you periodically to make sure the radios are working and that you're okay. When we talk, keep the conversation short and be as vague as possible. If they have a scanner, we don't want them locking in to our channel. In the same vein, pretend like someone else is listening in. You don't want to say anything that you would want them to hear, so put it in words that I'm likely to understand, but difficult for anyone else. If you do call me and I don't respond right away, don't panic. I'm probably not in a area from which I can talk without compromising my position. I'll call as soon as I can. Just like last night, if it's been more than two hours without hearing from me, leave and call Nick Giovanni."

He took out a pen and paper from the glove compartment and wrote down Nick's personal cell phone number. He handed it to Emily. "Here is a number that I know Nick will answer. If anything happens, call it and tell him what has transpired. He'll know what to do next. Do whatever he says. Got it?"

They arrived at the spot near the woods. Tears were streaming down Emily's face and she was visibly shaken. She threw her arms around him. "Please be careful. Can't we wait a little longer? Do you have to do this now?"

He returned her embrace and attempted to console her. "I told you, I can't wait any longer. I have to determine if she's in there or not and if she is, we have to get her out. I have new information that they know who I am and may even know I'm up here. I may not have much time before they decide to bail. It's now or never."

He backed away from her, opened the door and got out. He squatted down to her level and looked at her again. "Ready?" She nodded tearfully. He retrieved his pack from the trunk, donned a camouflaged hat and walked into the tree line. As she watched him go, she was struck by the fluidity of his movements as he picked his way forward. He advanced through the woods like a wild animal, natural, at home in his environment. Then, suddenly, he was gone, as if he had become one with the forest, which for all intent and purposes, he had.

CHAPTER
18

John walked a short distance before coming to a stop. He inhaled a deep breath and took in the aroma of his surroundings. It smelled good, natural, the way things were meant to smell. No exhaust fumes here. Not a trace of the stench of civilized life. He listened. The sound of birds and there! The clucking of an angry squirrel whose refuge had been disturbed. *Sorry little buddy*, he thought as a smile came to his lips. *I'll be out of your space shortly*. He stood there a while longer, listening, watching. If someone close had spotted him coming in, he hoped he could have his first clue by hearing their approach on the carpet of dead leaves and branches that littered the forest floor. In tune with nature, he also listened for its own distress signals, like the one he was listening to now in the form of the enraged squirrel.

Nothing much moves through the woods undetected by its inhabitants. Wildlife of all types had some form of sentry that protected their own by announcing to all that there was an intruder in their midst. By and large, almost all humans had forgotten the ways and language of nature and ignored it's cries of indignation and alarm. John had learned this dialect at a very young age.

He had been fortunate enough to live near a large expanse of wilderness quite similar to the area where he now stood. He had become aware that if he sat still and quiet, it did not take long for the creatures around him to come to life. He loved to watch them go about their daily routines, communicating, loving, fighting, playing, and he would sit for hours in rapt delight.

As he became older and more independent, he took great delight in spending many days and nights in the woods. He discovered a whole new world, available to all, but seen by few. Hidden lakes and streams. Waterfalls and natural water slides that were just as much fun as their man-made counterparts and with no lines of jostling, eager children awaiting their turn. Pools of water tens of feet deep, carved into solid stone by centuries of the pounding by pure, cold, crystal clear water, some as small as a foot or two in diameter. All of these enchanted sights were there, to be savored by those who chose to adopt, at least temporarily, the ways of their ancestors.

After a while, when he detected no indication of any person other than himself, John removed his binoculars and began to carefully examine as much of the area as he could from his position. He was looking for more odd shapes that protruded from trees, or from the ground for that matter. Given Harris's military training and the funds provided by Coeptus Guild, there could be any number and type of sensors out here. This could take a while, he decided.

He took some time and began assembling dried leaves and small twigs. He began to use strings that hung from his clothing to tie these pieces of forest floor to himself. Known as a "Gilly Suit," it allowed the wearer to adapt his camouflage to whatever surroundings he was in. Once completed, he would totally blend in and his own movements were the only things likely to betray him.

When he was finished, he keyed his radio and spoke the pre-designated call sign he had given to Emily. She responded immediately. "I'm here."

"Okay, just doing a radio check."

"I hear you fine," she said.

"Good. I'll call you again in an hour or so." He put his radio away and began to, ever so slowly, move forward. He carefully inspected each spot where he would put his foot. He was looking for things that would break, causing a noise that would reverberate through the woods in the still surroundings. He was also looking for manmade disturbances on the forest floor, such as small wires or mono-filament lines. Disturbed leaves or vegetation could indicate a hidden sensor or worse that had been placed there by Harris or his cronies.

As he got closer to his target, he went to a prone position and restricted his movements to a stop and go crawl. Inching his way forward, punctuated by stops as he carefully examined his surroundings, both directly in front of him as well as off in the distance. It still bothered him that he had seen no detection equipment at the rear of the house, only around the area of the driveway. It just didn't make sense that Harris would leave this area vulnerable. There must be something! But he could see nothing, so he continued his forward progress.

The man was eating an early lunch. He was due to be relieved in another hour, but he was starving now and decided not to wait. He went to the small refrigerator that sat in the corner of the room, all the while keeping his eyes on the bank of monitors that hung from the ceiling. Not that an audible alarm wouldn't warn him if someone broke one of the security perimeters. However, he was taking no chances. He had been warned that some guy would be approaching the house from the rear and it was his job to detect him. He was, quite frankly, afraid of Harris and he was not going to provide any excuse for Harris to vent his rage on him.

The large areas to the sides and the rear of the house, were covered by a series of cameras that had been mounted high in the trees. Each camera had its image displayed on one of the small monitors now displayed in front of him. They were equipped with motion detectors that if tripped, would cause the image from the camera to be switched to a large, fifty inch, high definition display in the center of the room. Harris himself had placed a lot of these devices and the man had helped him. He was amazed at Harris's ability to conceal the cameras in knot holes and using the bark of the trees to conceal the wires. Even standing a foot away and knowing where the wires were, it was difficult to detect them.

That's why he was surprised at the relatively clumsy installation of the systems covering the driveway. He eventually got up the nerve to ask Harris about it and was perplexed by the hearty laughter that followed.

"That's to deceive any would be snoopers if they should come a calling." he responded. "Any half way competent snoop should be able to spot them. They won't see anything else and they'll think that we've been remiss in our duties and only covered the driveway. They'll be lulled into a false sense of security and come in the back way, which is just where we want them. We'll have plenty of time to decide how to react and respond accordingly."

But the man had seen nothing yet and had pretty much decided that Harris's information was wrong. Either this mystery man wasn't coming today, or he was going to wait until the twilight hours to make his move, which was what the man himself would have done.

What he didn't understand, was why *one* man was coming. He had expected that if there was an assault, it would come in the form of a massive, coordinated attack. The man and his companions had been well versed as to what to do on that occasion. They were to begin by killing whatever captives they had at the moment. Except the woman, Harris would decide what to do with her based on the circumstances. Then they were to take the tunnel they had built, to the garage, where Harris's armored Mercedes was parked. After getting in, blowing through the garage doors and heading down the driveway, they would blow the house with the explosives that had been packed throughout the building.

The garage would follow shortly thereafter.

The man smiled, he had seen the amount of plastique that had been placed. It would make quite an impressive blast. It would be safe to say that any helicopters in the immediate area, as well as any men, would be knocked flat by the force. They would make their great escape in the stunned, chaotic confusion that would follow.

If by some chance they were pursued, they would head into town where other plans known only to Harris had been made. Once again, the man smiled. Harris had thought of everything. However, he would not have smiled if he had known that as a last contingency, Harris had orders that if their capture was imminent, *no one* was to walk away alive. The Mercedes itself was packed with explosives and if for some reason that didn't work as planned, well, there were other ways. There were to be no ties back to Harris's shadowy employers.

The man was just finishing the last bite on his sandwich when suddenly, the stillness of the quiet room was shattered by the main alarm. It came as such a surprise, the man began choking on the last remnants of his food. Instantly the view on the High Definition monitor changed. The view from the camera showed a view of the forest floor. He didn't see anything.

Harris and the man known only as, "Carl," burst into the room. Harris barked out his first command. "Turn that damn noise off." The man seated at the console promptly obeyed and all three looked at the huge monitor before them.

"I don't see anything," said Carl.

"Keep watching," Harris whispered. He knew that Harvard had just hit his last line of defense. It was an Electrostatic Field Disturbance Sensor that surrounded the rear and sides of the property. This sensor created a terrain following field approximately eight feet high and several hundred feet wide. It could be set to detect only objects within a certain weight range and that were proceeding outside the range of preselected speeds. It was high tech to the max and had a detection reliability of ninety-nine percent. This had been Harris's ace in the hole and he hadn't been sure he needed it. The fact that Harvard had reached it undetected, was proof that it had been a wise addition to security.

"There! He's right there," fired Harris as he approached the screen and jabbed a heavily muscled finger at Harvard's prone figure.

"Holy shit!" said Carl. "How did he get that close?"

"I'm sorry Mr. Harris," said the man at the console. Though he was a combat vet himself, he was trembling. He was absolutely terrified of Harris and his worst fears had just come true. "I swear I've been watching and I never saw him."

Harris's smile resembled the evil grin of a wolf that knows that his prey was as good as his. "That's alright Dave." His grin got wider. "He's good. Very, very good." He watched Harvard inch forward. "As good as I've seen in a long time. A pity that he couldn't be bought."

As soon as John Harvard's name had come to their attention, an extensive background search had begun. It was learned that he had been an exemplary cop. He was smart, tough, and his ethics were above reproach. As a matter of fact, he was pretty much the exact opposite of their current employee at Harvard's old department, Deputy Chief Ramsey. Harris loathed the man and didn't trust him at all. No man that could be bought off, in Harris's opinion, could be trusted. To top it all off with, Harris could recognized incompetency when he saw it and Ramsey was loaded with it. He understood why Harvard and Ramsey hated one another. They were polar opposites. But he also recognized the Ramsey's of this world were a necessary evil for the plans of Coeptus Guild.

On the screen, Harvard stopped and slowly brought a pair of binoculars to his eyes. "Pan back." Harris ordered.

Dave, the man at the console, complied and the view on the screen widened. They could see their cabin in the background.

"Christ!" exclaimed Carl. "He's watching us right now. Go out there and kill him."

"No!" Harris shot back.

"What do you mean, no. I am in charge of this operation and I am ordering you to kill him, now."

Harris turned and glared at Carl with a look that paralyzed most men with fear. Carl felt a tingle in his spine, but to his credit, he did not turn away. He was accustomed to giving orders and having them followed. Still, Harris's gaze made him take a step back.

Harris answered in a tone that made Carl feel like he was being scolded by a school teacher. "Listen, Carl, when it comes to security, that's *my* purview and *you* will listen to what *I* say."

"But I was told..." Carl protested weakly.

"I don't care what you were told. As long as everything was going according to plan, you got to be in charge. But the shit is about to hit the fan and my authority now supersedes yours, so shut your fucking pie hole before I shut it for you."

"But if you just kill him, the danger will be over." Carl insisted. Dave, the man at the console, thought Carl must have a death wish.

Harris was contemplating doing exactly what Dave was thinking, but instead got control of himself and answered, "Listen you stupid shit. Killing a man like that probably wouldn't be as easy as you seem to think. Not only that, but he may be making regular check ins with someone and they probably have orders to bring in the marines if he doesn't check in. That means if we just let him amuse himself out there for a while, it gives you time to convince the princess in there to fork over her work. I suggest you get to work on that. NOW!" he shouted.

Carl flinched as if he had been struck and looked over at Dave, as though Dave would be irrational enough to come to his aid. He decided that maybe it would be a good time to re-interview Susan. He turned and left the room without another word.

When he was gone, Harris turned back to the screen in front of him. Harvard was moving again, this time toward the garage. "Where's he going?" Dave asked.

"He's checking the garage to have a look see. He's probably trying to find what goodies we have in there. He's also still looking for alarms. I'm sure it bothers him that he's been unable to find any. He's not the type to fall for our, 'Oh I'm sure that the cameras we have along the driveway are good enough,' routine.

Harris went to a closet in the room and returned with three guns. All three were HK MP5's. The weapons were designed for the Secret Service and were deadly. These were the newest versions chambered for 10mm rounds. They could be fired on full automatic, or in single or three round bursts. Light weight, synthetic magazines could provide up to sixty rounds of ammunition without changing clips. Dave looked up at Harris and asked, "Do we need that much fire-power?"

"You don't know anything about Harvard or you would-n't be asking. There are a lot of men planted six feet under right now that made the same mistake. I don't intend to be one of them. Where's Bart?"

Bart was the fourth member of their little enclave and was considered to be off duty at the present time. He alternated with Dave, watching the consoles for signs of trespassers. Like Harris and Dave, he was ex-military. "I don't know, he was sleeping, but I thought I heard him a little while ago."

"Well go find him and get him in here," Harris commanded.

Dave left and Harris turned his attention back to the screen. Harvard had worked his way over to the garage and was out of view of the original camera. The motion sensors on those cameras still had not detected him. But he was visible on one of the other monitors. Harris punched a couple of buttons and brought him up on the big screen.

"Shit!" muttered Harris. A blinking light showed that the missing Bart was outside, apparently wandering aimlessly around and he was making his way toward the garage. The motion sensors on those cameras had no trouble detecting him. Harris had no doubt that if Bart accidentally found Harvard, the outcome would not be beneficial to Bart. Harris remembered his own brief encounter with Harvard outside of Susan's apartment. His throat still ached from the blow he'd received. Though Bart was competent enough, he didn't think he'd be able to best Harvard in a hand to hand contest. That was assuming that Harvard didn't just slit his throat and be done with it.

Dave came back into the room saying, "I can't find him. Maybe…" he stopped short as he saw Bart on one of the smaller monitors. He quickly saw where he was headed and said, "Oh no. I've got to stop him," and headed for the door.

"Wait!" Harris shouted. "We can't alert Harvard that we know he's here. Try him on his cell phone."

"But there's no signal out here." Dave protested.

"Try it anyway. Better than just sitting here twiddling our thumbs."

Harris watched the big screen as Harvard slowly rose and peered into one of the windows of the garage. Suddenly, Harvard froze. He must have heard Bart. Harris knew what Harvard was going through, been there himself on many occasions. He was deciding if he had time to back out of the area and blend into his surroundings, or if he should just take Bart out.

Though Harris knew that Harvard had no formal military training, he also knew men like John Harvard. They were natural hunters. They didn't have to be taught what was instinctive to them. Men like Harvard taught themselves the things they thought were, "interesting." His training as a policeman and his training in the martial arts, had taught him how to survive. Certainly, military training would have honed those abilities to a frightening level, but it would only have refined what was already there.

"No answer sir," came Dave's distressed voice. "What if I just open the front door and shout out to him. I can say that we need help with something in here. Harvard won't know any different."

"Fine! Do it quickly," Harris barked. Dave moved toward the door. "Wait!"

Dave halted and returned to the monitors. He immediately saw why he'd been told to stop. Harvard had elected to move back into the grass along the tree line. In his haste, he must have made some sort of noise because Bart suddenly stopped and looked toward the corner of the garage. He couldn't possibly see Harvard from his position, so he must have heard something.

Bart quickly moved to the garage, drew his weapon and slowly began to creep along the front of the structure in the direction of Harvard. To Dave, it was like watching a movie. "Sir," he said pleadingly.

Harris knew what he wanted. Without taking his eyes off

the screen, he quietly said, "No son. Whatever is going to happen, will happen. If you call to him now, it will only serve to distract him and he needs his complete attention on the task before him. If we go rushing out there to help, either Harvard will take him out, then go for us, or Bart will get Harvard. The outcome is the same. Anyway you look at it, the die has been cast."

The drama before them unfolded. Bart came to the edge of the garage and quickly stuck his head and gun around the corner. He saw nothing that alarmed him, but that obviously didn't relax him as he just as quickly retreated his head back around to the front of the garage. It was plain that Bart was trying to decide what to do next.

The answer became obvious as Bart slowly brought his gun up to firing position and stepped out into the open. He was concentrating on the grass in front of the tree line, where Harris and Dave both knew that Harvard had gone. But Bart didn't know that, so he was keeping a watchful eye on the opposite corner of the garage as well. Harris wished that there was some way to let him know he needn't bother wasting any of this attention on the corner He needed to keep his full attention on the grass before him.

Bart began moving toward the grass. Even on the big monitor, Harris had difficulty seeing Harvard. But Harvard had equipped his gilly suit with mostly leaves, twigs and only a little grass, so it was possible to detect him. Harvard didn't quite have the time to make it back to the woods where, given his current camouflage, he would have been much harder to detect. Harris fervently prayed that Bart would not spot him and would give up his search, thinking he had been mistaken in whatever it was that had attracted his attention.

On the screen, it was evident that Bart had decided that the most likely threat was in the grass in front of him and began to move slowly but deliberately toward that area. He still kept the corner of the garage in mind but most of his attention was concentrated before him. Harris didn't see that he, himself, would have played anything Bart had done thus far, much differently.

Bart reached the edge of the grass and began to scour the area with his eyes. "Come on Bart," Dave cried. "Don't you see him? He's right in front of you."

Bart inched forward, Closer, closer until it seemed impossible for him not to see Harvard. Bart looked back toward the corner of the garage. That was when John Harvard made his move.

He had been lying prone, facing Bart. When Bart turned his head, quick as a ferret, Harvard spun around and struck Bart's ankles with his own, whirring feet. The move even surprised Harris who calmly watched the next few moments in professional admiration.

Bart managed to keep his footing, but his equilibrium was knocked off and he fought to regain it. Harvard took this opportunity to rise to his feet quicker than anyone either Dave or Bart had ever seen. Harris had seen such speed and agility before and though Harvard had only made two moves thus far, Harris knew how this was going to end.

All three Coeptus Guild men saw that Harvard had a

knife in his right hand. He was not holding it with the blade sticking out, but rather, with the blade of the knife ran alongside Harvard's forearm with the cutting edge facing out. The mark of a professional knife handler.

He brought the blade up in a move that would slice Bart's throat. But with a speed born of pure desperation, Bart managed to deflect the blow with his gun. The trigger guard caught the tip of the knife and it went flying from Harvard's hand.

"Yes!" Dave shouted. Harris's stone faced expression never changed. For he knew it was but a moments reprieve.

The look on Bart's face showed that even he was as surprised at the success of the maneuver as was Harvard. But that didn't slow Harvard down. Without missing a beat, as though the entire event was choreographed, Harvard continued his forward motion and planted a knee deep into Bart's groin. Bart doubled over. Quickly, Harvard grabbed Bart's lowered chin with this right hand. His left fingers gripped the back of Bart's head. Then rapidly, forcefully, Harvard moved both hands away from each other, twisting Bart's head to one side, much further than nature had intended for the human head to pivot on the spinal column. A deep crunching sound came from Bart's neck and he dropped to the ground, his head looking up at an unnatural angle. It was over. First blood had been drawn.

Harvard looked around quickly and then grabbed Bart. Like a lion scurrying off with his fallen prey, he took Bart into the woods and out of sight. A moment later, he returned, sans Bart, and retrieved his knife and Bart's gun.

Then, he was just... gone.

Harris turned away from the monitor and looked at Dave. Dave was as white as a ghost. "I... I never saw anything like that before," Dave said slowly, hesitantly. "I was in Iraq and saw a lot of shit, but nothing like that."

"Nor is it likely you ever will again. I know you're shaken, but watch the monitors. He's obviously to this side of the Electrostatic Field. One of the motion detectors should pick him up shortly. Don't wait for that. You know what area he was in so start bringing up each camera on the high definition monitor and study it. You know what to look for now. Once you find him, keep track of him and let me know if he tries to come any closer. Things have changed and I have to start making plans. Be ready to move out."

Harris's voice was steady and he appeared to Dave to be as confident as ever. For the most part, that was still true. When he had started this operation, he never dreamed of coming up against someone like John Harvard. A civilian! From his research, he knew Harvard's record, but his record never gave him a clue that he was capable of what Harris just witnessed. Truth be told, Harris was a bit shaken.

Fortunately, years of professional army service and combat had given him the tools necessary to move on. That's just what he was going to do. Even now his mind was formulating a plan. Things were not good but far from hopeless. He was still going to try to salvage the operation.

He thought of his options. What were the weak points, the strong points, and how could he take advantage of each?

Strong point, Harvard was most likely still unaware that he'd been spotted by anyone other than the unfortunate Bart. In addition, he was still trying to go it alone. That meant that the strength of Harris's numbers, though now diminished, coupled with his advanced planning, gave Harris the edge.

The weak point? John Livingston Harvard. He'd shown himself to be brave, resourceful, cunning, and more than capable of handling most situations. The question now became, could he handle Harris's next move?

CHAPTER
19

At that moment, John Harvard lay on the ground, breathing heavily. He had hastily covered Bart with sticks and leaves and was now attempting to regain his composure. He had never done anything like that before. He'd been taught how to break a neck in his martial arts training, practiced it in fact on numerous occasions using a variety of methods. Even as he practiced, he had wondered if it was as easy as they made it out to be and he wondered what kind of situation would he have to be in to resort to that kind of violence? At the time, he couldn't think of a likely scenario that would necessitate it. He had found one.

Not only that, but he was surprised at how quickly the thought, rather, the instinct, had come to him to do it. He hadn't really thought about the naturalness of it until just now, as he lay there collecting himself. It had just happened. Like so many times in the past in perilous circumstances, John's body seemed to take control from his conscious mind. Like a hand that retreats from a hot object without the brain thinking about it, he had just reacted to the situation, unthinking, like a preprogrammed killer robot.

He replayed the event in his mind. John felt like he had been moving excruciatingly slow. His multiple layers of clothing had made it feel as though he was trying to move through a big bowl of Jell-O. He knew from past experience that treacherous situations seemed to cause time to slow to a crawl but he also knew that didn't entirely explain the slowness, nor did it explain the fact that as he had risen up to confront his foe, he had been slightly off balance and he was attempting to correct this instability even as he was pressing his attack. He didn't have the time to do otherwise. A large portion of his brain had been concentrating on the problem when his foe had swung his gun around and dislodged John's knife.

Since he was moving forward already, kneeing his opponent in the groin had seemed the logical next step and had actually helped him to regain his balance. As the man doubled over and his head had come down to waist level, pure instinct born from hours of training, took over from there. It was classic, for that was exactly the way most of his practice sessions had gone in class. Kick the opponent in the groin and when he bends over… "Finish him!" his instructors had yelled. He'd given no forethought to breaking his opponent's neck. It was just that the man's head was suddenly exactly where John's opponents head had always been in practice. And so, without thinking, John had simply done what had been drilled into him in training. It had worked with marvelous efficiency.

Now, he had to get control of his breathing. Controlled breathing was the key to overall control. He breathed in and held it, only for a moment. He then exhaled in a controlled manner. He repeated this several times, each time holding his breath a little longer and exhaling a little slower. He could feel his heartbeat returning to normal.

He began to reassess the situation. He didn't think anyone else was aware of his presence, otherwise they would have come at him with a lot more firepower. Still, it did bother him greatly that he'd been unable to detect any other devices. He was also aware that he probably didn't have long before they missed their companion and came looking for him. He decided to move around to the other side of the house, away from the body to where he could view the cabin and the front of the garage. Anyone moving from the house to the garage or vice versa would have nowhere to hide if gunfire erupted.

It took him some time to move to his new location just on the other side of the driveway. When he arrived, he found it was a fine spot for surveillance, but not so good for a fire fight. He didn't want to move around too much but he looked around and began to move several large rocks to form a barricade. He feared that bullets striking those rocks would cause shards to fly that could be as deadly as the bullets themselves but decided that they were better than nothing. To counteract the possibility though, he found a semi-rotted log that he put between the rocks and himself. He finished his fortification by spreading leaves and small branches over it, in an attempt to make it look as natural as possible, and settled in for what could be the final run.

As a final preparation, he removed his .45 and retrieved

all of his clips from his pack, which he then placed into easily accessible pockets on his suit. He ate his lunch, drank some water and lay there, playing out all of the conceivable ways for this to go down.

There was still the off chance that Susan wasn't in there, in which case all hell was about to break loose for no particularly good reason. If she wasn't on site, once the shooting started, she was as good a dead. John couldn't think of a good reason not to call in the troops now. If Sue was in the cabin, fine, it was time to go get her out. If she wasn't here, well… by killing the man, he had now pushed up the timetable and there was no going back. The scale in John's mind tipped to the side of calling Nick.

Before he could place the radio call to Emily, the front door of the cabin opened. A small, wiry man in his late fifties came out and walked toward the garage. He moved quickly but seemed nonchalant as he opened the side door and walked in. A moment later, the overhead door of the garage opened and John watched as the man drove Clemmons' Jeep out and down the driveway.

John remained still for several minutes as he waited for something else to happen. Why on earth would they be using Clemmons' Jeep? Because of Ramsey, they certainly knew that Clemmons' body had been found. Why take a chance on using his Jeep? He was beginning to get a very uneasy feeling about this.

He picked up his radio and called Emily. No answer. He tried several times, but to no avail. What the hell? Maybe she had to go to the bathroom. Had she fallen asleep? He didn't think that was likely. What if they had found her? The thought sent shivers down his spine.

John began to think of numbers. How many people was he up against? He had taken out the curious one. One had just left in the Jeep so their numbers at the present time were reduced by two.

Harris was in there, and most likely Peter. Not knowing Peter's intentions, he had to assume he was hostile. That meant at least two left. He looked at the cabin again. It was fairly small, so he really couldn't see too many more people staying there. Maybe one more. If his calculations were right, that meant he would have to go up against at least two, possibly three men, all before they had time to kill Susan.

He thought of the look on Peter's face when he talked about Sue. Peter would probably be willing to kill him, but not his daughter. If he could quickly take out the others, he might be able to convince Peter to give it up.

He was still debating his next move when he heard the crunching of tires on the gravel driveway. He looked up and saw the Jeep returning. Instead of pulling into the garage, it stopped in front of the cabin. The wiry man got out and hastily moved to the passenger side. He opened the door, reached in and yanked out Emily!

"God damn it!" he groaned to himself. This morning, he'd been feeling pretty confident. Now he felt his control over the situation rapidly slipping away as the man half dragged Emily into the cabin and slammed the door shut.

John put his face down on the ground and sighed. Nick

had been right. This was too much for one man to handle. He could only hope that he would live long enough for his friend to cockily tell him, "I told you so." He raised his head again and shook his self doubts away. He had to think!

In the cabin, Harris asked Dave, "Have you found him yet?"

"No! He just fucking disappeared."

Harris quickly scanned the monitors before saying, "Forget it. Time to move. You know what to do?"

Dave nodded. He turned to Carl. "What about you? You ready?"

"I… guess so," he stammered.

"Look, you god damn well better be. I don't like putting this kind of responsibility on someone like you," he said contemptuously. "But with Bart dead, I don't have a choice and I don't think Harvard is going to take a time out while I call in replacements."

"What if he just starts shooting?" Carl whined.

"He won't *just* start shooting." His dislike for Carl was growing. When this was all over, he considered killing Carl, just for the hell of it. Maybe make him squirm a little first, so he would know it was coming. He would kill Harvard because he was in the way and for the professional satisfaction of knowing he'd taken out a worthy foe. He would kill Carl for personal reasons. He shook off his momentary daydream and added, "We have his girlfriend as well as the woman he's trying to rescue. He's too professional to *just* start shooting."

He didn't add that if Harvard thought he was cornered or he thought he could take Carl or Dave out without hitting Emily or Susan, he'd do it. It's what he would do in Harvard's position. Harvard was aware that he'd lost control of the situation and only a bold move on his part would stand any chance of giving him back the edge. Harris knew he'd have to move fast, before Harvard made that move.

"Alright," said Harris to Carl and Dave. "Get going."

John gathered himself and prepared to move out. He had decided that he was going to quickly move to the road and flag down the first car he saw. He was going to run along the edge of the driveway where he knew all the monitors faced the drive. It would take time, but his only chance to save the girls now was to get in touch with Nick. But he didn't have time, for at that moment, the cabin door opened again. A man appeared with Emily. Another man came out right behind the first with another woman and John recognized her as Susan Browning.

The first man, the one with Emily, held a hand gun which was pointing straight down toward the ground. John recognized the wiry man he'd seen earlier. He held Emily tight against the front of him by squeezing her neck with his left arm. His face and body actions revealed that he was not comfortable in his current predicament.

The second man held Susan by the hair with the left hand of his extended arm. His right hand held what John recognized to be an MP5 machine gun, pointed at Susan's back. His body actions spoke of professionalism and John instantly knew that this second man was the far more dangerous opponent.

The second man closed the door behind him with his foot and John thought, *where's Harris*? Could it be that for some reason, Harris wasn't here? As he watched, they moved past the Jeep and toward the garage.

John immediately assessed the situation and came to a conclusion. Whether Harris was in the house or not didn't really matter. The women were right in front of him, in the open and as close as they were going to get, not more than thirty feet. If he acted fast and was lucky, he could get the women and get to the cover of the garage before Harris had time to react. Not only that, but he would hopefully have the second man's MP5 added to his arsenal.

John slowly, so his movement wouldn't attract attention, brought his .45 up in front of him. He was just taking aim at the second man, the more dangerous of the two, when that man spotted John. He reacted quickly and brought Susan up in front of him as he turned to face John. The MP5 was just beginning to spurt when John fired.

As the bullets from the MP5 tore into the leaves around him, the .45 boomed a deafening roar and a bright red hole instantly appeared in the second man's forehead. John rose quickly as the wiry man let go of Emily and began shooting wildly in John's general direction. John's mind was registering that the man's aim wasn't even in the ballpark when his .45 bellowed again, hitting the wiry man in the torso.

Not knowing exactly where the man had been hit, he fired once more and the man went down and was still.

John began to run. "Move to the garage," he shouted at the women. They stood in stunned silence. "Now!" he shouted again as he moved to the second man and picked up the MP5. He saw that the man had at least one more clip sticking out of his pocket and he quickly retrieved that as well before moving toward the garage himself, all the while keeping his eyes on the cabin for signs of Harris.

When he got there, he found both women huddled in one corner, holding each other and crying. His senses were alert for combat now and he felt absolutely no compassion for them whatsoever. "Check the car for keys," he barked harshly as he moved to a window and looked out. No sign of Harris yet.

He quickly looked over at Susan and Emily. They hadn't moved. "Is Harris in there?" he demanded.

Susan responded with a sob, "I don't know who Harris is. I do know that there was at least one more man in there."

"What about your father?" he bellowed.

"I don't know!" she screamed back. "I've been kept in a bedroom with no sunlight and no clock for days. I don't know anything about what's going on or who's there."

He could see that Susan was on the verge of hysteria. He couldn't afford that right now. He went over to her. "Listen," he said soothingly, taking precious time to calm her. "I know you've had a rough time of it. But we're a long way from being safe, especially if Harris is the one in the cabin. It's important, for all our sakes, that you stay as calm as possible. We need to work together so we can get through this."

He froze when he heard a gruff voice behind him. "I think you've caused quite enough problems for one day Mr. Harvard. Now kindly drop your guns and get down on your knees and... no heroics please. Otherwise I'll be forced to open up on this entire garage and kill everyone in it. I'm sure you don't want to be responsible for that, now do you?"

As soon as everyone had gone out the door of the cabin, Harris had quickly moved to the tunnel entrance that led to the garage. He had come up the other side just in time to see the gun fight. If you could call it that. Dave had reacted quickly and appropriately but Harvard was far too accurate, far too quick. No doubt about it, the man was dangerous. He was disappointed but not at all surprised when Harvard took out Carl. He really had wanted to do that one himself and now Harvard had spoiled that too. One more reason to kill him.

Harris had a feeling that things would turn out exactly this way. Dave was a good kid and Harris was as close to sorry about his death as Harris could possibly be. Not that he'd had a lot of it before, but any lingering feelings of compassion had been pretty much stomped out of him in Iraq. What was left was a cold, calculating, killing machine. He did what was necessary for the mission and if that meant that Dave had to be sacrificed to give him time to get here from the cabin, so be it.

He had to find out where Harvard was and then he had to be somewhere that Harvard would not expect him to be. Dave and Carl had drawn Harvard out and in addition, they gave Harris the time he needed to move through the tunnel.

Now, he watched as Harvard moved about and gave orders. Harvard was looking out the window but he didn't get too close so that any bullet coming through wouldn't send flying glass into his eyes. Harris wanted to give Harvard's combat senses a little time to cool. He wanted him to begin to relax just enough to let his adrenaline rush pass and to where Harvard thought Harris wasn't coming after him immediately.

Then he saw his chance when Harvard went to console Susan. He slowly raised his gun and aimed at Harvard's head. He was going to take him out right there but at the last second, he had another thought. Maybe he could use him later as a sacrificial lamb. He could threaten Susan once again with the death of her father and mother. Only this time, he would throw Harvard into the mix as well. When she still refused to cooperate, he would blow Harvard's brains all over the wall and floor, right in front of her. Then, he'd do Emily and then Peter. If *that* didn't show her what she was up against, nothing would. At that point, he'd kill her, blow the place up and be done with it.

So instead of pulling the trigger, he told Harvard to drop his guns. He had a great respect for Harvard and if the man had so much as twitched, he would sprayed the area with

10mm rounds, Susan Browning be damned!

John couldn't believe his ears. Where the hell had Harris come from? He briefly considered pushing Susan to the floor and jumping to one side. Then, he reminded himself who he was dealing with and reconsidered. That decision was punctuated with another harshly given order from Harris.

"Drop your fuckin' guns, now!! You got one second before I open up!"

John dropped his gun, fell to his knees and assumed the position, hands behind his head, fingers intertwined. Harris barked again. "You Miss Browning, move away from him." She complied. John risked a glance in her direction. Strangely, as he watched, her hysteria seemed to vanish, replaced by a look of cool serenity. Something had just clicked with her, whether it was a complete breakdown into insanity or a move to something else entirely, remained to be seen.

When Carl had opened the door to her room, Susan had known that something was wrong. He had a look on his face that she had never seen before. Fear? She wasn't sure. He was blunt.

"You're running out of time! I have been patient with you beyond measure but my employer's indulgence is at an end. That is unfortunate because I really do like you and would like nothing more than for us to work together. However, there is a timetable and that timetable is now at an end.

For the sake of yourself, your father, your mother, and all you hold dear, please, I implore you, please agree to work with us. Not only will nothing bad happen to you, but you will receive wealth beyond your imagination. Neither you, nor anyone in your family will ever want for anything again. Will you and they have a beautiful life from here on out, or will all of your lives end now, today? Susan, please, this is your last chance."

It had come to this. She knew it would and she'd been agonizing over her alternatives. She didn't want her father to die, let alone her mother. On the other hand, how could she live with herself if she unleashed such evil on the world? For it truly was evil these people were planning, no doubt about it. Men who were willing to go to such drastic ends were obviously not god fearing men. Say what you will about religion, believe in it or don't, those who abided by its teachings normally had some boundaries to their behavior.

Of course, that didn't always apply. The Crusades and the Spanish Inquisition being prime examples. There were always some who used their religion to justify their own moral decay. Muslim terrorists were another illustration, the vast majority of whom were nothing more than common street thugs who would have used another venue to express their depravity if one hadn't been so conveniently provided for them in the form of their religion.

However, by and large, religion at the very least, stood as a beacon, a moral compass whose teachings helped to guide a lot of people through the treacherous shoals of life. The people responsible for her capture, Susan was convinced, had no such moral compass other than their own unfathomable greed. She could not, would not be responsible for feeding that appetite and allowing them to obtain lord only knows what heights of power.

She did not want to die. Her only other option was to stall as much as she could in hopes that somehow, someway, she would be rescued. At the present time, she could not imagine how that could occur. She had few friends and spoke to no one on a regular basis other than her mother. Even that had no pattern that would arouse suspicions for at least days, if not weeks. In spite of all of this, her indomitable spirit refused to succumb to the weight of these depressing facts. So she began to negotiate with Carl in the hope that she would buy time and be saved before he realized that she was bluffing.

She was doing just that when her door burst open and a large man strode forcefully into the room. He left the door open and for the first time in who knew how long, she was able to get some rough bearings as to the time. It was daytime. She could also see why the mere opening of the door hadn't been a clue as to the time of day before. There were a double set of doors. Both doors were never opened at the same time thus preventing a view of the outside world.

"Come here!" the new intruder demanded of Carl. "We need to talk, *now.*" With that, the man turned and marched out of the room without looking at Susan once. Carl rose and without saying another word to Susan, meekly followed, closing the door quietly behind him.

She was stunned. Up until now, besides Carl and her father, she had seen no one and Carl had given every impression that he was in charge, that he was the mastermind behind it all and he knew everything and could do anything. She knew about the hidden microphone he had, but she had assumed that there was a group of nerds somewhere telling him what he should ask. She never dreamed of an encounter like the one she had just witnessed.

She thought again of the big man. He frightened her to the core, for there was a feral look of a savage hunter in his eyes that she imagined could only come from one who has killed, often.

She sat down and recalled the urgency in Carl's voice when he had entered the room and the insistent demand of the big man just now. She concluded that her time on this earth was probably very short indeed. She thought of her father and began to regret the lost years. Why had she been so unyielding and self-righteous?

She jumped as the door flew open once again. Carl and the big man entered. Carl remained timidly by the door as the big man approached, roughly grabbed her by the arm and stood her up. "Listen you prissy little bitch. You're going to go for a walk now. You do exactly what you're told or we will shoot you. Don't try to escape or I will kill you myself... slowly."

He looked at her face and then his eyes drifted downward as he began to look at the whole of her. She could see his attitude change slightly, to one that made her fear grow even larger. He was now looking at her as a man looks at a woman and she could feel his eyes probing every part of her until she felt as though she stood naked before him.

A look of pure sexual depravity came over his face and he added, "Of course I will make sure that you leave this world well satisfied and feeling like a true woman."

Then the wild feral look returned and he shoved her over to Carl. "Get going!" he commanded.

She looked down and saw a gun in Carl's hand. It looked out of place and she noted with apprehension, his hand was shaking; This obviously was not part of the original plan. What had happened to have caused this sudden restructuring?

Carl led her to the front door where another man stood next to a blonde woman. Who was she? Was she with them, or a captive like herself? Who was this other man? He looked serious and quite capable, though he didn't frighten her as the big man had. He held a huge gun in his right hand that she recognized as being some sort of rifle or machine gun. *His* hands looked as steady as a rock. She didn't have time to think about it further because the man gruffly ordered Carl, "Go."

Carl grabbed the woman and guided her out the door. Susan could tell he was attempting to give her a show of force. But his hands and grip looked weak, timorous, and it was obvious that he was unsure of himself.

The other man roughly grabbed Susan's long hair and instructed her to follow Carl and the other woman. "If you try to run, I will shoot you. Understand?" She nodded as best she could considering how tightly he held her hair and started out the door. The sunlight, the first she had seen in she didn't know how long, struck her eyes with a blinding ferocity that made her hesitate. Her captor savagely pushed her forward and whispered brusquely, "Keep moving."

She observed a garage ahead and saw that they were in a wilderness area. A movement in the woods to the right, caught her eye. At the same time, her captor violently pulled her back toward him, released his grip on her hair, wrapped his left forearm tightly around her throat and spun both of them around toward the direction of the movement she had just seen. Obviously he had spotted the motion as well. She then heard a brief, staccato sound of a machine gun next to her, quickly followed by an ear splitting roar coming from the spot in the woods. The sound of the machine gun stopped and the man's grip on her throat abruptly loosened as he fell to the ground. Even still, he almost dragged her down with him.

As she fought to regain her balance, she stumbled past the still form of the man that had been behind her. There was a cherry sized hole in his forehead and he was indisputably dead. She looked up and saw Carl push the other woman to one side and turn to run. She reverted her gaze back toward the woods and stood stock still in amazement as a bush rose up from the forest floor. A branch was extended from the bush and she heard the same deafening roar twice more. Carl had fired his weapon but he had been too busy trying to vacate the area to have been very effective.

The bush, who she was just beginning to realize was actually a man, quickly approached and roughly ordered her to the garage. Only now did she see that the blonde woman was standing over Carl, who was obviously just as dead as her captor. She stood transfixed, taking in this unexpected turn of events. The bush/man yelled at them again. This broke her trance and she obeyed the order immediately.

Once in the garage, she went to a corner where the blonde woman embraced her and said, "Oh Susan, I'm so happy you're okay." The blonde woman began to cry, which in turn brought out tears in Susan as well. *Who was this woman?* Susan wondered, *and how does she know my name?*

The bush/man ran into the garage carrying the big gun that he had taken from the other man in his left hand. He held a large pistol in his right. He quickly looked out a window in the garage and then ordered them to check the big black Mercedes sitting next to them for keys.

When they didn't comply, he began firing questions at Sue and that finally broke the emotional dam that had been building up pressure for days. She couldn't take it anymore. She felt the last vestiges of sanity breaking away like icicles from a warming gutter. The bush/man approached and tried to calm her.

As her hysteria was gaining strength, like a massive hurricane engulfing her psyche, she was trying not to look at the bush/man and was instead looking over his shoulder at the far wall of the garage. That was when she saw the big man from the cabin raise his gun and order the bush/man to drop his weapons. Always a quick learner, she learned a lot in the next few seconds.

She learned the bush/man had a name, Harvard. She also saw the anguish on his face as he dropped his guns on the floor beside him. The anguish was not for his own plight. As he went to his knees, Harvard looked Susan directly in the eyes. She imagined that passengers from the Titanic in the freezing water of the Atlantic, saw the same look as some person in a lifeboat reluctantly let go of their hand and let them slip away to die in the chilly embrace of the sea. She saw sorrow and compassion from the painted face of Harvard.

She was ordered away from Harvard. She backed away and lost the eye to eye connection but couldn't take her eyes off him. Then, like the tranquil aura of a young child lying in bed as a soft blanket descends as part of the final good night ritual, peace flowed through her. After days, no years of being independent and alone, she suddenly felt she had an ally. A trustworthy ally. A strong ally, from the look of him.

Her sanity returned with a speed that astounded even her. She was smart. Though small physically, she was no slouch. She was tired of running, tired of being ordered about, tired of feeling helpless, tired of being alone. This man had come to save her. Now, he needed her help and she was god damned well going to give it to him.

He looked up at her suddenly and she could see confusion in his face. She couldn't help the smile that lightly crossed her face. But she held back a much larger smile, for she didn't want to confuse the poor man any more than he probably already was. She was sure he thought she'd lost her mind. He had seen the change in her, but he had no idea what it meant for him.

CHAPTER
20

John had indeed been coming to the conclusion that Susan had lost it. *Great*, he thought. *As if things aren't bad enough already, now I have to try to get a basket case out of here.* He heard Harris approaching behind him.

Harris was a little vexed as to what to do next. He was going to tell Harvard to lie on his stomach as he searched him. But he remembered how Harvard had spun quick as a snake on poor Bart and decided that the kneeling position was best. "Cross your ankles," he ordered Harvard.

"I'm going to search you now," he continued after John had crossed his ankles. "I just want you to know that if you try anything, the first thing I will do is shoot your girlfriend over there. I guarantee that you won't be able to stop me. Then you and I can dance."

With the threat to Emily looming over him, John decided to put up no resistance as Harris searched him and removed his Walther and the knife. When he was finished and had retreated back to a safe distance, Harris spoke again. "Here's what we're gonna do. You are all going to walk over to the side door and stand, facing away from me. I will tell you when to move, as a group, back to the house. Emily, you will go first, then Susan, who will have her hand stuck into Emily's waistband, fingers and palm deep inside the pants. Harvard, you will go last and your right hand shoved down Susan's waistband, all the way, no fingers and palm for you. If Harvard or Susan lets go of the person in front of them, I start shooting. Does everyone understand how this is going to work?" They all nodded.

"Good, then everyone move to the side door." When they had all complied, Harris instructed them to form a line as he had described. "I want the fingers of those hands deep into the pants of the person in front," he yelled.

When he was satisfied, he told them to move out. It looked like a short line dance for a wedding, but John could see no possible way he could do anything without them all being cut to pieces by Harris's MP5.

They reached the cabin and went in. John looked around and was taken aback when he saw the bank of monitors. He looked at each carefully and the realization dawned on him that they must have known where he was the entire time.

"Nice little setup, eh?" Harris said with a grin.

"You knew where I was the whole time," replied John. "I guess I'm a little confused as to why you didn't react sooner."

"Oh, you don't give yourself enough credit Harvard. You're very good. Dave, the man you so callously shot in the head a little while ago, didn't spot you until you crossed an electrostatic field, which in turn set off an audible alarm and zeroed in one of the cameras on to your position. Even then, it was difficult to spot you. If it hadn't been for that last sensor, you probably could have succeeded, in spite of the fact that we knew you were coming and when."

Though he tried not to show it, a look of shock and confusion spread across John's face and Harris laughed. "Yeah Harvard, not that it made a whole lot of difference in the end, but we knew you were gonna be creeping around in our backyard."

How? John wondered to himself. *Peter? He doubted it. Peter didn't know enough about his current movements. Ramsey!* He must have learned enough to deduce what John would do. Ramsey had seen John in action before during his brief stint with the department's S.W.A.T. exercises. He looked at the monitors again.

"Trying to figure out how much we saw? Well, we saw your little altercation with Bart, that's the guy whose neck you broke. Then we lost you again until you killed Dave. You know, I'd really love to have you on my team, but I know better than to waste my breath, Mr. Goody Fucking Two Shoes."

John studied Harris a moment. Clean cut, good looking man that any father would be happy to have his daughter bring home. However, the clean, wholesome look of the exterior hid the moral decay beneath that had ravaged the man from the inside. What had made him like that?

He had seen his type before. He remembered a killer they had arrested for the murder of a twelve year old boy. The killer, who himself was only seventeen at the time, had broken into the victim's house to burglarize it. He didn't know that the boy was home sick.

The killer found him hiding under the bed and had taken him into the woods where he had proceeded to stab the boy to death. He didn't attempt to deny his vicious crime. Instead, he took great delight in reliving it, right down to the tiniest detail.

What had made it worse was the fact that he had known the boy and his family. He knew them well and had played with them on innumerable occasions. After the first blow of the knife, the boy had pleaded with the killer, calling him by his first name in a vain attempt to make him stop. It had done no good. In fact, most of the wounds had been caused by *slowly* pressing the knife in. He had laughed at the victim and had accused him of being a, "sissy," for crying so much. The poor boy had received twenty seven stab wounds and had eventually passed out and died from blood loss.

The pathologist who performed the autopsy said that the boy was conscious and aware of almost all of the stab wounds. It was a horrible way to die. That was one of John's first homicide investigations and he was only involved in it as a patrolman. The thing that amazed him the most was the total lack of remorse by the killer. In fact, when his picture was taken at the jail, he danced about, laughing and made the statement, "This is cool. I didn't know when I did this that I was going to be famous!" It was at that moment that John became a believer in the death penalty. A person like that was pure evil in its truest sense. No one was going to reform that killer. He would never change and if given even a half a chance, he would kill again. John just didn't see the reasoning for keeping a person like that alive.

The difference was that the man standing before him now was better at concealing his sickness. John suspected that the ability to kill without feeling had always been in Harris. If he hadn't joined the military, he would have most likely become a serial killer at some point. His military experiences had merely provided an outlet for his latent desires and had brought them to the forefront, much the same as the terrorist uses religion as an excuse for fulfilling their homicidal thirst. For Harris, killing wasn't just a necessary means to an end, it provided him with a satisfaction that he had most likely never known before and could experience in no other way.

Somehow, Harris must have guessed what John was thinking. "Don't you be looking down on *me*," Harris roared. Then, in a quieter, but sneering voice, he continued. "We're not so different, you and I. I saw the calm, efficient way you killed Bart, Dave, and Carl. You didn't bat an eyelash. You didn't run and puke, You didn't look scared. You killed and you moved on. I read your file. You've killed many times and you never had to take any downtime to, 'get yourself together,' as they say. You just took three lives," he snapped his fingers. "Just like that. Now you stand before me and dare to judge? You got some nerve asshole."

"Whatever, Harris." John replied calmly. There was no sense discussing the issue. There was a world of difference.

"Is that true John?" Emily unexpectedly interjected. Harris grinned as though he had scored a point in a debate contest. John looked at her and saw a pained expression that hinted that she felt she had been mislead. He didn't give two shits what Harris thought of him. Emily was a different matter.

"As I'm sure you already know, it's true that I have taken lives but no one who wasn't trying to kill me or someone else. When people are put in a position where they know that they may have to someday take a life, it forces them to think about it beforehand. Some give it a cursory once over and they're done with it. I think that those are the people who have the most trouble with it afterward. The forethought they neglected before catches up with them later, with a vengeance.

"With me, it was different. I thought about it... a lot. Each time I pulled my gun and didn't use it, I would think about it afterward and how I would have felt if I had pulled the trigger. Each time I heard of an incident involving another officer who had killed someone, I thought about how I would have felt if it had been me instead of them. Eventually, I came to the conclusion that if someone was depraved enough to try to kill me or someone else and I killed them instead, well, that's the way it goes.

"I've seen an awful lot of victims lying on a steel table who didn't deserve to be there. If I have to take a life to prevent that from happening, so be it. I would rather *they* be on that table than their intended victim. That's how I cope. I don't like killing. I don't even hunt animals. If I never had to kill again, that would be fine with me. In fact, I would love it." He looked at Harris and their eyes locked. "Some men," he continued grimly, "are nothing more than vermin, whose only redemption will be in death."

He turned his gaze back to Emily and was relieved to see that her face had softened. He felt better. Harris broke in. "How very nice. I'll have to remember that little speech next time I want to get laid. I don't believe a word of it of course, but it sure sounds nice. Just what the girls want to hear." He walked over to Emily, put his gun to her head and smiled. "Now tell me Harvard, if I was to put a bullet into her pretty blonde head right now, tell me you wouldn't take great pleasure in killing me."

John felt the blood draining from his face and it felt like the red fluid in his veins had turned to ice. It wasn't fear he felt. It was a deep primordial anger that threatened to completely overtake him and push him into an action that his civilized brain told him wasn't particularly wise at the moment. He held his emotions in check while at the same time noting that Harris's overriding arrogance appeared to falter as he saw the look in John's eyes. Like a lion handler who suddenly realizes that he's pushed the big cat a little too far and now has to deal with the consequences.

As much as it pained him to admit it, Harris was right. If he killed Emily just to prove his point, John would feel a great deal of gratification in killing Harris. Did that truly mean that he was more like Harris than he wanted to admit? Was he truly a killer at heart, the only difference being what side they had chosen? Had all his carefully thought out ideas on the subject been rendered meaningless by this one, thought provoking, action?

Harris laughed. "Wow. That's the most expression I've seen out of you yet. We might have to discuss this further, but not right now. We have other business to attend to." He lowered his gun and turned his attention to Susan. "Now Miss Browning, the time has come for you to make a decision. Are you going to cooperate or am I going to have to start killing people? I think you'll find that I'm not as patient as Carl is." He looked over at John. "Excuse me, I meant, as patient as Carl was."

Everyone's gaze turned to Susan, who stood there with the calm and slightly puzzled look of someone trying to decide whether or not to order desert. She looked at Harris and asked coolly, "Where is my father? I'll not answer any of your questions until I know that he is safe."

"He's safe!" Harris's voice was low, but venom dripped from every word as he continued. "But he's not going to be if you don't start cooperating right now. You are in no position to dictate terms to me. I'm tired of your stalling. I personally wanted to take a hot poker to you a long time ago, but I was overruled. I learned a lot of *interesting*, techniques in Iraq that I would just love to show you. Your time is up."

He moved away from Emily as he lifted his MP5 and pointed it in John's direction. "You have five seconds to start convincing me that you'll hand over your program, or I will pull this trigger. When I'm done with him, I move to Emily here. When I'm done with her, I bring in your father, who's quite alive by the way, though a little indisposed at the moment. So what are you going to do? I'm done asking."

For her part, Susan was quite sane, but the same tranquility that had come over her in the garage remained, keeping her as upright and sturdily moving forward as the stalwart keel of an old time sailing ship. Though she still had no intention of handing over her program, she also knew that she had to stall for time. For how long or for what, she didn't know. She just had to forestall Harris as long as she could. Every fiber of her being told her that things would work out if she could just keep the man called Harvard alive long enough. She approached Harris.

"Now Mr... Harris, isn't it?" she said with a tepid and collected voice. "Mr. Harris, I see no reason for anyone else to die here. No program is worth that. Carl said I would be very rich and to tell you the truth, I'm pretty sick of living the Spartan existence that I led before. To be frank with you, I don't like you and I certainly don't approve of your methods. However, at this point, I only want this to end as quickly as possible with these people," she motioned to John and Emily, " alive and free. I don't trust you so I want to talk to someone who can assure me that the conditions that Carl put forward will be adhered to."

Harris didn't reply as he attempted to sum up this new Susan, the one that had first appeared in the garage. Like John Harvard, he was quickly coming to the conclusion that her elevator no longer went to the top floor. He had seen people in stressful situations get hold of their fears before, but not the drastic change that this woman displayed. A glimmer of hope shot through him. He could take advantage of her shattered emotions and pull this assignment off yet.

Of course, neither she nor any of the other morons in this room would get out of this alive. It had gone too far but she didn't have to know that.

"Now Ms. Browning," he told her in a soothing voice, "I'm really not that bad a guy. Unfortunately, you've only seen my working side, brought out when I know I'm not meeting the expectations of my employers. I apologize if I've upset you but now that you see that the best way to handle this is to work with us, well, now you will see me in a better light."

Susan, softly, but firmly, responded. "I accept your apology, but I'm sure you understand that I would like to hear this from someone other than yourself."

Harris felt a surge of anger at her insolence but held it in check and continued with his soothing voice. "Unfortunately, we have no telephone service here and no cell phone signal either. Once you have given me the program, or at least convinced me that it works, we can all drive to my employers and discuss your compensation further."

Susan was standing very near to him now. "Oh come now Mr. Harris. Do you mean to tell me that with all this sophisticated equipment," she motioned toward the monitors, "and the money you obviously have at your disposal, you don't have a satellite phone?"

Harris desperately wanted to smash her face in. A thin line of doubt crossed his face as he began to wonder if he wasn't being played. He wasn't so sure now that she had indeed lost her mind. Maybe he'd underestimated her. If he had, he wasn't going to play anymore games. He would kill her, kill them all and leave. Still, he wasn't sure. "Yes," he slowly replied in an even monotone, "I have a satellite phone, but I won't bother them until you have convinced me that you're serious. Carl said that you told him the program wasn't finished yet."

"I told him that to stall him. I didn't want to give him the program." Susan had seen the sliver of suspicion that had crossed his face and knew that she had to allay his fears somehow to keep him calm. She let her face take on a slightly maniacal look as she continued. "That was before I saw the pretty red blood of course."

Her mind was racing. She had to be careful not to over do this or he would catch on and they would all be dead, including herself. "Don't you see?" she continued with an ever so slight amount of gaiety in her voice. "Before this began, I lived a pretty hum-drum existence. All dull and gray, black and white, ones and zeros. Then he," she pointed to John, "shot that man in the head. Suddenly, everything was colorful. Oh so very colorful and I realized that my stupid little computer program wasn't so important after all."

Harris nervously jerked his gun toward her as she moved over to John and took his hand. "Thank you for showing me that, thank you, thank you, thank you." She looked John directly in the eyes, only for an instant but suddenly he knew! Realizing that he was aware of what she was doing, she turned quickly away and moved back over toward Harris. In that fleeting glance to John, she had conveyed paragraphs of information. There was nothing wrong with Susan

Browning and she was intent on helping him. He tried to appear nonchalant as he carefully studied her every movement and understanding that sooner or later, she was going to make a move and he had to be ready to take advantage of it.

As Susan moved back over toward Harris, he risked a quick look at Emily. He wished he could somehow let her know to be ready as well but he didn't know how without arousing Harris's suspicions.

Susan approached Harris who had by now begun to relax once again. The woman had lost it, pure and simple, he decided. Having come to that conclusion, he didn't object when she clasped both hands around his right arm and tugged slightly downward as she said, "When this is all over, could you teach me to shoot a gun? That would be really amazing."

He smiled slightly as he answered, "Certainly! But right now, you have to show me your program and explain it to me the best you can. Convince me Susan. Then we can do anything you want."

"Oh, thank you!" Susan replied. She raised her head and mouth up, as if to kiss him. At the same time she brought her left knee up and with all the strength of the muscles she had developed from hours in the gym, kneed him in the groin and at the same time grabbed at the MP5 he held in his right hand.

Her strike had been well directed and totally unexpected, Harris doubled over in pain. She succeeded in snatching the gun from him. However, he recovered quickly enough to give her a vicious, powerful, backhanded blow across the face before she could move out of range. The gun went spinning out of her hands as she fell toward the floor. She hit hard, landed in a crumpled heap and lay still, her head angled upward.

Harvard was on Harris in three strides, his last stride launching him high up into the air. John meant to do a flying sidekick to Harris's throat or chest, but Harris, though in pain, was too quick and he fended off the attempt with an arm block as he stumbled to one side.

John landed, spun around and assumed a defensive posture as he assessed Harris's condition. He was obviously hurting from Susan's attack but far from out. Harris produced the knife that he had taken from John and both men stood facing each other. He held it the same way John had earlier, with the blade running along his arm, blade facing out. Both knew only one would walk away from this fight. Both respected the skills of the other. Both arrogantly assumed it would be them that would leave as the victor.

Harris lunged toward him and John skipped back, toward the kitchen. Harris made three more lunges and John skipped back each time until he was in the kitchen. There, lying on the table was a crumpled towel. He snatched it up just as Harris made a move for his throat.

John parried the move with the towel—that was now stretched between both of his hands—and attempted to wrap it around Harris's forearm. This would give him a way to move Harris's knife arm around safely and either disarm him or disable him. Unfortunately, he missed and the knife cut the towel in two with a ragged tearing sound. John used Harris's distraction with the towel to attempt a kick to the man's knee, Harris blocked that attempt with a downward stroke of his knife hand, slicing through John's clothing and finding the flesh beneath. The knife was sharp and while he knew he'd been cut, he felt little pain for the moment.

Though he missed Harris's knee and received his first wound as a result, the move succeeded in bringing him close enough to the man so that John was able to bring his right arm down to Harris's right arm, temporarily directing the knife away from him. He then used his left hand to deliver a crushing blow just below Harris's unprotected nose.

Harris staggered back with a surprised, disoriented look on his face. John ignored the growing pain in his leg and darted for the kitchen counter. There, he quickly snatched up a large kitchen knife from a butcher block. It was dull and not very sturdy, but it would give him some protection while fending off Harris's attacks.

He turned his full attention back toward Harris and found that the blow to his face had been more devastating than he had at first thought. Harris was moving slowly now and his movements appeared exaggerated.

John feigned an attack to Harris's left, causing him to twist to his left, leaving his right side exposed. John lunged in to take advantage of the opening, but slipped on an ever widening pool of blood caused by the wound to his calf. He went down, his forward momentum causing him to slide toward Harris while on his back, his entire torso completely exposed.

Normally, this would have been a very bad thing indeed for John, were it not for the fact that Harris was still moving a bit slow. The blows to his groin and his face were having their effects. John could see the indecision on his face. He was trying to decide whether or not to use this turn of events to back away from John, or to take advantage of his sliding, apparently helpless opponent and press the attack.

This moment of indecision was all John needed. As soon as he slid within range of Harris, he quickly turned on his side and put his hands on the floor to control himself. Then, he quickly delivered a kick to Harris's ankle, knocking Harris's left foot out from under him and judging from the look on his face, causing him immense pain in the process.

Harris fell forward and John twisted to one side as Harris plowed into the floor beside him. John quickly dropped his own knife and leapt to Harris's prone body. He swiftly grabbed Harris's knife hand and twisted the wrist to one side and back. John felt the bones and tendons giving way. Harris grunted in pain and dropped the knife.

John cocked his right hand, prepared to deliver a blow to Harris's nose with the palm of his hand that would have caused the parts of the nose itself to plow into Harris's brain, killing him instantly.

But before he could deliver the fatal attack, Emily's shrill, frightened, voice stopped him cold. "John, get off him." He looked up and in total disbelief, saw that Emily was holding the MP5 in her trembling hands. It was pointed at *him*.

Tears were streaming down her face. "Please John, please don't make me shoot you." Her voice was quivering and as she tried to hold back the torrent of tears, she added, "Greg, are you alright?"

Harris pushed the totally stunned man from him and rolled away. As he slowly rose to his feet, he shouted at Emily, "Shoot him! Shoot him now."

"I... I can't." she stammered and then the flood gates opened, into body shaking sobs.

"I said shoot him! Shoot him fucking now you fucking bitch!"

Emily lowered the gun and fell, weeping heavily, to her knees. "Greg, let's just leave... please. You said no one would get hurt," she pleaded.

Harris stumbled toward Emily, moving as quickly as he could on his injured ankle. John rose to his knees and moved toward Emily as well. But now he felt the weakness in his injured calf and he stumbled as he reached for her. It was a race of the injured, with Harris arriving a moment sooner.

Unexpectedly, Harris summoned the will to overcome the pain in his ankle and sent a side kick to John's stomach that painfully pushed him backward onto the floor. Grinning, Harris attempted to take the weapon from Emily, who had dropped to her knees in anguish. But she refused to let it go and rose back up off the floor as she fought to keep control of the gun.

"No! No!" she screamed. "Let him go. Let's just get out of here."

They struggled for the MP5 and suddenly it erupted, sending a stream of bullets in the direction of the floor.

Emily instantly went limp and fell, releasing her grip on the machine gun.

Harris took control of it, turned toward the prone figure of Harvard and raised the weapon to fire. Except, John was no longer there! Harris saw a motion out of the corner of his eye and turned toward the movement, just in time to see John's knife arcing downward. He tried to react, but he was way too late to prevent the knife from burying itself deep into the side of his neck.

While still holding the knife in Harris, John used his left hand to bat the gun to the floor. Then he twisted the knife rapidly back and forth before withdrawing it and jumping back, ready to deliver another blow if it was somehow necessary. It wasn't. Harris fell and blood gushed from the mutilated wound.

Incredibly, Harris's eyes looked up at John and smiled. "I told you," he croaked as his eyelids fluttered and eventually closed.

John looked down at him a moment longer, then moved over to Emily. Her leg was badly mangled from the stream of bullets and she was losing a tremendous amount of blood, but she was still conscious. He took off his outer shirt and used it in an attempt to staunch the flow of blood. It was no use, her leg had borne the full brunt of the short burst and there were too many wounds.

He then wound the shirt around the upper portion of the leg and used his knife to form a make-shift tourniquet. The blood flow slowed and he looked at her face for the first time.

She was still but crying softly. "I'm so sorry John," she murmured weakly. "It wasn't supposed to turn out like this. No one was supposed to get hurt. Please forgive me! Susan! Susan! Check on Susan! Please tell me she's not dead."

Knowing there was nothing else anyone could do for her at this point, he answered her quietly, gently. "Alright. Hold on and I'll check on her. Where's Harris's satellite phone? I'll call for help."

"I don't know," she answered quietly. "John, I'm getting so tired. Do you think it would be okay it I take a nap?"

"Try to stay awake," he said softly. "I'll check on Susan and then look for the phone. Hold on Emily." He stroked her hair. "Hold on. Everything will be okay." He got up and as she struggled to remain conscious, she watched him move away, fearing that once she lost sight of him, she would never see him again.

CHAPTER
21

Oh, how did this go so wrong? Emily wondered as she lay in the spreading lake of blood. She heard John call to Susan, but didn't hear whether or not there was a response. She prayed that Susan would be alright. She prayed that John would be okay as well and she tried not to accept that she wouldn't be around to find out. Though she had only known him a few days, she felt she could spend the rest of her life with him. She always felt safe when he was around. It felt like she was supposed to be there, by his side. And now, well, even if she survived, he would never trust her again. Would he? Could he understand how she had gotten into this? How she had taken the wrong fork in the road? That she had begun to regret taking that path even before she had become romantically involved with John Harvard? She had found that she was in a growing cesspool of quicksand and no matter what she did to try to free herself or correct her mistakes, she only got sucked in further. *It would be easier to go to sleep now*, she thought, *than to face John and see his devastated look of betrayal again. Oh god!*

She had lived a satisfied, if dull life, before Gregory Harris had come into it. Though she didn't know it, he had popped into her life in much the same way as Richard Clemmons had come into Susan's, and with good reason. The event had been planned in advance by the same people and for the same reason: to gain information and insight into the lives of Peter, as well as Susan. Actually, Emily had come first. It was information gleaned from her that led them to Susan.

Greg had told her that he worked security for an international firm. The intrigue appealed to her and he enthralled her for hours with stories of espionage and exotic places. He was so charming and he introduced her to a world that she had never experienced. Expensive cars, outlandishly extravagant yachts, parties where caviar was on every table and champagne flowed like water. She had made a comfortable living, but this... this was living life to its fullest.

Coinciding with these events, her best friend had recently married a wealthy entrepreneur. Like herself, she had come from humble beginnings and was now immersed in the same extravagant lifestyle that Emily was presently living. They took notes and laughingly compared their experiences in this new life. They decided that being one of the 'haves,' was definitely better than being one of the 'have nots!' They both rapidly became accustomed to this new way of life. In other words, she was hooked. She had swallowed the bait, as they say: hook, line, and sinker.

So, he had wooed her and she had, predictably, succumbed. He seemed to take an interest in her work and eventually began to ask more and more questions. At some point, she had brought up Susan and what a genius she was. He didn't start asking questions about her immediately. Oh no. He was far too cunning for such a crass move. He let her do the talking and only occasionally did he venture a question or two. Unbeknownst to her, he didn't ask too many questions because he didn't need to. Richard Clemmons had already been given that assignment.

Finally, he came to her with a vexing problem. He told her that he had gotten himself financially tied to a software company that was going under. He would be ruined and he feared that he might have to become a mercenary in order to pull himself out of this hole. Emily was appalled. She offered him what little money she had to start over. He refused, said he was too proud to accept such a proposition. Slowly, over a period of several days, he said there was a way out.

He started by saying that his company was going to approach Susan about buying her program. That program could easily get them on the right track. However, they were talking quite a bit of money and they wanted to be sure the price they were offering was worth it. They couldn't afford anymore losses or waste time on another useless venture. Maybe, he said, it would be possible for Emily to hack into Susan's computer and give it an evaluation as to whether or not they should pursue it.

Emily was troubled by this request on several levels. But he used just the right amount of tact and put it to her as giving her a taste of his world, with the danger and the intrigue.

He had appealed to the wilder side of her personality that had lain dormant inside her. His stories had fired her imagination and as with the new lavish lifestyle, she surrendered to it.

Emily really was a very good person. But she had reached a point in her life where she was asking the age old question, *Is this really all there is*? She felt that she was missing something and couldn't quite put her finger on what it was. When Gregory Harris had come along, she thought she had found the missing pieces. If she hadn't been at this point in her life, the money, the intrigue and the danger, none of it would have made a difference. She would have refused. Harris had been lucky because she was at a weak point in her life. Everyone has them. This was her time and Harris happened along at just the right moment.

And so it started. She was scared to death the first time she began picking her way into Susan's computers, doing the very thing that Peter Browning's daughter was trying to prevent. That only heightened the excitement, the adrenaline rush, and sucked her further in. She had a pretty good idea of what Susan was working on because of Tom Weaver, Peter's P.I. friend. She didn't know how Tom had found out about the program and she suspected Peter didn't either. He never asked Tom too many details about how he discovered the things he produced for Peter. He probably didn't really want to know too much about Tom's methods. The fact remained that they did know about it and because of that, Gregory Harris knew about it.

Once she had actually gained entry to the program,

Emily was awed by it. Even she couldn't begin to understand its inner workings. Greg quizzed her extensively about it, then didn't bring it up again for some time.

Gradually, things came around to the point where Greg began to discuss actually forcing Susan to give up the program. He said they had tried to approach her and she had flatly refused. Emily was flabbergasted. How could they even conceive of such a thing? Then things started to get nasty.

Harris reminded her, in no uncertain terms, that she had hacked into Susan's computer for the purposes of corporate espionage, a highly illegal action. That shook Emily, but didn't deter her resolve to correct this situation. When the threat of jail didn't bring her around, Harris resorted to vague threats to her and her family. He also stressed that no one would be hurt in this little venture, and that most likely Susan would come out of this a very rich woman. This added *enticement* was enough to bring her around to their way of thinking. However, she also decided that once this was over, she was through with the money, the danger, the intrigue, through with Gregory Harris and she let him know that in no uncertain terms. She was no good at this game and she didn't want to play it anymore.

It finally came about that Susan was kidnapped. Emily was shocked, but found that she was so deeply entwined by this point, that she felt she had no alternative but to continue on and see it through. Then they told her Susan was still not cooperating and that they needed Peter. Once again she had at first refused. Once again they used the classic stick and carrot method. The "stick," was a threat on her well being and possible imprisonment if she didn't help them. The "carrot," was the promise of a much easier, safer life, if she continued to help them. She did.

She gave them the key to Peter's private entrance and made sure that he was "available" at a given time. Things got worse. She gave them information about John Harvard and about the fact that he was going to Susan's apartment. She didn't think they would try to kill him. She gave them the information so that they could get whatever they wanted out of the apartment, so they wouldn't be there when he arrived.

It was then Emily realized just how over her head she really was. Things accelerated after that. It seemed like every move she made to try to protect Susan, Peter, and John, just got twisted into something ugly. She was the one to tell them that they were going to Susan's office. Later, she was the one to tell them she thought that John was working with someone at the police department. She was the one to tell them that they were going to Johnsonville. And yes, she was the one to tell them that John was going to creep in through the woods at the back of the house.

She had problems with that last bit though. Harris had a satellite phone. She did not and the lack of a cell phone signal had made her frantic. Once again, she had thought that if she could warn them, they could take steps to avoid John and to cover their tracks. When he had gone into the woods on that first night, she had desperately tried to call them, to warn them that they had been found. That was who she was actually trying to call when she told John that she was trying to reach her mother. When he suddenly opened the door to the car, she thought she was going to jump out of her skin!

This morning, was it really just this morning? It seemed like ages ago, when she had gotten out of bed and gone to the bathroom, where she listened while John talked on his cell phone. Before leaving the bathroom, she had called Harris again to let him know that they would be coming today.

She had also known that once again, her plans had gone awry when Carl came in Clemmons' Jeep to retrieve her. Seeing that Jeep drove home the enormity of what she had done, what she was a party to. Carl told her that John was somewhere near the cabin and watching, so she had to put on a show to convince him that she was their prisoner. Again, she was told that it was to prevent anyone from getting hurt. He failed to mention that someone already had been harmed, namely Bart, who was about as *harmed* as one could get.

As soon as she got inside the cabin, she realized that things were now totally out of control. She played along and wasn't really fearful for her own safety until Greg had threatened to kill her in the garage. He meant it. She could see it in his eyes. He wasn't at all charming any more. It wasn't until then that she realized that Harris would probably kill her before this was all over, and without batting an eyelash. That was the moment when she came to understand that this had been a total set up from the beginning and there was no graceful way out of this. She felt like the ultimate fool.

Which was how they had come to this point. She regretted so much, wanted to take back so much. Wanted to hit the, "Delete," button and start over again, rewrite the program. But she couldn't. And now her life was draining from her and onto the floor of the cabin. She cried, inside, because there didn't seem to be anymore tears left in her. She felt drained, tired. She wanted to be angry at her stupidity, angry that if she had handled things just a little bit differently in so many different places, she probably could have had a wonderful life with John Livingston Harvard.

She finally realized that it was too late for that now. She was too tired to be angry or regretful any longer. With an effort, she turned her head once again and saw John bending over Susan. She wished he was bending over her instead. She finally accepted that there wasn't time for that. So in lieu of that, she contented herself with staring at his form, watching him as she began to fade. It was the last thing she saw as life finally left her.

The driver of the speeding automobile was paying just enough attention to the road in front of him to prevent his vehicle from driving off the road or hitting something or someone. His concentration focused mainly on his thoughts. *Asshole*, he thought. *No, sanctimonious asshole! If Harris hasn't already killed him, I will. It will be a pleasure putting a bullet in Harvard's head. But I want him to see it coming. I want him to know who turned out to be the better man in the end. Fuck head. I'll have to be quiet though. I don't want him to hear me, he might get off a lucky shot. I can do it. I can be just as sneaky as that bastard. He won't ever see this coming.*

John looked down at Susan and felt for a pulse. Her head was at a funny angle, but there! Yes! She did have a pulse. He called her name. Once, Twice. Finally she moaned and her eyelids fluttered. He lowered his voice. "Susan, can you hear me?" She nodded. "Good. I'll be right back, I'm going to look for Harris's phone." She nodded again.

He rose to leave, but she reached out and grabbed his arm. "Harris?" she asked weakly.

"He's dead." John replied.

"My father?"

"I don't know, I haven't looked for him yet. Look, I'll be back as soon as I can, but I need to call for help. Emily has been injured and you need to be looked at as well."

He stood up and walked over to Harris. He dug through his pockets until he found the phone. That was the good news. The bad news was that it had been destroyed in the fight. He dug through his pockets again and found the keys for the Mercedes. He would have to drive it to get help. There was no other way.

He moved over to Emily to tell her he was leaving. Her head was twisted so that she was looking in the direction of Susan. Her eyes were wide open, but he could tell by the unfocused look that they would never see anything again.

He knelt down next to her and gently pulled her eyelids closed. He felt a lump in his throat as he quietly said, "I don't know if you can still hear me or not. I'm sorry Emily. I don't know how you got mixed up in this, but I know that you were a good person. You deserved better than this." He stood up and looked at her lifeless form a moment longer. Then he knelt back down and whispered in her ear, "Emily, I forgive you."

Wiping a tear from his eye, he kissed her softly and stood up once again before moving over to Susan. "I've got to use Harris's car to get help. His phone is busted. You okay here?"

She looked up at him and slowly nodded. It appeared as though she was going to say something and then decided against it. She looked sad.

John turned and quickly walked out the door and to the garage, passing the bodies of Dave and Carl along the way. He entered the garage and saw his .45 and Walther PPK lying on the floor. He walked over, picked them up, wiped off the dust and placed them into their respective holsters.

He took Harris's keys out of his pocket and approached the driver side. He was just about to put the key in the door when he abruptly stopped. He stood back and looked at the car. After studying it a moment, he turned and walked out of the garage.

Harris was ex-military and he appeared to be pretty buttoned down with his methods. John had been about to open the door when he had a thought. What if Harris had booby trapped the car to prevent someone else from using it? He wasn't sure if that was the case, but he wasn't going to take any chances.

After leaving the garage, he walked to Carl's body and began to rummage through his pockets. He retrieved the Jeep keys from one of them. He stood up and walked to the Jeep.

He was opening the door, when his right leg suddenly gave out. He heard the "crack!" of a handgun as he was going down. He began reaching for his .45 and found that his right arm didn't seem to be working. As he realized that he'd been hit in the arm as well, he heard another "crack!" followed by another and yet another.

Successive rounds took him first in the side and then in the head. The round in the side was stopped by the bullet proof vest he was wearing. Though the bullet didn't penetrate his vest, the concussion knocked the wind out of him. The bullet to the head felt like he'd been hit by a brick, but it hadn't been a killing blow.

He lay on the ground, bleeding and barely conscious. He was slowly, painfully, trying to get his left arm around to his .45 when he heard a sound. He looked up and saw Deputy Chief Ramsey standing over him, his face filled with a huge, clown like smile. He was reloading his gun as he was looking down at John.

"What's the matter Bucko? Having a little trouble are we?" The smile suddenly left him and his face turned to an ugly sneer. "You cock sucker. I've waited a long time for this. I wanted to make sure that you knew who was going to give it to you."

John was having trouble forming his words, but he managed to say, "Fuck you Ramsey."

"Fuck you?" Ramsey screamed at him. "Fuck you did you say? Well fuck this." Ramsey snapped another shot off and hit John in his right leg.

"Ahggg." John grunted, his face contorted in pain.

"Oh, this is going to be so much fun." He danced a little jig around John's body and then added, "Come on big man! Try for your gun, go ahead." Then in his best Clint Eastwood voice he said, "Do you feel lucky, punk? Well, do you?" He laughed again and continued, "Go ahead, make my day."

John was losing consciousness. He knew he was going to die. *What the hell*, he thought, *might as well go out shooting*. He began to renew his efforts to reach his .45.

"I don't fucking believe this," said a dumbfounded Ramsey.

Ramsey watched as John actually got his gun out and tried to raise it with his left hand. He failed. He tried again and failed. He tried and failed once again. He didn't have the strength. All the while, Ramsey watched him in amazement.

"What's the matter sissy? You actually gonna make this easy for me?"

With a last burst of energy, John was actually succeeding in bringing the weapon to bear on the Deputy Chief. The smile fell off from Ramsey's lips. "Okay, good enough for me," he said and raised his own gun.

John's strength gave out and his gun dropped before he could fire it. He lay there and waited for the end. He was looking up, straight into his executioner's eyes, when suddenly Ramsey's head seemed to explode, literally. One second it was there, the next second, it was gone and a headless corpse was standing over him. John was instantly covered with bits of blood, bone, and gray matter.

As he lost consciousness, he heard men shouting. He heard radios and he thought he heard a helicopter. *What the hell?* he thought. *Shit! This sucks!* Then the blackness took away his thoughts.

One Week Later

He had been shot in the back and it had been a through and through. He was looking at the wound in his chest, wondering who had done this to him. It had been someone he trusted. He fell to his knees wondering who it had been. He twisted as he fell to the floor and landed, facing the ceiling. He looked up and saw Emily approaching him. She had a gun in her hand and the barrel was smoking, just like in the old western's. He looked at her face. She was crying. She was saying something and he strained to hear what it was. He studied her lips and finally understood. "I'm sorry," she sobbed as her apparition faded.

He heard voices. At least one man, no two, and a women. Emily? He wanted to open his eyes, but couldn't. Why was Emily here? For that matter, where *was* here?

Three Days Later

His face itched. Then he realized that someone was gently stroking his face. Who? He opened his eyes and then closed them immediately. The light hurt. He laid there, trying to get his bearings. He felt weight on his arm. Not a lot of weight, but a familiar weight. About the weight of the head of a six year old girl.

He opened his eyes slower this time to let them become accustomed to the light. He moved his head slightly and looked down. It was Mary Kate. She had pulled a chair up next to the bed and piled pillows on it to bring her head up level. She appeared to be sleeping.

He moved his eyes to the other side of the bed. Susan Browning was sitting, stroking his face lightly while she watched a television at the end of the room. His movements had been so slight that she hadn't noticed them.

Where's Emily? he wondered. Then he began to remember. He remembered her betrayal first. Then the final battle. Then he remembered Emily dying. He remembered Ramsey. Eventually, after a period of some minutes, he recollected nearly everything. At the end, he remembered his dream of being shot in the back, and he remembered the sobbing face of Emily, saying she was sorry. Was it just a dream? Or had Emily somehow found away to come back long enough to express her sorrow and regrets? He guessed he would never know.

His eyes looked around a bit longer and finally, he attempted to speak. But all that came out was some sort of a croakish grunt. But Susan heard him. Her head snapped away from the television and she half yelled, "John?"

He wasn't looking at her. He was looking at Mary Kate. Upon hearing Susan, her head popped up like a jack-in-the-box. "Daddy!" she screamed. No half yell there.

She jumped up on the bed and threw her arms around him. "Ouch!" he croaked. His right arm hurt like hell.

"I'm sorry Daddy," she screamed, equally as loud. Normally the realization that she had hurt him badly enough to make him say something, would have sent her to tears. But she was so happy to have her Daddy back that she didn't give it a second thought.

"It's okay sweetheart," he managed to get out. He held her in his arms as he noticed Susan running out of the room. A few minutes later, a smiling Susan, Nick, and Peter Browning came rushing back.

"God damn buddy! You gave us a scare," said Nick when he reached his side.

John gave them all a return smile. "What can I say?" He looked over at Peter. "I see you're all right. Where the hell were you anyway?"

Peter grinned. "I was all trussed up like a turkey in the trunk of that Mercedes."

"Yeah," Nick cut in. "That was almost the end of him. Harris had enough explosives wired into that car to take out an M1 tank. Fortunately for Pete, that didn't include the trunk. The guys were just about to open the driver side door when they heard him pounding on the lid with his feet. They opened that first. They got him out and noticed some strangely open wiring. They looked further and found that if they had opened any of the passenger compartment doors, boom. That would have been it."

John remembered how close he had come to opening one of those doors. He shuddered slightly and rolled his eyes. His gut instinct had been right on once again.

Further conversation was cut short by the team of doctors and nurses who came filing into the room with enough equipment to start a medical clinic. They spent some time poking, prodding, and asking questions.

When they had finally gone away, with much congratulatory patting of each other on the back, John's initial elation at being alive had passed, replaced with a warm, comforting euphoria that made the bland hospital, "suite," seem like a family dining room at Christmas, complete with seldom seen kinfolk recounting old times.

John learned that Nick had fortunately decided not to listen to his insistence that he didn't need any help. Ramsey had disappeared and that worried Nick. He went to the Chief and it was decided that they needed to call in the state's S.W.A.T. division. They had their own, but they didn't know who could be trusted.

They collected the team, but had some problems locating exactly which cabin John was at. They were reluctant to use the helicopter for fear of alerting Harris. They had found John's car at the spot where he had gotten out and had narrowed their search area pretty well when they heard the first shots.

But the sound ricocheting through the woods made pinpointing the exact location difficult. However, "Ramsey himself did a good job of spacing his shots for a long enough period that we were finally able to get a fix on you," said a grim faced Nick. "Sorry we couldn't get there sooner."

"Hey," John grinned, "you won't find me complaining. Glad I could help out by having Ramsey shoot me *slowly*."

"Well," Nick grinned back, "I do have some other news you might be interested in."

"Really? What would that be? Must be good cause you're standing there grinning like a Cheshire cat."

"As you might expect, Ramsey's involvement in all this kind of caused a stir. It's difficult to blow the head off a Deputy Chief without attracting some attention from just about everywhere you can think of.

"You know what they say about shit rolling downhill. The Chief has taken quite a beating about this. Everyone wants to know how someone so corrupt could have been in the department so long and obtain such a high rank. The mayor is insisting that Ramsey was exceptionally deceptive and it was no one's fault. On the other hand, the Chief does hold the ultimate responsibility. So the mayor asked him to tender his resignation, which he did." Nick's smile got even broader. "You're now looking at the new Chief of Police for our fair city."

John broke out in unbridled laughter. "Well I'll be damned! Oh, that hurts. Congratulations Nick. Really, I couldn't think of a more qualified guy."

After a brief pause in the conversation, John asked, "So

what's going on with Coeptus Guild?"

"I was wondering how long it was going to take you to ask. You just came out of this, so I wasn't going to bring it up. But since you did... The F.B.I. has been all over it. They're scrambling like Osama bin Laden is here in the U.S. of A. They are pulling up all sorts of old cases, everything from death investigations, kidnappings, and mystery cases like the guy who turned up down on the border and didn't know who he was or how he got there. Everything.

"They're going through corporate records, checking patents. I shudder to think of the man hours being spent on this."

"So the lid's off this thing huh?"

Nick nodded. "Oh yeah, in a big way."

"And what about Sue's program?" John queried.

Susan approached the bed. "What program?"

"What do you mean, 'What program?'" John asked incredulously.

"I don't know what you mean, Mr. Harvard," she replied.

He stared at her a moment. "Oh. I get it. What are you telling the F.B.I.?"

Nick interjected, "Sue's just telling them that she was working on very big program that they were interested in."

"That's it? And they're buying that?"

Nick, Sue and now Peter all grinned. "No," said Peter. "But I think they realize that Sue's never going to reveal that information. They know that whatever it was, a lot of people died for it and it forced Coeptus Guild out of hiding. I think they figured out that for it to be worth that much, it must be a very dangerous program indeed. I believe they have decided to let a sleeping dog lie and just go after what they have."

A nurse came into the room. "I'm sorry everybody, but I think Mr. Harvard has had enough for one day. It's time for everyone to leave so he can get some rest."

John was feeling exhausted. He wanted everybody to stay, but he wasn't about to argue.

Later, when he was alone and the room still, he lay there in his bed, thinking. Mostly, he thought about Emily. He was going to miss her. He'd only known her for a few days, but it had seemed much longer than that. More importantly, she could have been his friend and more, possibly forever. Even though she had been working for the wrong side, he didn't really think that truly represented who she was. In the end, she'd given her life for him. That had to count for something. He began to think of her smile, her laugh and the few good times they had together...

Two Months Later

"Daddy, Sue says it's time for dinner."

John sat on his deck, looking out at the sun setting on the lake. The rays were shimmering across mild, rolling waves, sending up sparkling arrows of light into the darkening horizon. A fisherman was trolling his way along the bank, hoping to catch one last minute fish before the light finally surrendered to the night.

He looked down at his daughter's smiling face. "Come here a minute sweetheart, sit on your father's lap." She promptly complied.

"Daddy, is Sue going to always live here?"

"I don't know little one. She's living here right now because I haven't been able to get around very good."

"But you like her don't you?"

"Yes, I like her. But that doesn't mean that she wants to stay once I get better."

"But you're better *now*."

"I know, so I imagine she'll be leaving soon."

"I don't want her to leave. I like her."

"I know you do sweetheart."

Susan stood in the doorway behind them and listened to the conversation. She'd been giving the matter a great deal of thought herself lately. Did she want to leave? Did *he* want her to leave?

There really had been nothing between them since she moved in to help him while he recuperated. She liked John. A lot. And she thought he liked her. But still, there was an invisible wall between them. She knew what the wall was. Emily.

The wall was crumbling, she could feel it. With his recuperation and the last vestiges of that wall dwindling away, a moment of decision would soon be upon her, be upon *them*.

John stood up with Mary Kate in his arms and began

walking toward the door in which she now stood. He finally noticed her and their eyes locked and Sue knew that he realized that she had heard everything he and Mary Kate had been talking about.

He walked up to her and they continued to gaze into each other's eyes until Mary Kate yelled, "Hey. What are you guys doing? Are we going to eat or what?"

They both laughed and John said, "We're going to eat right now angel." He put her down and all three walked into the house.

Yes, Susan thought as they entered the kitchen, *I think everything really is going to be all right.*

The End?

The Twisted Series
Continues in…

Twisted Pieces

The saga of John Livingston Harvard continues as he recovers from the wounds inflicted upon him by the Coeptus Guild thugs. Physically, he's back to normal, better than normal actually, pushing his physical training to the limits as he struggles with his failure to save Emily and to come to grips with the moral conundrum left him by Gregory Harris. Is there really no difference between two men who kill, regardless of their reasons? Are they really cut from the same cloth? He finds that the only way he can sleep is to train until he is exhausted and when he's not pushing himself, he is at the firing range, always thinking of the next time. Slowly, day by day, John, much to the dismay of Sue, the woman who is living with him as he recovers, is transforming himself into a lethal killing machine.

Whether he's ready or not doesn't really matter as his best friend, Chief Nick Giovanni, approaches him with his own problem. Two bodies have been discovered and though they were far apart, Nick feels that they may be related… and they may involve the Guild. Unfortunately both men have first hand knowledge of how the deadly group has a history of placing their own members into police departments and government. It's a matter of trust and if the Guild is involved, it almost certainly will involve John and Nick. Events move quickly, with their worst fears coming to fruition. John suddenly finds that he has little time to put the Twisted Pieces of the puzzle together as he realizes that all that are dear to him are in mortal peril.

For more details and information,
visit www.SilverLeafBooks.com

ABOUT THE AUTHOR

Lew Stonehouse was born and raised in central New York and spent much of his youth sailing, canoeing, and wandering the backwoods of the Adirondack Mountains in moccasins. He is currently residing in a Chicago, Illinois suburb while raising a young daughter. After serving the public as a Deputy Sheriff for many years, he went into private practice and is the current owner of a successful private investigation agency.

The experience garnered from his eclectic career in the law enforcement and private sector, from gruesome homicides to gut busting humor, has provided him with a fountain of knowledge from which he can draw upon when writing his suspenseful crime thrillers.